Drinking Coffee
In the Shower

Pamela C. Sanford

Pack River Publishers
Sandpoint, ID 83864

ISBN: 0989639002
ISBN-13: 978-0-9896390-0-2

DEDICATION

To my Loving Twin Brother, may you continue to ride the stars and chase your dreams.

Many thanks to the greatest friend in the world for allowing her beautiful child to grace the cover of this book.

CONTENTS

INTRODUCTION

It is true that behavior is purposeful and willful. That is, we are each our own agents of change in a world that holds rewards and disappointments. In Paige's world, those disappointments often outweighed the reward. Paige's decisions had always been calculated ones. She weighed the good and the bad and chose from the most advantageous option. Despite the efforts she placed upon the actions she produced, someone else was always in control. Growing increasingly tired of always making the right decision, she soon learned how to make the wrong ones, despite everything around her getting in the way.

1 GOING DOWNHILL

Traffic was its usual nightmare. Paige fumbled around for the keys in her purse, clicked the button once and waited for the signature honk of the truck's horn to let her in. Just as it should, the locks released with synchronized precision and Paige climbed in.

Sighing briefly, she jammed the key into the ignition, found her favorite station on the radio and began the commute. She had to reach the bridge separating the two cities before 5:15 or else traffic would slow to a crawl and she would never make it to her kids' daycare by 5:30. "Who ever heard of closing a daycare at 5:30 anyway?" Paige asked herself. "Oh well, beggars can't be choosers. Quality childcare is hard to come by." She glanced over her shoulder at the car next to her. The driver was a balding, overweight older man who seemed to have a staring problem. "What's your issue?" she said looking right at him. "Haven't you ever seen a crazy lady talk to herself before?" The man with the weight problem and no name quickly looked the other way. "Hah, that's what I thought!" she said triumphantly, merging onto the concrete turnpike.

Everybody was in a hurry to get one place, away from work. Some headed to a bar for happy hour; others go shopping for groceries and head home to their families. Paige sung to the radio, turning it up when a song she really liked came across the airwaves. Singing helped the minutes tick by until she was finally off the interstate, only to come upon the marathon of traffic lights to get through. She went to change lanes, and in her hurry, cut off the guy behind. He honked and then proceeded to show her his IQ via his middle finger. There's always some idiot who thinks they not only need a green light but a flip of the middle finger as well to get them going. Patience was not one of Paige's strong points. Her mind usually worked two steps ahead of everyone else.

"One more turn to go, quick glance at the clock…5:23…just like that, yeah, I made it." With barely turning the ignition off Paige jumped out of the truck and clicked the door lock. Honk! the truck responds to the command. Everything in reverse.

She quickly made her way to the front doors and grabbed the handle. Drawing what would possibly be her last breath to call her own this evening, she put her suit of mom armor on and proceeded into the center.

"Oh, Mrs. Hayes, we're so glad you're here. Lindsay had another bad afternoon. You can gather her things and come back to my office. Aaron should be fine in the infant room for now."

Paige's shoulders felt heavy and dread began to seep in under the seam of her clothing. She popped into the four year-olds room. It was always the same with her daughter. Daycare after daycare had requested she be removed. If she didn't have this one, there would be no more working for Paige. She needed to work, if not for the money, then for the sanity it provided.

"Hi Mrs. Hayes!" a young girl with a mouth of perfectly lined white teeth, nearly shouted as she saw the young mother. It was Sarah, an insanely cheerful, perky 16 year-old who had yet to become jaded by the adult world around her. She stood there in her wide striped pink and white polo t-shirt with flared blue jeans. The sides of her smiled began to turn downward as she drew her next breath. "Lindsay had a tough afternoon. She's in…."

"I know," Paige replied cutting her off, "I know, she's in the office. I'm just here to sign her out. Paige picked up the pen and quickly inked her name.

"Thanks, see you tomorrow," said Sarah with a prom queen's wave.

Paige turned and looked down the hallway past brightly colored construction paper cut-outs and rows of blue and red wooden cubbies toward the office. She felt, quite simply, defeated – defeated as a parent, defeated as a woman trying to juggle a career and small children – defeated as a wife who could no longer bring her husband to make love to her.

Her legs felt weakened as she made the trek back down the hallway. The pinstriped industrial carpet seemingly stretched for miles. It made her nauseous.

Paige would deal with Lindsay first and then attend to her brother. This plan usually worked for her, much the same as receiving the bad news first so the good news covers feeling evoked from the former.

Okay, come on, it won't be that bad. Just another day, come on, you can do it. Positive self-talk is so over-rated. Just put your mind to it, you can do anything…yeah…bullshit. Not today baby.

Paige made it to the office door. There was her daughter. Her beautiful daughter in an orange and yellow calico sundress Paige had made for her last summer, long stockings, and boots. Her hair was pulled back in a braid and her sun silked bangs hung down to her brow. Paige had bought herself a sewing machine for Christmas last year. Derek apparently knew she was getting herself the machine, because he surprised her with a blue, wooden sewing box stuffed full of needles, bobbins, thread and scissors. It was a wonderful surprise, it really was. He could be so good. And when he was good, they were really good together, but that goodness was few and far between these days.

Lindsay was standing near a cabinet door of the daycare office. Paige stood there for a moment, transfixed by the calico dress, still engrossed in the memory of that Christmas.

The director bird-dogged Paige and went right into her tirade, ready to review the events of the day, as if they were going to be

3

some great surprise. "I have to tell you we tried everything today. Lindsay wasn't listening. Mrs. Hayes? Mrs. Hayes? Do you hear me Mrs. Hayes?"

"Huh? Oh yeah, yeah, I'm just tired that's all. Sorry for all the trouble, thanks again for your help. Lindsay? Lindsay sweetheart. Lindsay! Are you ready?"

"Hi mommy. See Kayla?" Lindsay thrust out her scantily clothed Barbie with the too small waist and oversized chest at her mother. "Mommy, look!"

"Yes, yes I see her honey. Mommy really wants to get going and I still have to get your brother, can we please get going?" The calico flowers stood up and in a flash rushed past Paige and made a beeline for the front door.

"Lindsay! Stop! You need your coat and backpack! Linddsssaayy!" It was no use. She was out the door and headed for the parking lot. Ugh! Paige hollered into the infant room as she ran past in pursuit of Lindsay.

"I'll be right back for Aaron. Lindsay got away from me again."

Breathless, Paige pushed past the other mothers coming in the front doors and scouted the parking lot. A chorus line of headlights and car alarms met her. Where was she? Don't they make leashes for kids like this?

Paige thought to herself, "I'm so tired; I really don't need this shit again tonight."

Seconds turned into minutes and those minutes felt like hours. Paige turned the corner of the building and there she was; calico flowers and all, her mouth and hands moving a hundred miles an hour. "Kayla is my Barbie. I got her for my birthday. She is best friends with Sarah. Would you like to hold her?" Lindsay thrust too-small-waist up into Mrs. Thomas' face. Mrs. Thomas stood there entranced by Barbie too-small-waist and the calico offspring of a broken couple. She was trapped and Paige briefly took enjoyment from that fact.

Mrs. Thomas was the mother of Caitlyn and Nicholas. She was the epitome of the successful working mother. Her hair slicked back and tightly clipped; she moved with the ease of sun tea steeping in the midday sun. Her high heels always matched her three piece business suit and her nails bore the mark of hard time served in the salon. In sum, she belonged to the world of the plastic people. Plastic people are those whose purpose it is on this earth to shine and look well on the outside. Yet, sadly, on the inside, just as their manufactured counterparts, there is nothing, just a space devoid of life.

"Lindsay, come on, we need to get your brother and go!" Lindsay looked up, but not at her mom. "COME ON!" There, she had done it; Paige had used her mommy voice. That voice only reserved for the most desperate of occasions, but seemingly overused as of late. Realizing the game was over, Lindsay reluctantly shifted Kayla to her other hand and grabbed onto her mom's coat, trailing behind like a reluctant pack mule headed up the final leg of a mountainous journey.

Paige finally made it back to Aaron's room. She saw him over in the corner sucking on a teething biscuit. His mouth was ringed with smashed cookie and his breath smelled of maple syrup. He gave Paige a big grin, showing off his newly emerged front teeth. His cheeks were rosy from the non-stop onslaught of drool which was in overtime due to teething.

"I'm sorry; it took me awhile to catch Lindsay."

"No problem" the daycare worker said through gritted, yellowed teeth ringed with fuchsia lips. She was, quite actually, old. She really had no business working in a daycare, and the infant room was unfortunately probably the best place for her. If you spent a moment alone with her she'd tell you about her ailments and how the government leaves seniors in the cold and that someday there will be no Social Security benefits for people my age, "just you wait and see." She was less than pleasurable to speak with on an adult level, but for whatever reason, in some grandmotherly way, the infants liked her.

Maybe the babies liked her because they had no idea what was coming out of her mouth.

Paige walked over to where Aaron was sitting and whisked him up off the floor. "Hi big boy, did you miss mommy today?" she asked with a high pitched, squealing mommy voice. It's as if when women give birth they gain an additional appendage and suddenly take on a repertoire of voices to accommodate literally any situation.

Aaron cooed back in response to Paige. She propped him up while stuffing his arms into his thick winter coat. Next the matching scarf and hat lovingly crafted by Aaron's great-grandmother and given as a token of acknowledgment of his birth, was positioned with precision on his head and neck. Last on were his overshoes. Satisfied that only his eyes were visible to the elements, Paige whisked Aaron up into the air and placed him on her welcoming hip. Yes, another part of the anatomy that was so conveniently placed on women by their creator. Hips were designed to be a perfect cargo hold for children.

Once in the truck Paige sighed heavily as she buckled the seatbelt for Lindsay. Lindsay's arms and legs were in constant rhythm with each other. Both moved like the second hand on a clock, perfect timing, never stopping. Doctors had hurled a number of diagnoses at Paige and Derek long ago – Oppositional Defiant Disorder, Attention Deficit Hyperactivity Disorder, Trichotillomania.

The list of disorders was seemingly endless, what didn't end; however, was the stress this little girl often placed on their marriage. Derek made it clearly known on many occasions that he wanted no part of this marriage or the raising of these children. He was "forced to have them." Paige chuckled to herself. "Yeah, *I made* you have them. Sure thing. I took down your 250 pound body, pleased myself, and became pregnant, not once, but twice!"

"If I had that kind of power over someone, I'd be ruler of a small kingdom" Paige thought to herself.

Finally, after what seemed like hours, Paige had both of her kids in the truck and began the final leg of the drive toward home.

Driving past the rows of houses with their neatly kept yards and painted shutters, Paige reached up absent mindedly and clicked the door opener to their garage. She glanced at her own yard. It had been such a beautiful house when they bought it three years ago. Now it revealed on the outside what it felt like to live inside behind those doors. The rough rocked terraces were falling in places and the weeds now outnumbered the shrubs ten to one. The grass hadn't seen a mower in nearly a month and the cracks in the sidewalk were now adorned with Jimsonweed filled ant colonies.

Paige pulled her truck inside the concrete cave and winced as she looked at the clock. "I've got so much to do." She reached around and snapped open Lindsay's seatbelt. Aaron began to coo louder in response to seeing his sister bound out of the car.

"Yes, it's your turn next sweetie. Be patient please."

Paige fumbled with Aaron's harness. For a moment his eyes fixed on hers and she seemed to look right into his soul. He was a wonderfully happy baby. His birth was both an accident and a blessing. Paige and Derek had tried to get pregnant for nearly two years after Lindsay's birth. Nearing divorce, one drunken night resulted in two lines on the pee stick test a couple of weeks later. Paige felt trapped by her pregnancy with Aaron. In fact, she often wished it had never happened, even as she felt him kick inside of her. She hadn't dared tell anyone how she felt. She already felt judged by literally everything else

Paige was good at that, putting on the stoic face. Derek used to tell her that she was the only person he ever met that could truly fake opening up an awful Christmas gift and acting as if it was what she had always wanted. Little did he know this façade was a culmination of years of practice, or, rather, survival in a bitterly cruel upbringing.

2 BEGINNINGS

Paige grew up in the Pacific Northwest, home to giant Evergreen trees and rain, lots of rain. Locals would often joke that one could truly identify a Washingtonian by their gills and webbed feet. Paige moved around quite a bit as a child. Recession was common, and her parents often had a difficult time making ends meet. Her mom, Judith, was a waitress at a local restaurant. She was of average build with short brown hair and brown eyes, in other words a fairly plain woman, nothing remarkable stood out about her at all really. Paige's stepdad, Dave, worked as a day laborer for a number of small industrial businesses in the area. His eyes were dull and his shoulders heavy. Paige later presumed his morose features were probably from having to bear the burden of being married to Judith. Paige's family was about as blue collar as they came.

Paige's own father, Roger, lived two hours to the south of them in a small lumber town. Her mother divorced her father when Paige was just four years old. Roger was a gentle man who doted on his daughter whenever he saw her. He had black hair with the grayest of eyes. Paige saw him one weekend a month and on holidays. Her memories of those weekend visits were quite vivid – at times, later on, too much so.

She had an older brother, James Michael. James lived with her, Judith and Dave until he was 13 years old. James shared Roger's hair color which he parted in the middle and feathered on both sides in equal sections. He kept his black comb (to match his hair of course) in his back pocket for any hair emergency which may arise. His nose was slightly turned upward and the bridge of it was dusted with freckles. It was the early 80's, feathered hair and pocket combs the size of a spatula were in, little sisters, on the other hand, were not.

James had two things which Paige was fixated on, his feathered hair and his tick. Yes, James had a tick. Paige didn't call it his tick. She wouldn't know that term for many years to come. Instead she just called it her "funny bruder." He would suck in air, squeak slightly in the back of his throat and then quickly shake his head to one side. One...two...three. The order never failed.

She loved him dearly, but to him, she was just the pesky little sister. He often told her that they were actually adopted and that their real parents were out there, somewhere, looking for them. At times Paige really wanted to believe that very statement. Her mom and stepdad fought furiously for years. The fighting became worse once James went to live with their father.

For a seven year old, Paige was quite in tune with her environment, keeping track of everything around her. She organized the clothes in her closet according to days of the week. Monday's metal hanger was ornamented with green cotton pants and a matching orange floral turtleneck. Tuesday's hanger revealed a knee length set of deep pink corduroy knickers, a green and pink checkered short-sleeved shirt and Paige's favorite fuzzy white painter hat. This was her "European look" just as she had seen splashed across the pages of National Geographic magazine. She would stuff it in her coat pocket on the way to school, taking it out only after her mother had drove away from the parking lot. She cocked it to one side of her mane of auburn hair, daydreaming of being a mysterious grown up woman with a complicated past. Judith always snapped at Paige for acting too grown up, so this ritual was reserved only for the school breezeway. It was funny that Judith damned Paige for being exactly what she created out of her.

On the wooden shelf above her clothes was a column of neatly stacked boxes of games arranged in alphabetical order. The second column contained shoeboxes, four of them, two empty and two full of Barbie clothes. Box one, on the bottom, was empty, the one on top of that was full, the third empty and of course the last full. Column three was bare at this point. Paige hadn't decided what would fit up there yet.

Below her clothes rack was the linoleum lain floor. On the right side were her shoes. Paige had three pairs, one blue and white pair of Stylon's – nylon in composition to the brand name leather one's that all the other kids had. Paige had wanted the white leather ones with the blunted tip, but her mom had said they didn't have that kind of money.

Her second pair of shoes was her "waffle stompers." Waffle stompers were brown suede lace-up boots with bright red shoelaces. The soles were a thick black rubber that looked just like the inside of a waffle maker. Waffle stompers were designed to take your feet anywhere muddy, snowy or just plain gross. James Michael had a pair just like them, only bigger.

Paige's last pair of shoes was very special to her – Boston Brown's with the polished silver buckle, straight from the shoe store. Paige loved the shoe store. She wasn't sure, however, which she liked more, the rows of perfectly lined shoes waiting in anticipation for a new owner, or the toy box stored behind the register containing a surprise just for her choosing.

On the left side of Paige's closet it was bare. What was there was a three by one space that Paige kept purposely devoid of any objects. It was a perfectly sized space for the little girl, when life became too scary, as it so often did on Friday nights.

Paige slid the heavy wooden closet door closed, turned around and quickly scanned the room for her notebook. It was over in the corner next to her box of pencils. Walking over to the spiral bound notebook, Paige picked it up, and flipped through its pages until she came to her list. All new stuffed animals that entered the domain of her room were checked in on the master list. Each new animal was then grouped by type and ability level. That's right, ability. Paige taught school in her bedroom and each animal represented a dutiful student.

Paige cleared her throat and began her roll call. "Bun bun, Dwar, Penelope, Missy," Paige continued on until she reached the end of the list containing nearly thirty stuffed animal students. Pairs of plastic and beaded eyes stared blankly back at her waiting for her request.

"Okay, let's get started. You, Dilly, please be quiet. Thanks." Paige stayed in her schoolteacher roll for the next hour until she heard the door slam to the room next to hers. It was James Michael, she was sure of it.

"Penny, please turn to page ten in your...." *SLAM* went the door next to her room again. This was followed by her mom's heavy footsteps coming up the stairs. Paige's heart began to race and with trembling hands she gave final instructions, "Okay, class is over, everyone put your books away," Paige said.

"James Michael, get your ass down here right now!" Paige's mom bellowed from the staircase. Stomp, stomp, two more steps up. Paige estimated five were left before she reached the top. Paige quickly went to her door and locked it for extra protection.

"Dammit James Michael, I've told you how many times and you just won't listen!" Judith shrieked. She was so tired, tired of not being heard or respected in this house. Sometimes she just wanted to go left instead of right onto the freeway when she got off of work. Drive far away and start a new life, just like in the movies. It would be so much easier.

Stomp, stomp, only three steps left. Paige backed up, held her breath and placed her hand on the grooved handle leading to her closet, ready to act at a moment's notice.

"James. James are you listening to me? You are grounded! That is it. I won't have any more of this," Judith continued to yell at the top of her voice.

Stomp, stomp, stomp. That was it. Paige's mom was officially at the top of the stairs. The end was here. This was serious business.

Paige flinched the muscles in her arm in anticipation of opening her closet door when the unexpected happened. All fell silent and the shiny brass doorknob of her own room began to shake.

"Paige? Paige are you in here? Paige please open the door for mommy," Judith asked, quickly changing the tone of her voice to get her daughter to comply.

Paige's own breath stopped halfway out her mouth. She was frozen with fear.

"Paige open this damn door right now." Patience was not one of Judith's strong points. "Do you hear me in there Paige? Are you just as stupid as your brother? If you aren't, you'd better open this door now," Judith ordered again.

Paige's voice emerged from somewhere deep in her stomach. "Yes mom," she cracked in a wispy voice.

"What? What? I can't hear you; speak up when you're talking to me. God, you are just like your father, spineless as hell. Find your voice and use it dammit," Judith said.

Paige relaxed just enough to allow the breath to escape from her stomach. At the same time she spoke, "Yes mommy, I'm in here, I'm coming." Paige's numb fingertips reached outward as she stiffly walked toward the bedroom door. The shiny knob connected with her fingertips. The door was pushed opened at the same time as the lock released thus allowing the knob to turn freely. There standing in the doorway was Paige's mother. Her feet squarely planted on the floor, arms resting on her hips and eyes staring coldly down at the little girl cowering on the edge of her bed.

"Get outside right now. Do you hear me? Do not come back in this house…no matter what," Judith said.

Paige's throat began to hurt. "But mommy," she began to cry, "I don't want to. Please mommy," she pleaded, almost begging, as the hot tears stung her cheeks.

"Paige, do not defy me. I said get out of here."

Paige began to sob. "No mommy, I don't want to." She didn't like being sent outside like this; nothing good ever came from it. What worried her most in her short life were the things she could not see, the things she could not control.

Judith raised her arm as she took a step toward Paige. Paige tried to duck to the side, out of her mom's way, but her mom was quicker. Judith's arm fell like a fine-tuned lever landing precisely on Paige's backside.

Paige yowled in a mixture of protest and pain. "Please mommy...please don't do it again...I'll go downstairs," Paige bargained for her release as she navigated the carpeted stairs, one hand on the railing, the other on her backside. It was not as if Paige was dealing with a rational being. Rather, she was negotiating with the devil herself. Her sobs grew louder as she took each step.

"Stop crying Paige. I mean it, stop that damn crying right now," Judith yelled.

Paige could hardly make out the end of the stairs. Her eyes were filled with wet tears making her vision blurry. Her breath heaved and contracted involuntarily. Her heavy footsteps were pulled along by protesting muscles in her legs which had to comply with Paige's every command.

The salty tears filled her lips. She licked them back and looked forward to the rectangular white steel door. In the center, next to the wall, was another shiny brass knob. Paige was able to make out the glimmer as it shown in the midday sun. She grabbed it and stepped outside to freedom.

She ran as fast as her legs would carry her to the wooded area across from the parking lot that housed the cars to the apartment complex she lived in. She entered the safety of the woods, hopping across bracken ferns and rotted wood, stopping only when her lungs began to burn and her legs would no longer hold her up.

She stood there, breathless, chest heaving in and out, waiting. "Field of flowers, fields of flowers," Paige repeatedly said to herself.

13

Finally, Paige collapsed onto the earthen ground. She breathed in the smell of mosses and decaying, dampened leaves. Her breathing, along with her thoughts, began to slow.

She waited for what seemed like an eternity. Peering through the dense underbrush looking past the rows of garbage cans, cars and white steel doors, she found the one with the number three on it and fixated her gaze on it.

Paige rubbed her eyes, growing tired of staring at the shape that would not change. After what seemed like an eternity, it looked as if the door to number three was opening. She squinted and looked again. Yes, yes it was opening. Paige braced herself against the rotting, wooden stump.

Judith and Dave emerged from number three. Dave was in the lead and headed right for the blue car in the corresponding number three spot in the parking lot. Judith, on the other hand, stood on the front porch and examined the area in front of her with soldierly precision. She drew a large breath and yelled for Paige.

Every bone in Paige's body told her not to respond. Just stay, stay in your fern covered shelter, away from everything, live in the flowers.

But Paige could not remain in her fairy tale hideaway for long. She watched herself slowly rise and take a step toward the entrance out of her forested haven.

"Paige, Paige, I know you're out there! Get out here right now, we have to go," Judith yelled.

Paige watched as Dave stood by the door to the blue escape vehicle not saying a word, letting Judith take the lead as usual. Paige would later learn that Dave's actions had a term which defined them – apathy. Later on Paige would unknowingly seek out that exact character trait in her own husband.

Paige reached the vehicle with rusty wheel wells as her mother held the door open. Her mother's eyes pierced right through her insolent daughter. Paige quickly ducked into the car with a cautious hand still over her backside. She anticipated receiving a swat, but none came, not this time.

They drove away, not saying a word until they reached Burgerworld. Once inside no words were uttered with exception of each family member taking their turn to order. Paige made sure to order last so she could sneak in a milkshake while Judith was distracted with the people around them. It was not until Paige was dipping her fries in the red sauce that Dave spoke of something other than the menu.

"We've got to do something Judith. It can't go on like this. Next time I'm gonna get hurt bad, real bad, and I hate to think what would happen to your daughter," Dave said.

"Paige? Paige? What about me Dave?" Judith asked. "Don't I count for something in this house? Why does it always have to be about you and these kids?" Judith inquired with selfish immaturity.

Dave was silent. Paige reached for her white plastic spoon and dunked it into the clear cup containing red gelatin cubes. She slurped the gelatinous lumps past her front teeth and felt its coolness slide down her throat. She was still entranced in her cup of gelatin when Judith abruptly stood up and announced that she was leaving. Curiously enough she didn't even care enough to look up at her mother. This was to be expected. Even she at such a young age had more insight into her mom's behavior than Judith herself.

"I cannot sit here with you two any longer. I cannot stand the sight of either one of you plotting against me." And with that, Judith whirled around on her heels and left out the door aptly labeled EXIT. Her red plastic basket of fries remained in their place at the restaurant table.

Paige looked up at Dave, who in turn looked back at Paige with a stunning amount of surprise in his face. He reached over and took a fry from Judith's basket. He was at a loss for words. What the hell was he still doing married to this woman, and worse yet, what was he going to do with these kids of hers. Paige wasn't bad, but she would end up just like her crazy mother, he was sure of it.

He watched the little girl gobbling up the last of her fries and then put her basket next to the others on the tray, nearly restoring the table back to its pre-family dining experience. Paige wasn't a bad kid he mused. James Michael was just as crazy as his mother though. Perhaps Paige would skid past the genetic anomaly which had taken ahold of this family. It was hard to say. If not, she would end up bitchy, bossy and out of control just like her mother.

"Come on Paige, we need to go. Finish up your lunch," said Dave.

She didn't question Dave, even though the average bystander could see that she was finished and the table was clean. Paige did as he requested, however, scraping the bottom of the small plastic cup for any last traces of red gelatin. She grabbed her toy and obediently followed her stepfather out the same door her mother had left through just a few minutes prior.

Once outside and back in the car, it was a silent drive home. Everyone in the car knew who was in charge, and they sat patiently waiting until she spoke. It wouldn't be long, Judith rarely let fires burn down into quietly glowing embers.

"When we get home Dave, we are going to give James Michael an ultimatum. He either shapes up or he is gone," Judith said.

Dave muttered something in response. Paige couldn't quite hear what he said but apparently her mother was satisfied with what he said as she sat quietly the rest of the trip home. This was a rare ember smoldering for an even greater fire yet to come.

Dave steered the car into its resting place on the concrete pad in front of their apartment. Embers turned to flame and Judith turned around glaring at Paige. "Stay outside until we call for you. I mean it Paige. Do not come in the house."

"What's wrong mommy? Why can't I come in the house?" Paige asked.

"Do not ask questions Paige. Just do as I tell you, now go," Judith replied.

Paige reluctantly did as she was told, running to the grassy field in front of the woods. She twirled and practiced her cartwheels until dizziness took its toll. She laid back and watched the white clouds do one last dance in the late day sun. Closing her eyes she listened as small commuter planes took passes in the blue skies overhead. Despite all the things wrong in her world, this was summer at its childhood best.

In the far distance a siren began to wail. Slowly at first, then it grew louder, until it overpowered the planes above. The sirens overtook her daydream and she rose up, resting her hands on her chin with elbows dug into the soft, green fall grass.

She took the scene in with wide eyes. Not one but two police cars came to rest right there in her apartment parking lot. It was just like on television, only live and in living color right in front of her eyes. *Wow, who's in trouble?* Paige said to herself as she watched with the intense curiosity of a child. She knew the police only showed up in an emergency, like calling 911. She learned that much in school from her teacher.

Paige's curiosity turned to horror as she watched the blue uniformed figures approach door steel door number 3. There had to be a mistake, something is wrong here. They're not at the right door.

She watched as the smallest of the three blue shapes knocked on the steel door. She could feel the vibration from his knock in the bottom of her stomach. Her throat began to hurt and her eyes started to tear up.

No, no, not my door, please God, Paige began to plead.

She watched her door open and the three uniforms slipped inside. She looked down at her Dynowoman watch securely fastened to her right wrist. Five minutes after six. Six o five. Six plus five was eleven and one plus one was two. Eleven, seven eleven. Oh how she wanted a freezee from the corner mini-mart.

Paige sat like an eagle waiting for prey perched near a rock in the grassy brush directly across from door number three. She checked Dynowoman again. It was now fifteen minutes after six.

Still longer she waited. Her legs turned numb from

crouching so long. After what seemed like an eternity to such a small child, the brass knob to door number three opened. Uniform one walked out followed by uniforms two and three. Between two and three walked James Michael, arms behind his back, feet dragging the ground, head bowed.

Paige's breath stopped halfway up her throat. A warmth spread down her legs and puddled around her Boston Brown's in the dirt. She opened her mouth to scream her brother's name, but the lump in her throat capped off any breath that tried to squeak by.

Paige's mind could not fully wrap around what was happening. All she knew is that the men in blue were taking away her brother, her protection from the world, the barrier between her and the rest of this messed up family. Paige was terrified that she would never see him again.

The police cars became fuzzy and Paige began to tremble. "Flowers, please, flowers. Orange, yellow, lots of green," Paige whispered to herself.

An awareness the police cars had left only emerged as she heard the roar of their engines. She looked upward at the sky for a plane, not wanting to believe that James Michael was actually gone. She looked further toward steel door number three and slowly stood up.

Dynowoman indicated it was now forty-five minutes after six. Paige was shivering. The sun was nearly down behind the mountain, promising an early evening, and her wet pants clung to her like a second skin. She put one foot in front of the other and counted her steps to door number three. Once there she drew a final breath and turned the knob to step inside.

She closed the door slowly behind her and turned to see her mom sitting cross-legged on the golden shaded davenport. "Hi mommy," Paige said in a small voice, trying to sound somewhat cheerful. "Where'd James Michael go mommy?" Paige asked.

Judith was silent on the couch. The only sound that could be heard was the clinking of the ice cubes against the sides of the glass cupped squarely in her hands.

Paige checked Dynowoman again. It was fifty-one minutes after six.

Judith finally spoke, and when she did, Paige regretted ever saying a single word to her mom.

"What you saw here today," Judith began hissing through clenched teeth, "is not to be repeated to anyone. Do you understand me Paige? I mean no one, not your father, not your aunt, friends at school, nothing."

Paige nodded her head in understanding. "Yes mommy."

"You know you can't keep your big mouth shut. Always gotta go around and blab about what happens at home. I can't stand the sight of you right now. Go to your room," Judith told Paige.

Paige took herself with the lump forming in her throat and went upstairs to her room. This time there were no tears, no sobs of pain. Only the silence of Paige's own thoughts meandering through whispering fields of flowers. Paige walked deftly over to her closet door, opened it and stepped inside. Just like Friday nights.

3 FRIDAY NIGHTS

Paige's life was one of patterns and order. Her brother's tick, her carefully arranged bedroom and Friday nights. Friday nights were supposed to be for adults to let loose from a long week of work while their children waited at home indulging in pizza, pop and b rated movies. This was partially true for Paige, who was picked up from daycare at 4:30 pm.

Daycare was no delight. She had great difficulty making friends. Paige didn't like kids her age, or, maybe yet, they didn't like her. "Hey flatface! What are you, Chinese or something?!" the kids would taunt. This especially hurt because Paige's facial features were a result of her being born with a birth defect, not due to some lineage, both of which were left to nature, neither of which Paige could control. At first she learned to ignore those jeers and taunts hurled toward her by her peers, but later she learned to loathe them. They became nothing to her, and as an adult, she chose relationships very carefully because of them.

Paige looked up at the clock on the far wall above long rows of institutional tables, anxiously awaiting the moment her mother would show up. She felt uncomfortable sitting amongst the other children like a heard of animals at a trough. The relief wouldn't come until Judith's face showed up at the front desk. Paige quickly dropped her snack of graham crackers and lumpy blue milk into the trash and grabbed her coat. The milk was powdered, probably to save money.

Paige didn't like real milk much less some fake copy of the white stuff. The daycare worker would grab the plain white box with black letters "POWDERED MILK" written across its face and methodically scoop out a tablespoon of white powder into each of the carefully arranged restaurant style glasses. Next a napkin for each child was placed beside the marbled yellow plastic glass and then a gloved hand would distribute the graham cracker. Feeding for the masses, memorable yes, spectacular no.

"Ready to go?" her mother's lips asked through ruddy cheeks as Paige ran to her with open arms. Paige hugged her long and hard, smelling her perfume mixed with grease from the grill at the restaurant where she waitressed during the day.

"Hey, I got my paycheck today, we need to hurry up and get going so I can cash it." "Okay mom," Paige said as she skipped out to the parking lot and got in the powder blue two-door vehicle.

Paige was excited. Payday meant a trip to Burgerworld and a frozen soda at 7-11 if she was lucky. The car door squeaked and groaned in protest as Paige used all of her might to get it closed.

As Paige buckled up, she listened to the whir of the windshield wiper motor. Its hum entranced her. It was raining, not a hard rain, but a gentle mist, the kind of rain that green lawns love and old black and white movies were born on.

"Hey mom, can I turn the radio on?"

"Huh? Yeah sure," her mom answered back absentmindedly as she navigated rush hour traffic in the rain.

Paige pushed the shiny black button on the radio to turn it on. Eye of the Storm by Survivor was the number one song and KJR was playing it. Paige hummed quietly to herself as she turned the radio up.

"Stop it! Just wait until you get home if you want to turn that crap up!" her mother snapped.

"Ok," Paige responded in a small voice.

She turned to the window and followed the rain droplets down the cold glass pane with the tips of her fingers. She retreated inward, picturing a field filled with large sunflowers with bright orange fronds surrounded by blades of grass crayon colored green. In the adult world there are several terms for it – splitting, dissociation, multiple personalities. It is here, the early experiences, where Paige believed she began to develop a penchant for just such an event.

They pulled up to the bank and waited their turn in line. The red lights from the car ahead of them shown hazily through the rain streaked window. It was as if the colors melted once they reached the warmth of the car inside. Paige's mom signed her check, popped it in the plastic cartridge and snapped the lid tight. She set it down gently back in the opening and pressed the bright green button. The door to the machine responded in kind and closed up with electronic precision. Whoosh! The cartridge was promptly sucked up through the long tube on its way to the inside of the bank. Whenever Paige watched this happen she often pictured herself doing the same thing, just like on a Star Trek episode.

"Thank you Judith" the bank teller said as she leaned into the microphone. A quick snap of the lid and whoosh; the money came back through the long tunnel. Judith grabbed the plastic cartridge from the ledge and handed the envelope full of green paper to Paige. Paige looked wistfully at the tube, hoping for a treat from the teller.

"Make sure you count this. Count it right. Banks can shortchange ya you know."

"Sure mom," Paige said eagerly, pulling herself back from her transporter daydream. Counting money was one thing she loved to do. At home she kept every dollar and cent she earned in an old wooden box that looked like a treasure chest. The chest was lined with red velvet and adorned with large metal knobs.

"One hundred, two hundred, three hundred, fifty, sixty, seventy-five and thirty five cents. Yup, it's all here."

"Good, be a dear and put it in my purse."

Step one, cash the check, was done. Now on to step two, food.

"Where do you want to go tonight? Burgerworld or Bob's Surf 'n Turf?" Paige's mom asked.

"Let's go to Burgerworld. They have the new Dynowoman toy that was on t.v." Paige replied.

Judith pulled the car into the drive-thru and waited her turn to speak into the dimly lit box. It was still raining and Paige was beginning to get nervous. Step two was half through and then on to step three.

"Welcome to Burgerworld. What can I get for you this evening?" a voice crackled through the speaker.

"Yes, I'll have a kid's hamburger meal with a rootbeer" said Judith.

"Will that be everything?" the metal box asked in response.

"Yes, thanks."

"Please pull ahead, your total will be at the window."

"Mommy, aren't you gonna eat? I would think you'd be hungry too."

Judith didn't mean to ignore her daughter as she pulled the lever down on the steering column and gently released her foot from the brake, but she was lost in thought. She was beginning to feel the anticipation of the evening. Fridays were her reward. A well-deserved reward for the long hours she put in at work. She shouldn't have to work at all, but, her husband, Dave, wasn't going to give her anything. As long as they stayed married, she would have to make her own way. She was proud of her income. Yeah sure she had made some mistakes along the way. Perhaps she should've stayed married to the kids' dad. Her life would be much easier now, that was for sure.

"Ma'am. Ma'am. Ma'am that will be a dollar fifty-seven."

Judith flipped through the stiff bills in the bank envelope and pulled one out with Lincoln's face on it. "Here…thanks."

The clerk handed her change back and then handed the paper

box of food to the anxious mother who passed it on in unison to Paige.

Paige quickly opened the box fishing past the fries and hamburger to the plastic toy. "Look mom, look what I got!" Paige grinned wide holding the red-caped Dynowoman up in the air. Food and a toy, step two was done.

Judith turned the wheel of the old car with precision, navigating the rainy streets as her daughter munched on her fries. She felt her pulse increase as a feeling of warmth fell over her. She was excited, she was almost there.

The neon lights of the green and white sign shown through the rain soaked car window beckoning those nearby.

"Here we are Paige. Put the fries away. You can finish when we get back from the store."

Paige complied with her mother's directive. She unbuckled the seatbelt and pulled on the lever to open the door. This was step three.

"Make sure you lock it. You never know who could be lurking in the parking lot, especially at night," her mother warned. As always, she dutifully complied with her mother's request. It was paranoia, but a healthy kind that keeps woman who are out alone safe.

Paige followed her mother into the store. As soon as the electronic door opened she was met by a strong smell. There was no air circulation in the store, so the odors hung thickly suspended by a mixture of positive and negative charged ions. It was difficult to describe, a mixture of something sweet, spicy and old – much the same as the smell of a lounge the morning after a good night. The cash register clicked in the background and a muffle of voices fought to occupy the space in the room.

Paige looked up at the rows of bottles. Each one was a different shape and size, holding its own special place on the metal shelves. Paige watched as her mother reached for the one which was wider than it was long. The front of the bottle was canvassed with a red and white paper label.

"This will do, come on Paige, don't dawdle. This is not the place to dawdle, and for God's sake, don't talk to anyone in here," Paige's mom said tersely under her breath.

She followed her mom up to the counter and patiently waited by her side, careful not to look at any of the strangers that her mother cautioned against. Maybe they were the ones that would wait in the backseat of unlocked cars.

The clerk picked up the bottle from the counter and punched the price into the register. Click, click, click, the register spoke in response to the clerk's entry. "That'll be five seventy five ma'am" reported the clerk, reaching for a crisp, brown bag, slowly putting the heavy bottle inside.

Paige's mom reached inside her purse finding the white bank envelope. She handed the clerk a ten dollar bill and waited in earnest for her change. Soon she would take possession of that brown paper sack. Her mouth began to water; the twinges that began in her toes were now to her stomach. She was on the homestretch.

Paige followed her mom to the exit door of the store. She rushed to go in front of her mom. She wanted to be the first to grasp onto the silver handrail and jump onto the black rubber floor mat. The door would then magically swing open; unbeknownst to Paige an electronic eye aided just such an action.

Swoosh, and they were out the door, mom in front, brown paper sack in hand, daughter in tow. Once back in the car, Judith handed the paper sack to Paige.

"Put it in the glove compartment," she said.

Paige did as she was told. After all, she had learned that if a cop was to pull them over, her mommy would get in big trouble if the cop saw the pretty bottle, and trouble was not what mommy needed.

"Check the backseat for me too; you never know who might be lurking in the dark around her," said Judith.

Paige dutifully turned around and searched the depths of the blue vinyl backseat.

"Nothing mom," she replied.

Paige's mother taught her to beware of much of the outside world around her, strangers lurking in dark places ready to steal little girls at a moment's notice. Unfortunately, what she didn't teach her was to beware of what lie on the inside, the demons that lurk in the very neurons of one's mind.

Judith turned the key in the ignition. It was time to go home and Paige's hands began to sweat. Step three was officially done.

4 THE CLOSET

As the tires of the old car turned into the parking lot of the apartment complex in which Paige lived, she began to feel around the dark interior of the car for her stuff. Dynowoman was clutched tightly in her left hand, leaving her right hand free to search. She grabbed her purple polka-dotted raincoat, tucked it neatly in the fold of her arm, and reached for the silver door handle to the car door.

"Wait for me Paige. You don't want to leave your mom out in the parking lot with strangers do you?" Judith asked.

"No mommy, I love you. I'll wait," Paige replied.

Judith reached across Paige's lap and popped open the button on the glove compartment. Just as if she was opening a treasure chest, Judith's eyes widened as she grasped the crinkly brown paper.

"There, I got it sweetie. What are you waiting for Paige? Get in the house now," Judith said.

Paige knew that sound of her mother's voice. As quick as her feet would carry her she was out of the car and onto the doorstep. Quickly stepping into the house, she listened for the sound of the door to close behind her. When it did she jumped just a little.

Dave was sitting at the kitchen table. He was hunched over a white, styrofoam container of fries and a greasy looking patty melt. This was dinner tonight. He knew he wasn't getting anything from his wife.

"Hi Dave," Paige said. "See what I got tonight?" she said thrusting Dynowoman into his face.

"Oh yeah, hey, that's great," Dave replied with feigned interest.

"More woman than you can handle there Dave?" Judith shot back at him. "You see Paige, Dave never had kids, so he has no idea who Dynowoman is," said Judith.

That wasn't the truth at all. In fact, Dave had three kids from his second marriage. Judith was his third wife. His second wife bore him three children, all of whom he had absolutely nothing to do with. Judith didn't understand why, they were three beautiful girls, and truth be told, his ex-wife really wasn't all that bad to deal with.

"Are you going to start your shit tonight Judith?" Dave asked. "Because if so, I want no part of it, okay?"

"No, no Dave. I'm not. Just relax, okay?" Judith responded.

Paige decided this was her cue to exit the room. She turned around and headed up the stairs skipping a stair with each stride, rounded the corner and went into her room. Closing the door behind her she walked over to her brand new 13 inch black and white television set and turned on the power knob.

Paige sat on her Prairie Friends bedspread, crossed her legs, and interlaced her fingers together setting her chin on them to rest. She let her whole body go limp and stared blankly at the black and white images dancing before her.

Some time passed before Paige grew bored of what she was watching and decided to venture back downstairs. It was fairly quiet right now, and she was starting to get hungry for a snack.

Tiptoeing down the stairs she entered the living room. Her mom was on the couch, legs tucked neatly behind her like a swan. She wore her silky black and pink floral nightgown and was covered with a brown plaid blanket made by Paige's great-grandmother. Dave was nowhere to be found.

"What do you need Paige?" Judith asked.

"I'm hungry mommy," Paige replied softly

"Look in the kitchen sweetie, there's stuff in there. If you can find it, you can eat it. Judith smiled sweetly between her puffy red lips, raising her glass up to them after speaking. She sipped long and slow, enjoying the slow numbness that was taking hold of her mind and body.

Paige walked into the kitchen and poked her head into the fridge and cupboards. She took down a small glass from the shelf. To that she carefully added three ice cubes. On top of the ice cubes she filled her glass as close to three quarters full as possible of apple juice. Apple juice was the best, not only when she was sick, but for making her drinks. To this she added a few drops of tap water. She watched how the water swirled and swooped its way through the amber colored liquid it met. She pretended the water was the same drink her mom bought on Friday nights at the special store. Paige swished the glass so the ice cubes clanked against the sides.

"Just like mom's," Paige whispered quietly to herself.

She took her drink back through the living room to head upstairs.

"Hey sweetie, where's mommy's girl goin'," Judith asked as Paige was almost passed her.

"I'm going back to my room," Paige replied.

"You don't have to go back right away do you? Don't you want to keep mommy company? Dave certainly won't," said Judith.

"I love you mommy. My show is almost back on. It's a good episode tonight."

Judith drew in a long breath. Her voice was slightly slurred, but not soaked with vodka as it would become later on in the evening.

"Alright, alright. You know I wanted you more than anything, right? I mean, I fought to keep you alive. Do you understand that Paige? Do you know what they told me? They were all so wrong." Judith had miscarried three times before finally becoming pregnant with her daughter. She had worried the whole pregnancy, and covered those worries with the occasional visit to her

Friday night store.

"Yes mommy, I know, thank you." Paige stood there and nervously fidgeted. She had tried so hard to slip past her mother.

Judith laughed and then turned on Paige with a stern look. "Alright, be like him, just leave me Paige."

"Good night mommy." Paige turned on her heels and headed up as fast as she could to her room, skipping two steps as she got closer to the top.

Once back in her room she turned on her blue and white lamp next to her bed and turned off her overhead light. She liked the way her room looked like a dimly lit movie cinema. She sipped her drink slowly, swirling the ice in her glass with her pinky finger. She felt so grown up.

Paige looked around her room. It was a mess. She checked Dynowoman, it was almost nine o'clock.

"Let's get started Dynowoman, there is work to be done," she said confidently.

She began with her clothes, picking up the dirty ones and tossing them into her white wicker laundry hamper. Next came any papers and books. Each book was picked up with care and placed back on her shelf; papers were placed according to subject matter (notes to her, schoolwork, teaching materials for her stuffed animals) in piles. Once each pile was made she placed the whole lot in a blue plastic milk crate. The crate was then placed neatly by her bookshelf.

Paige could feel the sense of urgency slowly subside as each step of cleaning her room was gradually checked off. It felt somehow soothing to have everything in order. Once finished, she put her pajamas on and peeled back the layers and cool sheets and blankets from the bed. She crawled in and proceeded to once again tune into the brightly lit screen before her.

Before she knew it the clock had nearly reached eleven at night. The final episode of Prairie Friends was just coming on as she heard her mother's footsteps come up the stairs and abruptly stop outside Paige's door. Paige held her breath in anticipation, but nothing happened. Judith turned around and went back downstairs.

Paige settled her head down deeper into her pillow. Her breathing slowed and her eyes glazed over as she fixated on the glowing square box in the corner of her room. She drifted off to sleep, a sleep that wouldn't last long, not on a Friday night.

Sometime after one in the morning Paige awoke. She had been dreaming as Judith's shrill voice pulled her consciousness to the surface, placing it abruptly on top of the Prairie Friends bedspread.

"I can't stand you. I hate you. Do you know that? I hate you!" Judith screamed at Dave.

Paige's heart skipped a beat signaling the start of a race of it beating in her chest. She sat up in her bed drawing her knees up to her chest and wrapping her arms tightly around her drawn legs.

"Please stop, please stop, I don't want this to happen, not again. Please stop, please stop," Paige chanted over and over to no avail.

The wheels were put into motion at quitting time earlier in the day and wouldn't stop until something or someone was hurt.

She got up from her warm bed and slowly moved toward the door. Judith and Dave's voices were reduced to mere muffles through the closed wooden barrier, but once opened, Paige would succumb to every syllable, every utterance made below.

Curiosity is innate in every human, and she was no exception. With everything in her small body telling her not to, she grabbed the handle to her door, held her breath, and opened it.

With the door opened the mute button flicked off and muffles became words. Words which were meant to inflict pain on the receiver.

"You're nothing but a drunk Judith, do you know that?" Dave said.

Dave loved his wife, of course he did, even enough to leave his own before they were divorced. He fell in love with Judith's drive, her tenacity which bordered on bitchiness. When she drank, however, he quickly forgot that woman he met in a corner

31

neighborhood bar.

Judith had come into the bar that day when Dave was still bartending. He took a long drag on a cigarette after finishing up with a customer and Judith's tight denim jeans had caught his eye. All it took was a hello, and he was hooked from there. Her brooding eyes were enough to lead Dave on a long road of adultery and poor choices.

Judith was in the process of her own divorce from Paige's father and missed the comfort that male company gave. Meeting Dave for her was like a bandage over her recently created wounds. He possessed edginess to him which she liked. It awoke something in her which had never been touched.

On this evening they were a million miles away from that first hello – Judith spewing forth venomous accusations and statements at Dave; Dave receiving those statements with increasing anger.

"Damn you Judith, just leave me alone. Enough is enough," Dave warned. His voice increased in volume with each passing moment.

"Please mommy, please just stop. Don't do it," Paige pleaded to herself. "Don't get yourself in trouble."

Paige began to tremble. Trembling turned into shaking so violent that if a person unknowingly stepped into the picture at that moment they would swear she was convulsing.

The powers that be were not in Paige's favor that night. Judith continued on her tirade until Paige heard her mother cry out in pain. Paige's bedroom door shuddered against the jamb as bodies thudded against the wall downstairs.

"Mommy, mommy no," Paige's voice faltered.

The stinging hot tears began to flow freely down her cheeks. The terrified girl spun around on her heels and headed blindly for the closet door. She felt for the door handle, flung the heavy wooden door open and swiftly closed it behind her. The dark, empty space she had skipped over earlier, now fulfilled its purpose.

She began bargaining with God. "I swear I will be a good

girl. I will do everything you want. Please just let my mommy be safe, please." Paige would make many more such statements in the years to come to no avail. And as such, she would continue to feel as if Friday nights were her fault.

Paige's breaths came in heaves as she pressed her hands as hard she could against her ears. She felt so alone. She wished that James Michael were back. Judith and Dave never fought like this with him around.

In the safety of her darkened closet Paige gradually released her hands from her ears. An eerie silence greeted her. She sat huddled in that dark corner of her closet until her legs turned to pins and needles. Her breathing slowed and her heart returned to a regular rhythm. The race was almost over.

Paige counted in a whispery voice to herself. First by twos, then by threes. She loved numbers. Numbers to her represented order; twisted and turned they could still be set straight again.

The house had been quiet for nearly a half hour. Paige knew it was time for her to emerge from her sanctuary and assess the damage. Uncrossing her stiffened legs she stretched each one out, first separately, then simultaneously. Pains shot up her legs as the circulation began to flow freely through her veins again. She crawled out of her closet staying close to the brown shag carpeted floor. Her room was dark except for the bright hallway looking for a way under her bedroom door. She emerged much like those tornado survivors do in the wake of a severe storm, standing on what was once a solid home, now only foundation showing for all the world to see.

As she did every Friday night, Paige drew a deep breath in and walked toward her bedroom door. She stopped just short of the door, tucked her hair behind her right ear and leaned inwards until the cool wooden door was pressed tightly against her ear. There was no ocean sound like when she put her ear next to a large conch shell. There was nothing, just silence.

She opened her door; the hallway light rushing into her room and surrounding her. But that was her only greeter. She poked her head into the empty space of the hallway and again heard nothing.

Turning the corner of the hall, she quietly tiptoed down the staircase. Reaching the living room she saw the glow of the television casting shadows on the white walls. Every light was turned off and there was no sound on the television. Paige hoped everyone had gone to sleep.

A few more steps and Paige reached the kitchen. Her hopes were dashed as Judith was found in the old wooden rocker in the corner. Small sobs were making their way from Judith's throat to the heavy, indoor air. She stared off into the corner, gently rocking.

"Mommy? Mommy? Mommy are you okay?" Paige asked.

Judith did not answer. She couldn't. The words would not come, no matter how hard she wanted them to. A combination of alcohol induced mental stupor and trauma from what just happened created a roadblock against any communication.

"Mommy, please answer me, I'm scared." Paige began to feel the lump rise in her throat. She did not like this, not one bit.

The rocker continued a back and forth motion in bondage to its human occupant. There was no stopping, not now.

"Mommy, I need to know if you're okay. Should I call Auntie?" Paige asked.

"No sweetie, no," Judith responded to Paige in a tiny voice. She clutched her left arm tightly. A blood stained towel was tightly wrapped around it. Of course there was no pain, but once the effects of the alcohol wore off there certainly would be.

Paige edged closer to her mom. "What happened to your arm mommy?"

"I'm so sorry Paige, mommy doesn't mean to have this happen."

"What mommy?" asked Paige.

Judith continued to weep as she tried to answer Paige's questions. There was no good answer. How do you explain to a seven year old that your husband beats you up because you're a chronic alcoholic and get in fights with him every Friday night when you drink to excess?

34

"Paige, I don't know what to say. I want to leave so bad."

Judith grew silent. As if her mind had willed it to be, the legs of the rocker froze midstride. Judith turned her eyes toward Paige, fixating on the little girl's coarse auburn hair falling lightly on her shoulders.

"Get your shoes on Paige, we're leaving."

Paige knew this part already; in fact, she had anticipated it ever since stepping out of her bomb shelter of a closet.

"Yes mommy." With the practice of a fireman prompted into action by the firehouse bell, Paige turned on her heels and flew up the stairs as quickly as her long, narrow feet would take her.

She flung open her bedroom door and making her way to her closet to slip on her Stylon shoes over socked feet. Paige dropped to her knees and felt under her bed for her duffel bag.

Judith went into the utility room and stared at herself in the mirror. She hated how she looked. In one word she summed it up - old. No, two words, old and fat. "That's why he doesn't like me. I deserve every bit of this," she said to herself. She removed the blood soaked rag and wrapped it up in a paper sack, stuffing it as far down into the laundry hamper as she could. As she pulled her arm up from the bottom of the clothes, she brushed her hand against a cool, glass liquor bottle. Her hand grabbed the bottle and finished pulling it up from the depths of the soiled laundry. She held it up in front of the light, just as a fisherman pulls his prize catch from the lake. It had the same red and white label on it that Paige had become too familiar with.

Judith became entranced in the label of the bottle and for a brief moment became lost in time. "Paige, hurry up for god's sakes," Judith bellowed from the bottom of the stairs.

"I'm coming mommy," Paige replied.

Paige stuffed Dynowoman and her pillow into her duffel bag and went back downstairs, not wanting to be left in the house alone. She grabbed her coat off of the armchair by the front door and followed her mom out the door into the cool night air. The air was damp and the ground slick with dew.

Judith started the car and Paige arranged her pillow next to the door.

"Paige, don't be so stupid. Lock your damn door and don't lean against it. It could come open you know. We never have anything nice to drive thanks to Dave." Judith had no regard that her blood alcohol levels were nearly twice the legal limit. No, all Judith cared about was some neurotic ritual her own mother had taught her as a young child. Locked doors. Locked doors in a car, just like the locked doors in their house. Memories neatly tucked away, out of sight and only opened by the owner.

Paige double checked the lock on the door, pulled her pillow from the duffel bag and moved the soft cotton rectangle to the space between herself and her mom in the car. Settling her head down on the pillow, she watched the glow of the dash lights until her eyes became heavy. It wouldn't be long and she would be safe; it would be okay.

Judith's heavy breathing was drowned out by the sound of the tires on the pavement. She focused hard on the broken yellow lines in front of the car's headlights.

Paige drifted off to sleep; awaking to the dome light of the car's interior shining down on her face. As her sight came into focus, she fixed on the face in front of her. Judith was staring down at Paige.

"Mommy? Mommy, what?" Paige asked.

Judith did not reply. She had only wanted to capture this moment, a snapshot in time, of her beautiful daughter sleeping. She couldn't even get that right; Paige had woken up as soon as the dome light shown. Judith thought to herself about how much she didn't want Paige to end up like her – dependent on some man, afraid to take chances, just plain stupid and uneducated.

"Come on sweetie, we need to get going in," Judith said, her breath powerfully pointed at her daughter.

Paige grabbed her pillow and stuffed it into her duffel bag.

She followed her mom across the stone steps and up the wooden stairs to the small house. Judith knocked on the hollow steel and plastic front door until the porch light flickered on. Paige heard the sounds of someone unlocking the chains and then the door handle clicked and turned.

"Auntie, it's you," Paige said from behind her mom's coat, upon seeing her Aunt's face behind the opening door.

"Judith, oh my gosh, do you know what time it is?" Paige's Aunt said in response to seeing them on the front porch.

"Yes, I do sis, I've got Paige here with me, please let me in." Paige came out from behind her mom's coat and stood square in front of her Aunt Janice.

Looking down at Paige standing there cloaked in innocence, Janice's voice softened. "Yeah, I'm sorry, alright, come on in. Paige, you know where to go, the extra bed is always made up in there. Jude, you've got some explainin' to do girl."

Judith was grateful that her sister had chosen not to hold a full inquisition there on the front steps, rather, she would wait until later, and it would be twice as lengthy.

Janice took their coats, hung them on the coat tree, and headed behind the partition to the kitchen. "Are you hungry?" she called from behind the wall.

"No, we're fine," Judith replied for both of them.

"It's late Paige," Judith said turning to her daughter, "you need to get in bed."

"Is the spare bed still made up in the girls' room?" Judith asked her sister.

"Yeah, go ahead Paige, its waiting for you honey" Janice replied. Janice was much different than her sister. They were only a year apart, but Janice was still the older of the two, and certainly the wiser.

Paige made her way down the long paneled hallway to the last door on the left. In the dark she felt the cool metal knob and turned it to open the faux door into the room. Her cousin's snores were barely audible as she made her way to the twin bed on the opposite side of the narrow room. Paige sat on the edge of the bed and pulled her pillow from her bag and placed it neatly at the top of the bed. She lay down on the bed and pushed her shoes off of her feet. Her blue Stylon's dropped with a hollow thud to the floor.

With one heavy sigh her body began to relax. Paige closed her eyes and waited for the words in her head to slow down. She hoped her mom didn't come back until Sunday. In secret she hoped her mom never came back and she got to live here with her Auntie forever. At her Auntie's, Paige never had to enter the field of flowers. The words in Paige's head never really slowed down, something that would become a hallmark of her personality in years to come, but she eventually drifted off to sleep anyway.

5 SPILLED MILK

"Good morning Omaha, this is your favorite morning crew, the John and Ron show. Great to have you with us this morning, hope you're waking up to...."

Paige reached over and succeeded in silencing the morning radio wake up crew which had haughtily invaded the last moments of any real sleep. Sleep eluded Paige on most nights, coming on only in the last hours before she was due to wake up and start her day.

"Derek," Paige's voice crackled.

She cleared it and tried again. "Derek hon, come on, the alarm went off, time to get up." She rolled over and looked at the back his head. His short, sandy brown hair always looked the way it did before he went to sleep. "*Lucky*," Paige thought to herself. She poked her finger into her husband's shoulder. There was no response.

"Derek?"

"Fine, I'm not your mother; if you're late you're late. I have plenty more responsibilities in this house besides making sure you're up" Paige continued on, talking to Derek's back.

Paige swung her legs over the side of the bed letting them hang until the blood pulsated in protest at the tips of her toes. She looked out the window over the tops of the tall trees across the street. How she longed to be a bird flying above the treetops, so free, so light.

"Hi Mommy." It was Lindsay, bright eyed and wide awake as always, peeking around the corner of Paige's now open bedroom door.

"Good morning sweetie," Paige replied.

"Hi Daddy."

"Daddy?" Lindsay asked again.

Paige stared at Derek under a mountain of covers moving up and down in rhythm to his breathing.

Lindsay waited momentarily and then she was gone again, down the hall with lightning speed, not waiting around for a response from her father.

"Jesus Derek, you don't have to talk to me in the morning...that I get, but your own daughter? Really? You just want to ignore her?"

Derek continued to lay there shutting the world out around him. He hoped Paige would grow tired of his silence and eventually leave the room declaring defeat. And that she did, precisely two minutes after that thought entered and then left his mind.

He groaned in protest as the long fingers of morning light made their way into the heavily shaded room. He rolled over onto his back and stared up at the gently turning blades of the ceiling fan. "This is my life? Humph. What shit." Derek rolled back onto his side, pulling the covers tightly over his head and hoped for sleep to take back over. It didn't, reality set in, he was awake. Another day, much like a nightmare that didn't end. How he hated life.

Paige pulled her long, curly hair back into a ponytail and slipped into her silky white robe. Shuffling down the hall, letting her feet absorb the cool tiled floor underneath, she made her way to the kitchen. Flipping the switch on the coffee maker she watched the little orange light glow with anticipation of a freshly brewed cup of coffee.

Paige glanced down the hall at Lindsay, sitting in front of her television in her room. It was 6:30a.m. and Paige knew it would only be a matter of time before Aaron awoke as well. A shadow appeared in the hallway, it was Derek, making his way to the shower.

Paige knew it was now or never. She took a coffee cup from the cupboard and carefully poured the dark liquid, into her favorite mug, which would soon course through her veins. One last look at Lindsay glued to her television, and Paige made her way to the basement.

This was perhaps the highlight of Paige's day. In the doldrums of housewife suburbia, Paige had found her outlet, her comfort in this world, one that was neither moral nor ethical, but for Paige it gave her a reason to look forward to the next sunrise.

Paige toggled the mouse connected to the computer. The machine whirred and whined in response to the command and soon the screen lit the dark basement like the morning sun. The family cat, Butterscotch, yawned, stretched and gave a scowl Paige's way presumably for disturbing his early morning slumber.

"What?" Paige asked the ball of fur on the couch, "You are just a cat you know."

She picked up her coffee cup with her left hand, slowly sipping the java while quickly executing a series of clicks with her right hand on the mouse. Ah, the beauty of multitasking. Her eyes darted left and right until she came to her login screen. With the precision of a brain surgeon, she quickly entered her user name and password. The icons on the screen danced in front of her. Endorphins in Paige's brain joined the dance in response. The screen stopped moving, she held her breath, and then the welcome screen arrived. There, she was in. Just a few more moments, Paige would know how her evening would play out.

"You have new messages," displayed the banner across the computer screen. "Yes," Paige squealed in delight. Butterscotch was quite done with the interruption and promptly jumped off the couch. Giving Paige one last dirty look, he lumbered up the stairs until he was out of sight.

Paige clicked on the messages and scrolled down the screen until she found the name she was looking for – lonleyguy38. It was him. Her heart skipped a beat in excitement.

She read his message in earnest. "Hi sweetie, I hope your night was well and your morning was even better. I am looking very forward to seeing you tonight. Can you still make it? I'll call you just before I leave work. See you soon, Len." Paige read his words over and over in her imagination, matching his voice to the written images on the screen.

Pulled away from her mission, Paige heard Aaron's screams funnel their way downstairs to where she sat at the computer desk. Her solitude – her moment – was broken. She grabbed the mouse and closed out programs in reverse of her actions of just three minutes ago. Careful not to leave any tracks, Paige pushed the chair into the desk, grabbed her coffee cup, and headed back upstairs to get Aaron from his crib. Morning was in full swing, Paige taking on the brunt of the duties while Derek continued on in his own world.

Paige rounded the corner of the basement steps into the kitchen. There she found Lindsay, still in pajamas, hair uncombed, clutching her stuffed rabbit in one hand and twisting her long locks of hair with the other.

"I'll get you breakfast in just a minute sweetie. Would you please go into Aaron's room and talk to him for mommy so he won't scream all morning?" Lindsay dutifully whirled around on her heels and skipped off towards her brother's room.

Meanwhile Paige poured a bowl of rainbow colored Fruit Rings, added some milk and placed it on Lindsay's tray. She walked down the hall towards her room calling for Lindsay.

"Come on, it's ready. You can watch TV in mommy's room this morning."

Lindsay appeared around the corner and climbed up onto Paige's tall poster bed, sinking in the large down comforter.

"Please don't spill Lindsay, I really don't want to have to deal with your daddy this morning." Derek was in the bathroom getting ready for work, oblivious to his family activities.

Still in her robe, Paige focused her attention on Aaron.

42

Glancing at the clock, she was already running fifteen minutes behind.

"All right little man, mommy's here to get you."

Paige pulled Aaron from his crib. The house was slow to warm up in the morning and his cheeks had a red chapped complexion from crying in the cool indoor air. He sucked on his lower lip, still giving Paige that look of complete forlornness of having been ignored for so long.

"I'm so sorry Aaron. Mommy tries to do everything for everyone. Sometimes that just doesn't work out."

Paige went to the fridge with Aaron attached firmly to her hip. She grabbed a pre-made bottle, shook it and waved it in Aaron's face.

"Is this what you've been waiting for big boy?" Aaron's eyes lit up and a smile shown on his face.

"I thought so," said Paige as she gave the bottle to its eagerly awaited recipient.

She walked past the clock in the kitchen on the way back to Aaron's room.

"Crap, I've got to get going."

Hurriedly she made it to the nursery and placed him on the floor to change him into his clothes for the day. Aaron continued sucking on the milk with complete contentment. Once finished, Paige picked him back up and placed him in his crib while she headed for the shower. Derek was out of the bathroom now making noise in the kitchen. She checked on Lindsay who was still happily chomping down her Fruit Rings while watching the images dance on the television set in front of her.

Paige slipped her robe off in the bathroom and pulled her nightgown over her head. Turning toward the mirror she ran her hands lightly across her collarbone and then further down across the area which socially defined her as a woman. She stared at the image momentarily and then looked away in disgust. How she hated her own body. No longer was she that young woman who could run like the wind. No, Paige now felt her mortality, she was a mother, a wife, part of the herd, part of the masses – just Paige – not really even feminine anymore, certainly not desirable to her own husband. He made that very clear. Stepping into the shower she continued on with her self-defeating thoughts, plucked from them only when the water started to run cold.

She stepped out of the shower, dried off with the beige terrycloth towel, put her robe back on, and headed into her bedroom. Lindsay was still glued to the glowing square box in front of her.

"Come on Lindsay, go to your room and get dressed, mommy is really running behind now."

Lindsay remained lost in the animation in front of her, completely unaware that her mother had even entered the room.

"Lindsay. Lindsay, please." Still no response.

"Lindsay!" Paige barked in desperation.

Lindsay jumped, spilling the bowl of milk onto the tray which in turn funneled itself to one side, forming a milky white river until finally making its stop on the pink and lime green down comforter below it.

"Dammit Lindsay, you're gonna get mommy in trouble," Paige hissed under her breath.

At that same moment Derek walked into the bedroom to get his sports jacket. Paige froze in place as she waited for Derek to lower the boom once he realized what had happened to the comforter.

Lindsay started to get up from the bed, the edge of her nightgown soaked in cereal encrusted milk. Holding her breath Paige looked at Derek who in turn was studying the comforter. Time was slowing to nearly a halt. She braced for what was coming next.

It was too quiet in the bedroom. Derek turned away from the closet and studied his wife and Lindsay for clues to the silence. Paige's eyes darted to the comforter and back to the floor. Dammit, she knew she had given it away right then.

"What the hell happened here?" Derek asked.

Paige's legs felt heavy as she tried to move closer to Lindsay with the instinctive protection of a mother bear over her cub.

"Lindsay, what did you do? Tell daddy now," Derek demanded, his voice rising with each syllable.

Lindsay's eyes welled up with tears and she started shaking. Heart thumping, Paige jumped in rapidly spewing out words as fast as she could spin the tale in her mind.

"Nothing Derek...I was reaching for Lindsay's tray when I...I...tripped over these shoes at the foot of the bed. I knocked the milk over, not Lindsay."

Derek stood squarely in front of Paige, studying her unwavering stance for what seemed like eternity. He was reading every square inch of her body looking for some sign of deceit.

"*Damn time, why doesn't it move?*" Paige thought to herself in this standoff.

Satisfied she wasn't lying to him, he reached for his sports coat in the closet, turned, and walked out of the room without another word.

Paige's legs unstiffened thus buckling underneath her. She caught herself on the edge of the bed, gripping hard onto the wooden footboard. Another crisis averted.

"Lindsay, please go to your room and get dressed. Mommy already laid your clothes out on your dinosaur chair," Paige asked this time in a much smaller, pleading tone of voice. For once, Lindsay did as she was asked.

Paige heard the front door close a few minutes later. Peering out from the window shade she watched her husband head down the steps and out onto the street where his car was parked.

"Bye to you too," Paige said to a now empty room.

Collecting her thoughts, she gave one final glance at the clock and hurriedly finished getting herself ready for the morning. She went into the kitchen and checked the coffee pot and stove. Scooping up Aaron from his crib, she hollered for Lindsay to come downstairs and get into the car. Another check of both appliances and she grabbed her purse from the landing as she hurried out the door. Children safely in the car Paige felt the urge to go back in one more time.

"Lindsay, please don't touch a thing, mommy will be right back." Anxiety driven compulsion plagued Paige relentlessly.

The now frazzled young mother went back into the house and headed straight for the kitchen. Unplugging the coffeemaker she went to the stove next. Out loud she announced to the house "The stove is off. No burners are on. No light is on to indicate a burner would be on. I can leave now." With that she whirled around on her heels and dashed out the front door to her vehicle.

Paige arrived at daycare, now fully twenty minutes behind schedule. She dropped Lindsay and Aaron off, gave a kiss to each and headed down the road for her morning commute. Getting onto the interstate Paige tapped her fingers to the guitar clashing sounds emitting from speakers on either side of her. She was now on auto pilot, reversing her course of the night before, the herd surrounding her on all sides, jockeying for a position within the striped yellow lines.

Paige pulled her boxey black truck into one of the last spots in the parking lot. "Thank God for small miracles," she said to herself. Not only had she found the parking spot but she was also only four minutes late as of now. Pulling in right next to her was her co-worker Nate. She watched as he adjusted his sunglasses in the mirror, running his long fingers through his short black hair just before he opened his car door. Apparently satisfied, Paige pulled her gaze away from him and stepped out of her own car.

Paige liked to study Nate. Below his head of black hair lie two bushy eyebrows canvassing dark brown eyes with the longest lashes she had ever seen on a man. His nose flared out, at times almost matching that wide grin. A cleft in his chin finished his self-portrait. His voice deep and shoulders broad, Paige felt herself drawn to him, an emotional connection that she rarely felt with any human. He was unassuming, non-judgmental and completely accepting of Paige as she was.

"Good morning Nate, how ya doin'?" Paige asked.

"Oh hey there Paige, oh you know the cliché, another day, another dollar, or shall we say dime around here" he responded walking up to hold the door for her.

Paige and Nate worked together, along with six other co-workers at a social service agency providing assistance to low-income women and their families. It was a job that paid little in the way of monetary gains, but made up for it with intrinsic rewards. Paige's father simply called her a bleeding heart liberal social worker. He always told Paige she should've been an engineer, someone who used their mind, not their heart.

Paige walked in the doorway ahead of Nate. His stride was longer than hers, so he always overtook her by the third row of cubicles.

"Talk to ya later, have a good one," Nate said to Paige as they parted ways.

"Yeah, thanks, you too" Paige replied.

Paige navigated the beige and grey room dividers until she found her own assigned daytime residence. Before she sat down at her desk, she glanced over at her supervisor sitting just a few dividers away. Paige knew she was late and felt a twinge of guilt as her supervisor looked past Paige's shoulder length hair towards the clock behind her. Paige avoided direct eye contact and sat down in the stiff backed roller chair. She scanned her desk for the day's work. The orange message light on the phone blinked in unison to Paige's heartbeat. Her inbox looked as if it would scream out in protest if one more item was bestowed upon it. It was only eight o'clock in the morning, how was she going to make it through the next fourteen hours.

At a crossroads, Paige hoped for some interruption, something which would prevent her from having to tackle what lay on the metal and fake wood laminate table in front of her.

"Good morning Paigester, how goes it?"

"Oh, thank you God, that wasn't quite what I was thinking," Paige said quietly in response to seeing her melodramatic co-worker Rebecca walk in. The world, not to mention this office, revolved around Rebecca's life.

"What was that sweetie? I didn't hear you. Did you say something?" Rebecca asked Paige.

"I said good morning Rebecca. Did you find a parking spot okay?" Paige asked with feigned interest.

"Why yes I did, right up front in fact. Besides, wouldn't I still be in my car if I hadn't? And Paige, haven't I told you its Becca. Call me Becca. All my friends do."

Rebecca's overly rouged cheeks puffed out like a fish when she pronounced the 'b' sound in Becca. She was wearing a long sleeved silky print shirt tucked in at the waist of her nylon khaki colored pants. Blunt tipped black boots peeked out from under the cuffs of her pants. Her hair was tucked back off her shoulders with a matching silk scarf to hide the majority of her thin, mousey brown hair, rounding out her office casual outfit.

Phone ringing, Paige wheeled her chair around so Rebecca couldn't see her puffing her cheeks out as she replied, "Okay, yes, Becca, sorry."

"Good morning, this is Paige," she said into the mouthpiece. It was Lois at the front desk.

"Hey, there's a gentlemen calling on the line…I believe it's Leeennn" she drawled out slowly in the most teasingly seductive accent she could come up with.

"Crap, really?" said Paige straightening up in her chair. "I don't even have my lipstick on yet" she replied to Lois.

Lois laughed on the other end. "He's on the phone, not at the front door."

"I know I was just messing around, put him through."

Paige fidgeted in her chair feeling like she was watching eternity pass in the microsecond it took to connect the two phone lines.

"Hello?" she said in an upbeat, too much coffee type of morning voice.

"Hey there Paige, it's Len."

"Oh hi, you're calling earlier than I expected."

At that same time, Nate came around the corner trying to make a beeline for Paige's desk without Rebecca interrupting his mission. He was just about there, only one tan filing cabinet to go, but it was too late, she spotted him.

"Good morning Natester. I haven't seen you yet today. Were you hiding from me?" Rebecca asked her head bobbing from side to side like some dash ornament for a car.

"Good morning Becca. No, I wasn't hiding. Considering we're only eleven minutes into the eight hour workday, I haven't had my chance to make the morning rounds yet" Nate replied in a flattened tone.

"Oh don't worry Natester, I would've found you eventually."

It was funny how much a married woman would carry on flirtatiously to a married man. Certainly red flag signs of someone embroiled in a failing marriage.

Nathan dismissed her conversation as soon as he could. There were more important things in his day than listening to what came out of Rebecca's mouth. Worse yet was that Rebecca had no idea no one in the office cared what she said or did, only that she provided entertainment in her idiocy.

Nate hovered and then plunked down on a corner square of Paige's desk, his long fingers tapping quietly on his leg to a random song in his head. Nate was a would be writer moonlighting as a social worker by day. He actually shared a number of poems and short stories he composed with Paige that were pretty good. She always pretended his literary works were filled with mediocrity so as he would have to work for her approval. She loved it.

Paige hardly noticed Nate had come to rest on her desk. She looked up at him, covered the speaker part of the phone with one hand and whispered she would be done in a minute.

"No problemo," he nodded back. Nate was patient, especially when it came to Paige. Something about her brought him to a peacefulness he had not felt in years.

"So, are we still on for tonight?" Paige asked Len.

"Yeah sweetheart, we sure are. Say 6:30pm at the Iron Rail Restaurant downtown?"

"Yeah Len, I can't wait."

Nate sat there taking in the conversation, mouthing Paige's words as he wrapped his arms around himself making kissing motions with his ruddy lips. Paige playfully slapped Nate giving him that 'you're gonna get it' look moms are so famous for.

"Me too," Len replied.

"Bye."

"Bye," said Paige. She hung up the receiver, fighting to harness the butterflies swarming her stomach.

"Oh Paige, you are the greatest ever," Nate said with his wide grin.

"Oh Nate, you are the biggest ass ever," she retorted back.

"Only if I get to play the big, manly stud horse," said Nate.

"Sure, anytime," Paige replied. "Now if you don't mind, I have work to do. Some of us come to this establishment to work you know."

"Who…where…point them out and they will be tried and hung."

"Did you come to my assigned cubicle for a reason other than to harass me, or are you just bored?"

"I had a purpose, I'm sure I did. Forgotten now, way too much smoke last night – losing memory cells in the ole' noggin by the day you know."

"Yes I do Nate, I worry about you" said Paige.

"Worry, I'd say I rather worry about you Paige. Please be careful with this guy, dangerous territory you know. Don't wanna see you boiling rabbits."

"Okay dad."

"I mean it Paige," Nate said with seriousness in his voice that rarely shows.

Paige paused and then locked her gaze with Nate's, "Of course I will. I'm a survivor Nate, just like you. Don't worry about a thing."

Sensing the gravity of the conversation turned intense, Nate jumped up onto the industrial carpeted floor, flicked a pen off of Rebecca's desk and rounded the divider wall out of sight.

"I'll be careful, I promise," Paige said to the scented trail Nate left behind him. "I always am."

6 PREPARATION AND POLITE CONVERSATION

Paige stared at the matching black hands of the clock, one short, one long, sharing space with equally black numbers on a white background. Only five more revolutions on that face to go and it would be time to leave. She could hardly wait.

Now four minutes. Ring, ring. It was her desk phone. "What the hell? Really? Don't people know not to call this close to the end of the day?" Paige asked herself.

She picked the receiver up and put it to her left ear. "Hello?" she said into the plastic mouthpiece.

"Hey Paige, it's mom."

It was Judith. She was supposed to watch Aaron and Lindsay for Paige tonight. She hoped her mother wouldn't screw this up. There was no cause for concern though, because one thing Judith was good at was keeping secrets and telling lies. It was a family tradition – everything nice and good on the outside, but hollow and baseless on the inside.

"Hi mom, what's goin' on? Everything okay?"

"Oh yes, everything is fine. I just wanted to get it clear one last time. You're going out with the girls after work and then doing some Christmas shopping, right?"

"Yes mom, you got it. Thank you so much."

After a short pause, Judith continued, "I was there once

Paige, you know. I feel so much for what you go through. This is the least I can do."

Rather than risk any form of emotional connection with her mother, Paige abruptly ended the conversation.

"Thanks again mom. Call my cell if you need anything. I have to hang up now, it's five o'clock and I've got to lock up the building. Responsibility you know, it's a big thing."

Judith seemed satisfied with Paige's reason for ending the conversation and hung up without incident. Paige was relieved.

Little hand on the five, big hand on the twelve. Time to go. Paige picked up the receiver on the phone, punched in a series of numbers, waited for the beeps and hung up. The phones had been forwarded for the evening.

"Pity the client that calls now", she thought.

Paige grabbed her keys from her desk drawer and made her way out the back door where industrial office carpet met parking lot concrete. She caught her breath as the door opened into the chilly evening air. Clicking the alarm on the truck she pulled on the silver handle to open the door. In the back seat lay her blue striped duffel bag. Paige would soon make the same transformation in the office bathroom.

Paige re-entered the office building and followed the corridors of beige walls and fluorescent lighting until she reached the bathroom. She stepped into the women's restroom and quickly began to strip down. Slipping off her brown loafers, Paige unzipped her khaki pants and sat down on the edge of the toilet to push down her pants. They fell to the floor exposing her white ankle length socks. She slipped each sock off exposing freshly painted crimson red toes. Shivering as the bottoms of her feet touched the cold tiled floor beneath her, Paige pulled her white polo t-shirt over her head.

Her white cotton bra was next to go. A soft, lacey white bra was put on in place of it. Paige put on a matching pair of white lace panties; in fact, these were the same ones she had worn on her wedding night to Derek. The bra, however, was new. Apparently

53

Paige had not read the top ten list of surefire signs your spouse is cheating on you. If she had, she would've known that new undergarments, sexy or pretty, ranked high on the list, especially when worn in privacy from one's spouse.

Reaching further into the duffel bag, Paige pulled out her form fitting black slacks and a grape purple spandex and nylon shirt which hugged her body in all the places it needed to. She stepped into the pants one leg at a time and slowly pulled them up to her waist where she fastened the black button. Paige ran her hands down the front of her stomach and around to her backside as she admired herself in the mirror.

"Not too bad for near thirty" she complimented herself.

Next came the shirt. Paige studied herself in the mirror, glad to see her womanhood was still above the waterline. She finished her ritual with a full complement of makeup, hairspray, earrings and necklace. Stepping into her black high heeled shoes Paige emerged from the bathroom a new woman, one of superhero proportions. She needed to be in order to face what lay ahead that night.

Just as with the phones, she entered a combination of numbers on the alarm's keypad until it beeped back in response. Her heart fluttered just a bit as she stepped across the threshold out into the nearly dark evening sky; she was on her way.

Paige navigated rush hour traffic as if she was taking a country drive through the Swiss Alps. Visions of Lenny danced in her head. Paige wondered what the conversation would turn to tonight - sports, politics, religion, his wife, her husband?

Paige had met Lenny innocently enough one night as she browsed the personals on one of the Internet dating websites. She was only looking because one of her co-workers had just gone on a date with a man she had met online. Internet dating was in its infancy and Paige was curious to see what kind of people would put their lives on the superhighway for anyone to pick up along the way.

Lenny's sight was headlined *Married Man, lonely, looking for someone to share good times with.* His personal ad had a grainy, black and white dated profile picture of him. Paige was intrigued as to why a married man would so boldly advertise his needs in such a sneaky yet equally competing honest manner. She replied that night to his ad, and one meeting and several phone calls later, they were three hours shy of ending up in bed together.

She shook her head in disgust at herself and turned her attention back on to finding parking. It was dark now and Paige worried about walking alone very far from her car to the restaurant at night. Glancing down at the clock, she decided to suck it up and pay to park in the parking garage.

Pulling up to the red and white striped bar resting at eye level Paige greeted the parking lot attendant with a nervous smile. She scanned his face, hoping she didn't know him. Paige was always nervous meeting Len; she didn't want anything getting back to Derek. In her mind what she was doing was okay, it was necessary in fact for her daily survival, but she didn't think Derek would see it that way. In fact, Derek would quickly put an end to life as Paige knew it. He was smart, vengeful, and hated to lose; it was a deadly combination.

"That'll be five dollars ma'am."

Paige avoided direct eye contact with the attendant and stuck a crisp five dollar bill out her truck window. In exchange, the heavily clothed employee pushed the button releasing the striped bar from its horizontal position.

Paige pulled in to the first spot she found, wrote her spot number on her ticket and tucked the ticket into the zipper pocket of her purse. She checked her lipstick once more in her mirror, fluffed her hair and brushed some lint from the sleeve of her shirt.

She pulled her black pea coat tight around her and opened the truck door into the increasingly cold night air. Walking briskly over the cobblestone streets, Paige made her way to where Lenny had promised to meet her, an upscale bar and grill named the Iron Rail. Heavy wooden doors opened to warm air laden with the buzz of happy hour voices and the clank of silverware against dinner plates. Paige breathed in the aromas and scanned the dimly lit restaurant for her suitor. She didn't have to look far; Lenny was standing off to the left with his hands in the pockets of his leather coat and a smile on his face. He walked straight over to Paige and gave her a long hug.

"How's my sweetie tonight? Did you have any problem parking?" Lenny asked Paige looking straight into her eyes for the answer.

"Yeah, no problem at all. Parking always sucks; I had to park in the parking garage. How 'bout you?" Paige asked.

"Oh I found a place just around the corner, lucked out I guess," Lenny replied.

"Can I take your coat for you?" Lenny asked.

"Yeah, that would be nice, thank you."

Paige was hoping the whole night wouldn't be full of nervous small talk.

"Sir, your table for two is ready," the hostess said to Len. "You can follow me," she said leading them up the stairs to a cozy table with one lit candle on it overlooking the bar below. The hostess set the menus down as Len pulled the chair out for Paige.

"Here you are."

"Thank you Len" Paige said sitting down in the cushioned chair.

Len pulled the chair out across from her and sat down studying Paige's face. He was amazed by her style and presence, a far cry from his matronly wife who no longer took the time to fix her hair or impress him in the least. He nervously wanted to make a good impression on Paige; let her know that he was still a good man even though he was committing a mortal sin.

"So did you find the place okay?" Len began the dinner conversation with the polite "nice to meet ya" intro.

"Yes, I did" Paige said watching the busser pour water into the glass. As soon as the young girl walked away, Paige picked up the water glass and took a long drink. Her mouth was as dry as the desert Southwest on a midsummer night.

"Good, I'm glad you did. Have you been here before?" Len

asked.

"No, but I did read the reviews of the restaurant online before I got here. Apparently the eggplant parmesan is their signature dish. I've never had eggplant myself, but it has always looked appealing to me, especially pictures of it grilled" Paige replied.

"I've never had eggplant either, but I've heard it's good." Lenny looked around for the server. He spotted a woman with upswept hair in her late forties, with black slacks and a white shirt on. His eyes met hers and he motioned for her to come over to the table he and Paige were sitting at. Paige love how he took control, relieving her of the usual duty of doing so. It felt so great to be with a real man.

The server walked right over, pulled her notebook from a hidden pocket in her pants and smiled broadly at Paige and Lenny as she cleared her throat to give her speech.

"Good evening and welcome to the Iron Rail. My name is Glenda and I will be your server this evening. Our special tonight is the eggplant parmesan. It comes lightly brushed with a garlic butter cream sauce, seared to perfection over our hot, wood-fired grill and then laid in a bed of linguini noodles drenched in a white wine caper sauce. It comes with a side of lightly seasoned fresh vegetables and your choice of soup or salad. Our soup tonight is a creamy tomato basil made special by our chefs right here at the Iron Rail. What can I get you to start off with for drinks? We have one of the largest selections of on tap beers in the city as well as a variety of mixed drinks, or perhaps you'd like a soft drink" she said turning her head to Paige.

Ignoring the potential dig, Paige wondered if this woman had a stop or rewind button somewhere hidden in those black slacks as well. She was perfectly automated; didn't miss a single syllable in her introduction. "Bravo!" Paige thought to herself, *you are one of the herd.*"

Glenda the good server stood there, hovering over the table with pen to paper, waiting for either Len or Paige to speak first.

Len looked at Paige. "What would you like sweetie?"

"Um, water's fine for me for right now. Maybe I'll have something later" Paige replied. "I'm watching my figure you know, have to keep looking young somehow" Paige threw one back at her.

"I'll just have a beer on tap."

"What kind?" Glenda the good server asked.

"Um, surprise me," said Len. He wanted to show Paige that he had more to him than just your typical type A office personality. He wanted to be daring, bold, mysterious, and this was a start.

"Okay then, one water and one surprise on tap, coming right up" Glenda said with a peeled back smile showing over bleached teeth. Closing her notepad, she turned on her heels and walked away into the backdrop of conversations.

Lenny turned his attention back to Paige.

"Wow, you look amazing tonight. I'm not used to being out with such a professional looking woman." Lenny wished he could've come up with something better. *Really, professional, how stupid* he thought to himself.

"Thank you Len, you look pretty handsome yourself this evening. Don't smell too bad either."

They both sat there staring at the lit candle between them, absorbing the sounds which filled the air. Len reached his hand out to Paige's and fondly stroked her long fingers. He ran the tip of his index finger slowly up her hand and across her wrist. His touch, the music, the candlelight entranced Paige. She was taken back to a place that she had not visited in so long - intimacy.

The moment was quickly broken up by Glenda the good server. Her voiced seemingly boomed over the table, destroying the brief moment we both were sharing. Turning her body to Lenny, the server set a frothy glass of beer down on a cardboard disc.

"Here's your beer sir. I'm sure you'll be pleasantly surprised with the choice. I'm usually a pretty good judge of character."

Paige could not believe the irony here. *Are you serious?* she thought to herself. *Nobody but me could be cheating on their husband and have the waitress hit on the married man I'm cheating on with.*

The server turned to Paige, "Here's your water sweetie. Enjoy," she said empathically as she turned toward Lenny.

Still facing Lenny, the server asked "What can I get you to eat tonight?"

"Let's let the lady go first, shall we?" Lenny replied, motioning to Paige across the table.

"Certainly," Glenda replied stiffly, still not looking at Paige.

"Oh you're too sweet Len, such a gentlemen," Paige replied with satisfaction. Continuing on Paige looked straight at Glenda and said, "I think I'll have the special tonight Glenda. The way you described it was so out of this world, and I really think I'd like to try something new tonight." All the while Paige spoke, she slipped her high heel off and ran her silken stockinged leg up under Lenny's pant leg.

With much less drama, but a smile that equaled Paige's, Lenny ordered a steak, medium, backed potato and a salad drizzled in a raspberry vinaigrette. Glenda stood there for a moment, rocked back on her shoes and turned to walk away.

Lenny drew the glass of beer up to his mouth and took a long swallow. He set the glass down, took a breath and smiled at Paige warmly as he took her hands into his.

"I'm so excited to be out with you tonight Paige. Do you know that when I'm with you I feel ten years younger?"

"Good thing I don't feel the same Lenny, because that would make it illegal for you and me to be together."

Lenny laughed, "Ah, that's what I like about you, your quick wit."

"It's either a gift or a curse Len, I haven't figured it out yet."

Their conversation turned to their lives, their backgrounds, where each of them grew up. Words flowed easily and so did the alcohol. Lenny felt so relaxed with Paige, so wanted, something he hadn't felt in years with his own wife.

"So Len, I view you as the classic Type A personality, am I

wrong?" Paige asked.

"No, you are right on. I live by my planner."

"Really?"

"Yes, my life is sadly planned out for the next couple of months."

"Does that include your New Year's resolutions?"

"Why yes it does. I think the only thing I have in pencil still is whether or not to leave my wife."

Paige was quiet for a moment. She hadn't expected the conversation to turn to their spouse's. How could it not, after all, the two of them were breaking one of the most holy sacraments of marriage. "I guess that's where you and I are different. That part of my planner is in pen, there's just no date for it yet. I saw a lawyer before Aaron was born, but, well, Aaron sort of put a glitch in all that for now."

"Wow Paige, I haven't even gotten that far. To be quite honest, I'm afraid to. God, I want to leave her so badly, I really do, but she'd take me to the cleaners, she really would."

"Well, Lenny, I guess you need to make a list of priorities in your little planner there. What's it worth to ya? What means more to you, money or happiness? God knows money doesn't buy happiness, that's why we're left to choose."

Lenny took another drink of his beer. Glenda the good server appeared with their food. Perfect timing Lenny thought to himself.

Surprisingly Glenda was civil by this point. Perhaps there was another table with a younger couple to prey upon.

Paige and Lenny finished their meal the same way it had begun, polite conversation and plenty of handholding. Lenny ordered and drank two more beers, this time leaving no surprises.

Glenda the good server brought their check and placed the leather bound pocketbook down on the table cloth between Lenny and Paige. Paige reached out to grab it, but Lenny was too quick. "Allow me, please; it's the least I can do to repay you for the pleasure of your company."

"Wow Len, you'd better stop with those nice compliments or I might just start to like this a little too much."

"That's okay Paige, I want you to."

Lenny pulled out his billfold and thumbed through the plastic cards. Placing one inside the leather pocketbook for the server to take he leaned back in his chair and studied Paige. He didn't want this to end, not yet.

"Hey, what do you say we go for an after dinner drink somewhere? The night is still young, and I quite honestly am not ready for it to end just yet."

"Yeah sure, I know just the place - Mr. Hobbs'. It's right up the block from here."

Another server picked up Lenny's card and the bill and brought back the slip for him to sign. Apparently Glenda was either on break or done with her shift. Paige pictured her on a broom flying through the silver clouds on her way home. She giggled to herself.

Lenny signed the slip and put his credit card back into his billfold. "Ready to go?" he looked up at Paige.

"Yeah" she said taking her coat from the back of her chair.

"Let me get that for you," he said placing her coat across her shoulders.

Paige couldn't believe his manners. She felt like Cinderella waiting for the clock to strike twelve.

"Shall we?" Lenny said motioning to the front door of the restaurant.

"We shall," Paige said back with a smile.

7 CROSSING THE LINE

Paige and Lenny stepped out into the cold night air. They walked arm in arm past other couples seemingly in love. She led him along cobblestone paths past warmly lit windows. Lenny put his arm around Paige's shoulder as she snuggled in tighter against his chest. They walked in unison like two lovers who had been intertwined since the dawn of time. She felt so secure in his arms, a feeling she hadn't experienced in many years with Derek.

They arrived outside the cozy bar with inner lights shining warmly onto the street through heavy paned windows. Lenny opened the door for Paige and motioned with his arm for her to go first. She stepped into the bar and waited for Lenny to pick a spot. How she loved being with someone who wasn't afraid to make a decision.

Lenny pulled the chair out for Paige as she took off her coat and placed it neatly on the back of the chair.

"Thank you Len, you are such the gentleman," Paige said.

"Anything for you sweetie."

The cocktail waitress came over to their table and gave them both a quick "are you 21" glance. Paige was nearly 28, but still looked quite young. Seemingly satisfied she asked them what they wanted to drink.

"I'll have a beer," Lenny replied, "and the lady will

have…well, we'll let the lady decide."

"I'll have a hot buttered rum please."

The waitress walked away and the two of them sat in a comfortable, numbed silence. Just before the waitress came with their drinks, Paige excused herself to use the restroom. She stood up sucking her stomach in and pulling her shoulders back. She knew Lenny watched her walk all the way to the restroom, wanting her more with every step. She felt the lust coming from him and she couldn't wait to return it.

Lenny sat at the table and took a long drink of his beer. He too basked in the attention that Paige was giving him. Had his own wife done this for him, he wouldn't have to go elsewhere for it. It was she who had driven him to this point of having an affair.

Paige stood in the restroom and stared at her image in the mirror. She looked long and hard, as if expecting confirmation for the evening's events – what had and what was about to occur. Satisfied in the answer that only she and the image shared, Paige returned from the restroom and sat down to the table with a smile. She picked up the warm drink, first blowing slightly and then sipping it slowly as to not burn her tongue.

She looked up at Lenny who was watching her intently.

"Thank you for coming out with me tonight Paige. You don't know how much it means to me. I think about you constantly during the week you know."

"I wouldn't have missed it. I enjoy your conversation and your touch even more," Paige replied, basking in his adoration.

Len reached across the table with his other hand and stroked Paige's hair.

"Your hair is beautiful Paige."

"Thanks Len." She didn't know what to say in return. Women don't tell guys *their* hair is beautiful, and his was thinning at best.

Lenny seemingly read her thoughts and reached up to his own hair. "It's okay Paige, I know I'm a bit 'hair challenged'" he said with a chuckle.

Paige laughed in return and continued to relax more with every sip of her drink. A slow warmth began to grow in her stomach. She didn't know if it was from the drink, the warm room or Lenny's touch. Maybe it was a combination of all three; either way, she couldn't ignore what she felt.

Paige straightened up in her chair and continued on with superficial conversation, trying her best to contain her emotion.

"So, how was work today?" she asked Lenny.

Lenny paused and put his beer down. He grinned widely and spoke in measured tones. "How was work today you asked?" raising his brow.

"Um, yeah."

"Really Paige, we're back to that?"

"Back to what?"

"Back to the 'hey, nice to meet ya' conversation. Oh, we are way beyond that," Lenny said leaning in closer to her. He was so close she could feel the warmth of his breath on her shoulder. "Tell me what you really want to ask Paige."

Butterflies swirled in Paige's stomach. "I don't know what you mean Len."

"Oh, I think you do," Lenny replied with definition in his voice. "What do you really want to ask me?"

Paige's mind raced in quiet response. *Do I tell him how I want him to take me as far away from here as we can get, or do I simply play the muse and make him guess? Dammit, I deserve this. I need this chance.*

Finally, Paige leaned in to Lenny until their faces almost touched. She felt her bosom lay heavily on the table. Parting her moistened lips, she spoke from the very depths of her emotions which had been quelled for far too long.

"Len," she said, looking him straight in the eye, "I don't have any questions for you, that's where you are mistaken. What I do have for you is a request," Paige hesitated for a moment and then drew another breath in before letting out another sultry line of measured verbiage, "I want *you* to take *me*."

There, she had said it. Six little words magnified times ten thousand. Both of their bodies stayed there, temporarily suspended in animation.

Lenny drew his chair back and sat upright, a look of concern drawn on his face. Paige coiled back in response. Suddenly she was frightened. Had she said too much? Did he not understand? What just happened? Up until now they were simply two people who had found each other on the internet, had some engaging chats, and met for dinner and a drink, all harmless enough. Paige's invitation had now upped the ante.

Finally Lenny spoke, "We need to go."

This was not the reaction that Paige had expected. She felt the lump start to rise in her throat. *Oh God, not now,* she quietly whispered to herself. She fumbled in her purse for her keys as her eyes filled with tears. Lenny got up and quickly paid the bill at the bar counter. He walked back over to Paige and hurriedly helped her on with her coat. She looked around the table again for anything that might be left behind. Then she checked her purse. Nervousness and fear was giving way to her checking behaviors.

Lenny put a gloved hand forcefully around her waist, leaned into the side of her face through parted hair and hissed into her ear, "We need to go Paige, I mean it."

They both quickly exited the tavern. Once outside, the night air stung Paige's face, causing the hot tears to turn to steam. Lenny did not let go of her waist. Rather, he tightened his grip and turned her in the opposite direction of where she was parked.

"Where are we going?"

Lenny did not respond.

"Lenny, please, tell me what's wrong!"

They continued on down the sidewalk, hurriedly past the couples in love that just hours before Paige had felt a kindred bond with.

Finally, in a darkened part of the street, they reached a newer cream colored sedan with slightly tinted windows parked by itself on the street. Lenny pushed Paige up against the side of the car and pressed his body into hers. He cupped both hands against her cheeks and positioned her face directly at his. Paige's heart was beating wildly.

Clearing his throat, Lenny spoke in broken sentences. "My God Paige, do...do you know...do you know what the hell you're doing?" The end of his sentence came out much better than the beginning. "Better yet...do you know what you've done...what you have done to *ME*?"

Lenny was fuming, not at Paige, but at himself. He was the picture perfect image of control. He had control of his company, control of his finances, and most of all control of his emotions. And here she comes along, out of left field, and he completely loses his control for the first time in over twenty years. He didn't know what to do next but react with his emotions - the same ones he'd kept hidden away.

The tears were streaming down Paige's face. The lump in her throat broke and gave way to small sobs.

Between breaths Paige spoke, "I'm...I'm sorry Len...I didn't mean to...I'm so sorry...." She couldn't finish her last sentence; her weakened legs caused her body to collapse to the ground.

Len released his hands from her face and held her up with his arms. "Paige, I want this...I want this so bad...I don't think you know how bad I *need* this."

Without further hesitation Lenny pressed his lips to hers, and instead of drawing the life from her, which Derek did on a daily basis, Lenny breathed life back into Paige. Like a wilted flower come to life, she slowly felt a warmth fill her body and tension release from every tip of her very being. Time had ceased and the world's spotlight was on these two stolen lovers huddled against steel on a cobblestone street.

Without another exchange of words, Lenny released his lips from hers and reaching behind her, opened the car door that she had been leaning against. He motioned for her to enter, which she willingly did. Stepping around the car, he got in the other side and put the key into the ignition. The car started right up. He was in control now, that's what he wanted, and that's what Paige gave him. They were seemingly perfect for each other.

The two of them drove in an eerie silence down the lamp lit streets. When the street lights began to dwindle, Lenny directed the car onto the main highway, taking it until they were out of the city limits. Paige watched the green and white mile markers with an odd mixture of anticipation and dread. Light snow was beginning to fall. She hadn't been out this far on the county highway before. There hadn't been a reason to, until now.

It was funny, here she was with a man that she barely knew, and there wasn't an ounce of fear in her entire body. Yet, she had been with her children's father for years, and fear never left her body. Finally, after complete darkness, a light began to show in the far distance. As they got closer, Paige made out neon red VACANCY letters. Above that was the phrase, "Motor Inn." It was a motel. Paige knew what people did at motels like this. She half expected to see rates by the hour in the office window. This was blatant foreshadowing.

Lenny turned the car into the graveled parking lot. The motel was single story, painted a dull brown. There were twelve white doors, each with a gold number on them and a matching window next to the door. A small light fixture was perched between each door and window combination. Paige sat motionless, waiting for Lenny to pull into the parking lot and simply turn around. Certainly this was a mistake, right?

There was no mistaking tonight, everything was purposeful and the large, cream colored sedan came to rest at the side of the motel office door. Lenny looked across the seat one last time at Paige. Her face peeked out of the shadows, eyes widened with fear for the very first time. It wasn't him she was afraid of, it was herself. She knew full well what was about to happen, and the worst part of all, she *wanted* it to happen.

He placed his hand on hers, "It's okay, I'll take care of you."

"Yeah, I know Len." She wanted to believe his words so badly, but years of emotional abuse from Derek and Judith had taken its toll. Paige felt like a child again, listening to the adults in charge.

She watched from the car window as Lenny went up to the small door highlighted with red neon OFFICE letters. He stepped in to the small foyer, flashed his businessman smile and opened his wallet.

He'll probably write this off on his taxes, Paige thought to herself.

Lenny emerged from the office a short time later, took a quick hop down the two steps and was at his car door in no time. His hand trembled as he pulled on the vehicle's door handle.

Control. I'm in complete control of me, he said to himself. He could say it a hundred times over, but he would never believe it.

Lenny got back into the car, put the shift lever into drive and proceeded to gold numbered room four. The graveled parking lot was nearly empty except for an old pickup near the end of the row of rooms.

Lenny handed Paige the key. "Here sweetie, go ahead and let yourself in. I'm gonna park the car in a bit better place."

Paige knew what Lenny was talking about. His nice car parked out in front of a motel known by locals for its hourly rates, which was like a flashing sign stating 'Hey everybody, cheating couple right here.'

Paige looked down at the hard plastic tag attached to a dull, brass colored key. On the plastic tag the number three was inscribed in white. Paige looked up and scanned the row of numbered doors until her eyes stopped at door number 3.

"Do you think these doors are steel Len?"

"What?"

"The doors Len, do you think they're made out of steel?"

The question completely caught Lenny off guard. "Um, I don't know, why do you ask sweetie?"

"It just matters to me Len, please don't ask why. If you think they're made of steel, then we have to get a different hotel room."

Lenny was confused. What the hell did it matter what composition the door was made out of? He gave it his most political answer he could think of.

"Well Paige, if I had to guess, those doors are made out of a composite wood based upon the age of this motor inn. I'm sure they are safe and up to hotel standards of our area."

"I don't care about safety Len. Listen...oh...never mind."

Paige hesitated for a moment and then opened the car door into increasingly falling snow. She stepped across the curb up onto the broken sidewalk. Fumbling with the key, she managed somehow to insert it into the lock and release the springs causing the door to open. She blindly walked inside the dark room, stepping onto shag carpet. She left the door open behind her and sat on the edge of one of two double beds in the small room. There she waited for Lenny to come. Her mind was blank, not a thought to be found. She continued to sit, her arms folded across her, not realizing she had begun to shiver.

Lenny's footsteps crunched in the snow as he approached door number three.

"Hey sweetie, why'd you leave the door open? It's freezing in here."

"I'm sorry Len, I guess I just must've forgot about it. I'm really sorry."

His voice softened. "It's okay, I was just worried about you Paige, and you're shivering."

He shut the door and double locked it. Taking a quick peek out the windows he closed the rubber backed blinds. "Let's get some heat on in here for you," he said walking over to the thermostat on the wall.

"Okay, thank you," Paige managed between chattering teeth. Her muscles began to ache as she tensely held down her spot on the edge of the green floral bedspread.

"I'm sorry it's not fancy for you Paige, I wish we could've found something better, but...well...you know."

Yeah, she knew alright, there were no fancy 'by the hour' motels for married, star-crossed lovers.

"I feel like I'm in a movie right now Len."

"How's that Paige?"

"Like this isn't real, you know?"

"Yeah, I know. Keep this as a dream, keep this as yours and my dream. That way, we having something no one else can take away from us."

Paige started to respond as Lenny knelt down in front of her. "Ssshh," he said gently, placing a single finger over her lips. "It's okay." And with that, he cupped her chin with his right hand and kissed her gently on her cheek. Without further hesitation, he drew in a breath and kissed her fully on the lips. They stayed like that for fully a minute, breathing in unison.

Paige opened her eyes and pulled back first. Lenny followed suit. An uncomfortable silence began to fill the room as Lenny stood up. The two of them had watched this scene in the movies before, but never had they played the characters in real life. He began to empty his pockets out onto the table beside the bed, just as Derek does every night before he goes to bed. He pulled his wallet out last. As he laid it down on the plastic topped table, it fell open to a picture of his kids. Paige intently watched his every move.

With curiosity she asked, "Are those your children?" of the picture laying there.

"Um, yeah, this is Jonathan and this is Myra."

"They're really beautiful."

"Thanks."

Paige stiffly reached down to the ground below her and pulled her black leather purse from the clutches of the dense, shag green carpet.

"These are my two."

"Gosh, they look like you. How old are they?"

"Lindsay is five, and quite excited about starting Kindergarten this year. Aaron is just 7 months old. He's my happy one." This is really weird Paige thought to herself. We're at a sleazy motel, about to consummate our affair, and we're talking about our kids. Is this how the middle-aged have affairs? Unfortunately there wasn't an answer book readily available on this one.

Heavy silence again filled the air. Paige felt frozen to the bed as she heard Lenny begin to unbuckle his belt behind her. Everything in her mind told her this was not right; she needed to leave now. For the first time in many years, however, Paige was not going to listen to her mind. No, instead she was going to listen to her heart. She stood up and turned around, walking slowly towards Lenny. The two of them stood there, in the dimly lit room with its dark walnut paneled walls, eyes locked onto one another. She reached up with fumbling hands and unbuttoned her heavy, woolen coat. She slowly turned around and placed it on the bed. Turning back to Lenny she reached for the waistband of her shirt, and with both hands, slid it up over her head. Her wavy, auburn hair fell softly to her shoulders and rested on her bosom.

"My God Paige, you are absolutely beautiful," said Lenny.

Paige looked shyly down at the floor below them. She no longer knew how to take such compliments; her femininity was not something routinely observed anymore.

Lenny raised his hand and stroked Paige's soft skin. Goosebumps rose up in response. Her breath deepened and she felt lightheaded. She grabbed Lenny's arm to momentarily support her. He unbuttoned his shirt cuffs and moved his hands to begin work on the long row of white buttons. Paige stopped him and took over the delicate work of separating buttons from cloth herself. This very small act excited Lenny beyond imagination. A man in charge relinquishes his control only under the direst of circumstances - the eroticism of being taken by a beautiful woman was almost more than he could bear.

Paige undid each button with quiet determination. She got to the last one and then ran her hands fully up his hardened torso. She stopped short of his neckline and pulled her hands away. The two of them proceeded in a dance of sorts, each shedding an identical piece of clothing one at a time. Paige knew this was it, she about to cross the line, and as Lenny reached down to turn off the light, she did just that.

8 NO GOING BACK

Paige's decisions had always been calculated ones. She weighed the good and the bad and chose from the most advantageous option. This time, she had gone against that. There was no predetermined calculation; there was simply action in the heat of the moment. Quite honestly, it felt good.

She lay between the crisp white sheets of the hotel bed, staring at the tiled ceiling, all the while enjoying the warmth of Lenny's skin next to her. She was pulled from her dreamlike state by the ring of his cellphone from his pants on the carpeted floor. Oh how she silently wished he didn't have to answer his phone, and the two of them could lie there together all night. Alas, her wishes were seldom answered, and Lenny pulled back the sheet and hopped out of bed. She watched the silhouette of his naked body fill the dense void of the lonely hotel room. Paige wondered how many other couples had stolen hours alone in this very spot.

"Hello?" said Lenny into the gray cellphone. "Yeah…okay…right now? Alright, I'll be there in about an hour."

Lenny turned to Paige with disappointment on his face. It was nearly 10 o'clock at night. Time had gotten away from the both of them.

"Listen sweetie, work calls, I need to…."

"Don't say anymore Len, I know, you need to go." Paige felt

73

the lump begin to rise in her throat. She didn't want the night to end, not this way, not with someone else dictating how they spend their time together.

Lenny walked over to the bedside and sat down next to Paige. He gently stroked her cheek and looked into her eyes.

"Thank you Paige."

She didn't understand. "Thank you for what?"

"Thank you for tonight." With that Lenny stood up and reached down to the floor, gathering up his clothes.

Paige's body began to stiffen. The lump in her throat acted as a cork to her whirlwind of emotions that were often hard to control once they were unleashed. Paige told herself repeatedly, *This is not the time. Not now dammit. You feel nothing Paige because you are nothing.*

With a few deep breaths, Paige got out of bed and began to collect her own belongings. Her mind was racing. She felt as if Lenny had thanked her with the same enthusiasm the local fast food guy says when she goes through the drive-through – forced by necessity, not by goodness. She looked up from the floor when she heard the water running in the bathroom. Peering through the crack of the door, in the thin sliver of light, she watched Lenny as he stood looking at himself in the mirror.

Lenny took a washcloth from the towel rack and turned the water on as hot as it would go. Steam began to rise as he watched his reflection slowly disappear in the mirror in front of him. He felt no guilt or remorse for what he had just done. No thought was given to his wife and children waiting at home. He rubbed the bar of soap vigorously on the washcloth and then began to wash himself.

Paige watched with disgust through the doorway. *How can he do this? What is so wrong with me that he must wash every trace of tonight away before we even leave?*

Paige backed away from the doorway and reached for her coat and purse. Not caring if her coat was buttoned, she opened the motel room door and stepped outside onto the snowy sidewalk. She hurriedly walked down the path until rounding the corner of building. Lenny's car was parked there – three inches of snow already piled on the roof. Paige tried to open the door handle. It was locked. *Of course, its locked dummy, we're in the country in the middle of a snowstorm, great place for people to break into cars.*

Lenny emerged from the bathroom, cleaned and dressed. "Alright sweetie, are you ready?" Lenny asked of an empty room.

"Paige?"

Lenny quickly glanced around the room. There was no sign of Paige or her stuff. He walked over to the door, opened it, and was greeted by a whoosh of snow that blew in on him. He followed Paige's footsteps down the walk in the direction of his car. Lenny walked faster, finally finding her standing next to his car. Snowflakes were clinging to her hair as she stood there motionless.

"Paige? What the hell…" said Lenny, nearly speechless and quite confused by this point.

"You've got to get going Len, I was just trying to help you save time, that's all," Paige said flatly.

Lenny fumbled with the keys, trying to get them out of his coat pocket. "Yeah, okay, well, I appreciate that, but it's not that much of a hurry."

Lenny let Paige into the car and closed the door behind her. He walked around the other side, still wondering what had happened. *Why had she so quickly changed her mood?*

The two of them drove back into the city in silence. Paige watched the wipers go back and forth across the cold, glass paned windshield. She listened to the radio softly play in a bath of green glowing light from the dash. She felt seven years old again, sitting in Judith's car on Friday night. Paige continued to block out the elements surrounding her, until she was completely locked in her own mind. Brick walls, she was building brick walls. In her view, it was the safest place to be when everything else around her was falling down. It wasn't until the sedan stopped, and Lenny spoke, that Paige came back to the present.

75

Lenny reached over to Paige and gave the top of her leg a quick squeeze. "We're here," he said with the tone of a bus driver announcing the next stop along the route.

"Um yeah, thanks Len for driving me back to my car."

"Sure Paige, have a good night."

"You do the same." Paige got out of the car and began the trek through the snow back to the parking garage where her own vehicle was parked. She trudged along the sidewalk, not even realizing how cold or miserable the conditions had turned outside. Her phone started to ring in her purse, but her mind didn't register the sound as important enough to fully come back to reality at this point.

Paige got to her truck and began brushing the snow off the door with the ends of her scarf. There wasn't much to do because most of her vehicle had been under a carport of sorts. She clicked the locks open and stepped inside. Her breath formed clouds in front of her face. She turned on the ignition and waited for the truck to warm up before disengaging the transmission. Remembering her phone had rung, she took it out of her purse and checked the caller ID. The display read MOM. She pressed the green CALL button and Judith answered on the first ring.

"Paige? Paige is that you? Where are you, are you alright?" Judith fired off a series of questions.

"Yes mom, if you would let me answer the first question you ask, you wouldn't have to ask me the other six questions."

Judith sounded irritated, "Well, I worry about you out there with some stranger at night."

"Mom, Derek isn't around is he?"

"No Paige, do you think I'm that stupid? He's out in his shop as usual. I'm with the kids upstairs. I figured that's the best way to stay, far away from him. I knew he wouldn't want to be around the kids."

"Alright mom, well, I'm gonna go do some Christmas shopping quick and then I'll be home, okay?"

"Yeah Paige, take your time, we're find here."

"Thanks mom, bye."

"Bye."

Judith no sooner clicked the phone shut and Derek appeared in the kitchen.

"I heard voices, is my wife home?" Derek asked a surprised Judith.

"Uh no, she's not, that was actually her on the phone just now."

"Oh, what'd she want? Why didn't she call on the home phone?"

Judith was not one for quick thinking on her feet, but she was good at covering up the truth if she was prepared beforehand.

"She probably didn't want to wake the kids up or something. Her candle party is finished, and she wanted to stop at Supermart to get a couple last minute presents for the kids I guess. She'll be home soon I'm sure."

Derek studied Judith, taking in her body posture, movements and tone of voice. Something wasn't adding up. Then again, it was Judith, not much ever added up about her.

"Do you think Paige is having an affair on me?" Derek threw out to Judith.

Judith's heart skipped a beat and she turned away as if to look for something. Her voice lightened into a sickening sweet pitch. "What makes you ask a question like that Derek?" She couldn't look at him as she asked.

"I don't know; things just aren't the same between us anymore. And then you factor in these late nights, and well, I don't know, I just thought I'd ask."

"That's between you and Paige, I don't get in the middle of these things. She hasn't said anything to me." That was classic Judith, stay out of it when *she* didn't want to be involved, be in the middle of it when *others* didn't want her involved.

"Just thought I'd ask." Derek stood there for a moment, still studying Judith. Satisfied, he walked back out of the room.

Judith sat down on the recliner and waited for Paige to get home; hoping Derek didn't come back into the room with another line of questioning before the night was over. Thankfully he didn't.

Meanwhile Paige was waiting in line at Supermart with a cart full of toys. She had done this every year for Lindsay, and now for Aaron too. She always went shopping for birthdays and holidays by herself. It was not something which Derek wished to be bothered with.

It was her turn and the green vested checker looked at Paige, "How is your evening tonight ma'am?"

It was a simple enough question, harmless really, after all, the clerk was only doing her job. Paige looked up, "Well, checker person, my evening is going fabulous. Let's see, I'm having an affair on my husband, just had a round of sordid hotel room sex, and now I must live with the life altering guilt of sleeping with a married man for the remainder of my years on this earth. How about you, how is your night going?"

Checker person stood there with her mouth gaping wide open. She managed a meek, "Fine, thanks," and continued to proceed with running the toys across the scanner. Paige swore the checker's hands were shaking. She laughed to herself in her mind, *Teach her to ask questions. What do people expect; the same canned answer to the same questions they deftly asked a hundred times over in one shift?* Paige finished paying for her purchases and bid the still shocked clerk good evening.

Paige enjoyed shopping for her kids during the holiday season. What she didn't take pleasure in was the season itself. So commercialized and full of unfilled wishes and disappointments, especially for her clients at work.

As a child Paige loved holiday get-togethers at her grandparent's house. She remembered plates full of brown sugar glazed ham and sweet potatoes encrusted with mounds of marshmallows and bits of walnuts. After dinner the men would settle into overstuffed recliners in front of the television set while the women picked up the dirty dishes and leftovers. The kids would usually play rounds of board games in the den adjoining the kitchen.

Those were visions of good days gone by. Now, Paige faced an onslaught of in-laws armed with fake smiles and stories which they used to try to one-up the other. One Christmas Eve Paige had even begged her boss to stay at work after all the other employees had been allowed to go home early to celebrate the holiday with their families, just so she wouldn't have to do the same with Derek's.

Paige returned home twenty minutes after having hung up with Judith. She took one sack of toys out of her truck and left the rest in there for later. She didn't want to hear Derek complain about how much money she had spent or where she had gotten it from. She walked into the house and made a beeline right past Judith into her room. Judith got up from the recliner and quickly followed, coming to rest in the bedroom doorway.

Paige felt Judith staring at her. She knew what her mom was expecting, a full report on the evening's events.

"Thanks again mom for watching the kids tonight. The girls and I had a lot of fun at our candle party. I was surprised at how few people were at the store though."

"Yes, well, you're welcome, anytime for the kids and you. You know that, don't you?" Judith responded.

"Yes mom, please don't get all emotional or mushy on me. You know how I hate that."

"Yes, my cold, ice queen of a daughter, I know."

"Thanks mom, for the continued compliments which you have so kindly showered me with my entire life."

Paige looked up at Judith. She looked hurt.

"I'm sorry mom, I'm tired, and I'm sure you are too. Are you going to stay over tonight, or make the trip home?"

"Well," said Judith with the "poor me" tone of voice, "I suppose I could stay here and then take Aaron home with me for a couple days; give you a break here."

"Oh, that would be awesome. I could use it. Thanks."

Judith turned and headed down the hall to the guest bedroom. Paige finished putting the toys in the back of her closet. Once satisfied that Lindsay wouldn't find them, Paige backed out of the closet right into Derek's chest.

"Jesus Derek, you scared the crap out of me," said Paige.

Derek stood there, looking at his wife intently, not saying a word.

Her heart was beating wildly in her chest. "Derek, I need to finish getting ready for bed," Paige managed to squeak out. Her hands started to tingle.

"So…how was the party with the girls tonight?" Derek began his inquisition.

Wild heart beats skipped in her chest causing her to catch her breath. "It was fine hon, I don't feel good now though, I think I need to get some sleep. It's getting late."

"So, who all was there?"

"You know, just the ladies from work."

"Which ones?"

"Myra, Toni, Shannon and Lois."

Derek continued to stand in front of Paige, not allowing her to go by. This was classic Derek. To all on the outside, he was extremely intelligent, good looking and well educated. He appeared to be the perfect husband and father. What people didn't know is that Derek used his intelligence to intimidate, control and eventually dominate those closest to him. People would never know this until Paige spoke up. Like domestic violence victims, Paige didn't have the physical scars to show, only emotional ones that she stuffed deep down inside her.

Paige watched Derek's chest heave in front of her. He clenched his fists open and shut, staring right through her.

Finally Paige spoke, "Derek, do you need anything else from me? Your laundry should be done for morning, and the coffeemaker is set. It's late honey." Paige tried to soften her voice and body posture as much as possible in an attempt to de-escalate her husband.

Derek started to back away, making a small escape route for Paige. "It's only late because you made it late Paige." She pissed him off to no end; always thinking she was better than him.

"Yeah, Derek, I know…you're right," Paige responded in an emotionless tone, trying her best to appease her husband. She felt detached from her body, almost as if she floated out of the room and into the bathroom to brush her teeth. She looked at the clock, it was almost midnight. She had to be up early for work tomorrow. She finished brushing her teeth and went back to her bedroom. Derek lay there on his side, with his back facing Paige like always. She climbed into bed and closed her eyes, praying for morning, praying for a new day, or better yet, a new life.

9 A SCHOOL FRIEND

Many people are accustomed to putting barriers between themselves and those around them. Some do so to keep others out; some do so to keep others in. Paige was of the former. It began really around the time she became a teenager. Her thirteenth birthday was ushered in by Judith's hand wrapped around a glass of rum and cola all the while telling Paige that there were no birthday presents this year because there was simply no money. When her daughter appeared hurt by the lack of gifts or fanfare, Judith accused her of being ungrateful and spoiled. Paige was neither, she was just a girl trying to be a kid, the perfect student, secret keeper, and whatever else the world threw at her.

Paige excelled all through school. She was Most Valuable Player of the softball team, standout track star and academic nerd. She was good at almost everything she tried - the envy of many perhaps, but she never knew that.

Socially, Paige felt like a failure. Her second grade report card was headlined with, "Smart, bright child, teacher's helper, won't play with other kids, prefers to be alone." School was a very lonely place until seventh grade however. That was the year Taryn entered Paige's life.

Taryn was a girl known to many as popular, a social butterfly, outgoing, and so on. Taryn held her status, in part, due to her older brother Reed. He had classic good looks and charm which lead to his popularity and Taryn's as well. Every girl in Woodview Junior/ Senior High School wanted to be Taryn's friend - so they could get closer to Reed. She knew this, but dismissed it all in the same thought. She didn't mind, she craved social contact any way she could get it.

Paige was a new student to Woodview Junior/Senior High School in the fall of 1987. The move to Woodview, Washington, would be Paige's last for the next couple of years at least, which was quite an accomplishment for her family. She looked forward to the moves though, a chance to start over and become another nameless face in the crowd. Staying one place too long meant getting too close to people, which always led to questions about her life.

The first day of seventh grade was marked by the usual excitement of seeing which new outfit's the popular girls were wearing and whether or not you were assigned to the same classes as your best friend. Paige's first day was different. She walked into the building following the other kids who had just gotten off the bus. She figured at least they would lead her to the right places. A couple of eight grade girls stood in the halls with their name brand outfits and matching haircuts. *They all look alike, no individuality,* thought Paige.

These girls were like the People Pleasers that greeted you at the entrance of Supermart. They waved their arms and bubblegum pink smiles, "This way...yeah...oh hi...like oh my God, I haven't like seen you like in forever!" They were chosen based on their 'natural ability' to help others. Paige felt they were chosen based on their natural ability to kiss the ass of others.

Paige made her way to the commons area and got in line according to her where her last name fell in the alphabet. Paige Miles placed her in line M-Z. She clutched her backpack tight and waited until she was next in line. A friendly teacher face greeted her. It was Mrs. Bellows the English teacher.

"Hi sweetie, what's the last name?" she asked. Her hair was

salt and pepper curly, tight to her head and punctuated with red ball earrings and matching necklace.

"Miles, Paige Miles."

Mrs. Bellows licked her thumb and began flipping through the pages until she came upon Paige's welcome packet.

"Here you go. You'll find your locker assignment and combination along with your class schedule in this envelope. Seventh grade lockers are back at the main entrance on your immediate left. There are a couple of forms in there for your parents to fill out and return as well, so make sure you don't lose them."

"Yes, okay. Thank you."

And with that Paige turned back to the sea of unknown faces and headed down to the seventh grade locker bay. She tried her best to follow the maroon and gold carpeted hallway glancing up only long enough to ensure she was still going in the right direction.

Paige made it to locker 703. She felt relieved, like it was home base in a game of tag. She got the locker opened and put up a couple pictures of her cats and a magnetic mirror. Once she finished moving in, she continued to stand there, pretending to be busy. This ensured Paige wouldn't have to talk to the others. It seemed like an eternity until first bell, but it did finally do so not three minutes later.

Paige double checked the schedule and made her way to her first class – Social Studies and then Language Arts. She entered the classroom hoping for either assigned seating or enough seats to be left open that she wasn't "that girl" that couldn't find a place to sit. Looking around the classroom, she breathed a sigh of relief; she was one of the first kids in the room. Of course she was, all of the cool kids were still out in the hall complaining that they weren't in the same classes together. Paige walked across the classroom and chose a seat in the far left corner. Reaching in her backpack, she took out a pencil from its new package and placed it on her desk next to her notebook so that they both matched up in perfect unison. Then she sat back in the chair and watched the door intently as the other students filed into the room.

Paige was a people watcher; people fascinated her. It wasn't so much solely the individual as it was the individual and how they interacted with others in their environment. Perhaps she was enthralled with human interaction based upon her own lack of such.

Kids continued to pour into the room well after the bell rang. Woodview was no different from all the other schools she had attended. There were your jocks, skaters, stoners, preps, popular kids, nerds and loners. Paige fell into the last category.

Loners were those kids that for whatever reason didn't fit in to the school culture. Often they were very bright, but socially couldn't adjust. Sometimes they had received so much ridicule in the early days of school they just gave up trying to fit in. They could be seen spending a lot of time at their lockers or with their nose in a book sitting in a corner of the school somewhere. Paige had her fair share of bullying and teasing when she was younger, but she also carried so much emotional baggage from home, she put up walls around her to protect outsiders from being part of it as well.

The majority of the morning was uneventful. Paige was one of the first kids in line to get lunch, thus giving her a head start on finding a seat in the dauntingly large lunchroom. There were fifteen plus round tables, each seating about five kids comfortably. Some tables were overflowing with kids, while others had less, depending on which crowd was there.

Paige took her tray of traditional school food – corndog, tater tots, orange wedge, green salad and milk – and found herself a seat. She studied the flecks of color ingrained on the hard plastic tray. Each morsel of food was savored like it was her last. Eating slowly was another trick often employed to use up as much time of the lunch hour as possible so Paige wouldn't look weird and alone, nor would she have to face the crowd of her peers.

She watched the other kids laughing at their round tables, obviously having known each other for years, envying everything about them, the way they dressed, their perfect hair, everything. She longed to be that girl that turned the heads of guys in the hallways.

She was down to her last tater tot. Even the slivers of carrot and red cabbage had disappeared from the tray. That is when she heard it – the laugh. The laugh that was so infectious, it actually brought a smile to Paige's face. It wasn't just once, not even twice, but almost continual, and not stupid or obnoxious, but genuine. "Who in the heck would laugh that hard or that much and still have a voice?" she thought to herself.

She cautiously turned around, trying not to let others notice that her head apparently moves like any other normal human being, and looked in the direction of the laugh. And that is when Paige first laid eyes upon Taryn. Taryn Grabonsky.

Taryn sat in the center of the popular kids table. She had bleach blonde permed hair which fell to the white fringed leather jacket that hugged her shoulders. She had a neon pink shirt on over her acid washed jean skirt. Dominating the conversation at the lunch table, she balanced her words with laughter in perfect harmony. Paige was in awe, so much so she hardly heard the lunch bell warning students it was time to get on to fourth period.

Paige got up and emptied her tray into the garbage can. Fourth period was Algebra. She loved math, having been in advanced classes as early as she could remember. She got her backpack from her locker and headed down the hall watching her feet move one in front of the other.

As it turns out, Taryn was in the same math class as her. Taryn was good at math, but anything she had in ability was lost in the lack of effort. That same theme headlined Taryn's entire school career. That was okay though, her rich social network helped with homework completion and test taking just fine.

Algebra began just like any other math class, and the teacher was no exception to the stereotype. He was a tall, thin man, with wisps of graying hair combed and cut short above his ears and neckline. His fingers were long, and Paige reveled in watching them work magic over the keys of the calculator when he became particularly stumped over a problem. He kept two mechanical pencils at all times in his left pocket of his short sleeved, business shirt. The pencils were snuggly nestled in a plastic pocket protector. He and Taryn equally held Paige's fascination.

The rest of the day was relatively uneventful with the exception of the bus ride home. The bus was just like the classroom and the lunchroom – seats went to the privileged with the rest scrambling for survival under a cloak of anonymity. Paige walked up the rubber lined steel steps of the bus much like a pirate must walk the plank. She walked down the aisle, not looking at the back, and found an empty seat just three rows back from the front. She sat down on the hard, green plastic seat and hugged her backpack like it was her life vest. The rest of the bus filled, doors closed, and the ride home began.

The actual ride itself was usually not too bad, it was when the bus stopped and Paige had to walk the remainder of the way home with the other kids that she dreaded. Paige's parents had managed to buy a house in a newly built neighborhood. Woodview was originally cow pastures and hay fields, but it was growing quickly. The school district, however, was still rural and didn't have enough busses for the number of kids in the school, so many kids were dropped off and picked up at similar spots as close to their homes as possible. As close as possible to Paige's house was a quarter mile down the road from her home.

As soon as Paige heard the "whoosh" of the air brakes, she darted off the bus and started to quickly walk down the road. Four other kids got off the bus, including two older boys, Mike and Robert. They were both freshman in high school, and neither had the maturity past the fifth grade level. They taunted Paige with name-calling even throwing things at her sometimes, despite her best efforts to "just ignore them" or cut through backyards to avoid them.

The bullying didn't stop until one day Judith got tired of Paige's protests about riding the bus and took care of the bullies herself. Judith parked on the corner across from where the bus stop was. She waited until she saw all the kids get off the bus, including

Paige. They paid no attention to the small, four-door, black vehicle parked across the street. Judith watched as Paige walked down the road heading home, her hands holding an open book, apparently reading. Paige had no idea that Judith was there, or what was about to happen next. She had adopted a new strategy. Rather than try to outrun the boys, Paige got off the bus last and tried to walk as slowly as she could behind them, hoping they would forget she was there. Instead of going on, Mike and Robert just walked slower. Today they were bouncing a basketball behind her. Suddenly, out of seemingly nowhere, Paige felt the hard rubber ball hit the back of her head, knocking her book out of her hands and sending her down to the ground.

Paige cried out in pain, crumpled on the ground, although more in shock than truly injured.

"Whatcha cryin' for flat face?" the boys taunted. "Get up, we'll give ya' more, come on."

There were no more chances for the two boys to say another word to Paige, for Judith jumped out of her car and marched right up to them. All three were stunned.

"God dammit, I swear if I see either of you two little shits ever touch my kid again, I'll kill you! Do you understand that? I'll kill you!" Judith snarled. Paige swore she saw Judith's eyes turn red and her nostrils flare with fire.

Mike reached to get his ball, his eyes fixed on Judith.

She took two steps toward him. "Don't you dare touch that ball. It's my ball now. Do you understand? Now get the hell out of here!"

With that, the two boys turned and ran. After that, the two boys never spoke to Paige again. Eventually Mike got his license as he was one of the older freshman; only because he had failed an earlier grade, so Paige didn't have to worry about the boys again.

A couple of weeks went by and Paige had begun to settle in to life at Woodview. Her grades were strong, still no friends yet, but the kids did talk to her in passing. Of course Judith continued to ask

Paige each day after school if she was invited to any birthday parties yet or friends' houses for slumber parties. Finally Judith quit asking. It was of no use, her daughter was never going to make friends, and quite frankly, she preferred it that way. She didn't let Paige know that, but in her mind, the fewer people that came around asking questions, the better.

The only student Paige ever mentioned by name was quite by coincidence. Judith had spent the afternoon cleaning out her cedar chest which contained baby books, mementos, letters, old clothes, and anything Judith felt held some sentimental value. Paige got home, changed her school clothes, and then headed into her mom's bedroom to see what goods the hope chest held.

Judith took a drink from her glass and looked up at her daughter.

"Well hello, how was school today?"

"Fine."

"That's good, do you have homework?"

"No, it's Thursday, they usually don't give us homework just before the weekend."

Judith paused, "Paige, are you lying to me? Thursday is not just before the weekend, Friday is, and it's not Friday."

"No mom, I wouldn't lie about that."

"Okay," she paused, apparently satisfied. "Take a look at these pictures I found in here from a long time ago."

Judith handed her daughter two large pictures. They were group photos from Paige's preschool classes when she was four and five years old. Paige took the pictures and studied them closely. One photo was from a play the children put on as a group. Paige couldn't remember the name of the play, but each kid had to dress up as an animal. Paige was a frog. There was also a bear, a cow, a pig, practically the whole animal kingdom, and then Paige came to the duck. The duck was a girl, a pretty little girl with blonde, curly hair, high cheekbones and…"Oh my God…no way," said Paige out loud.

"Mom, this looks just like a girl in my class at school."

"What's her name, the girl at your school?"

"Taryn."

"Yeah. What's her *last* name?"

"Taryn Grabonsky?" Paige replied.

"I was friends with Taryn's mother," Judith said.

That statement took Paige aback a bit. Her mother did not have friends. "Yeah? Is that her in this picture?" Paige asked her mom.

"Yes, you went to preschool with her when you were four and I think five, then we moved away. Don't you remember?"

Paige vaguely had memories of the play in the picture; she had been her favorite animal, a frog. Other than that, she recalled nothing.

"You should take the picture with you to school tomorrow and show Taryn that the two of you used to be friends," said Judith.

"Yeah, I think I'll do that." Paige walked out of the room with the pictures and put them in her three ringed binder. She rehearsed over and over how she would approach Taryn tomorrow. She was nervous, scared and excited all at the same time.

Later that evening Judith came in to Paige's room. Judith tucked Paige into bed every night. "Come on Paige, it's 8:30, time to turn off your light and go to bed."

"Okay," Paige replied turning off her light. She checked her alarm, kissed her mom on the cheek and turned over. She stared at the pictures on her wall until sleep paid its ritualistic visit.

The next day at school she couldn't wait until math class. The morning drug on slower than usual. Finally the lunch bell rang and Paige went to the commons to eat her lunch. Only thirty minutes left to go; she couldn't wait.

The warning bell went off and Paige rushed to her locker. She grabbed her binder, checked for the pictures and nearly ran to class. Her heart was beating hard in her chest. She entered the classroom and sat down. Tapping her fingers on her desk, she waited for Taryn's grand entrance. It finally came.

Taryn walked in wearing her fringed leather jacket, black leather skirt, oversized sweater and leggings. Paige watched as she sat down and immediately started talking to the person next to her. Paige felt sick to her stomach as she opened her binder and pulled out the pictures. She stood up and bravely marched across the room to where Taryn sat.

Holding the pictures in a shaking hand she stood there, towering over the seated Taryn.

"Hi, I'm…um…I'm Paige. Well, I suppose you probably already know that. Um, well, I have these pictures, well…uh…a picture in particular that I wanted to show you. I think you and I used to know each other."

With that, Paige handed the pictures to Taryn and waited. Taryn took the colored matte photos in her hand and studied them. When she realized that it was her, there in the feathered duck costume and yellow webbed feet, she nearly crawled under her desk. For once in Taryn Grabonsky's life, she was absolutely speechless. *What did this girl want, to embarrass me?* No, she had to play this cool. Here's this brand new kid, who hadn't said more than two words to anybody yet this school year, who has the guts enough to come up to her, with a picture of what appears to be some Noah's Ark scandal from their childhood. Well, Taryn felt she needed to give this girl a chance; and that she did.

Paige held her breath, searching Taryn's facial expression and body language for some sign of recognition, disgust, whatever, just something. Finally, she got just that. Taryn let out one of her signature, from the gut, laughs. She laughed so hard, tears came to her eyes and she started to cough.

"Wow," said Taryn, looking up at Paige, "Like, where'd you get this?"

"My mom found it yesterday when she was going through some old stuff in her cedar chest. I saw the faces and recognized yours. My mom remembered your name I guess from when we were in preschool together."

The two teenage girls were interrupted by their math teacher, "All right now students, let's go ahead and begin. It's your lucky day; I have a math quiz for you."

"So, yeah, like hey Paige, let's talk about this some more after class, okay?" said Taryn.

"Yeah, that's great Taryn."

Paige walked back to her desk and sat down. She took out her pencil and a clean sheet of white paper. She felt something inside of her, deep down in the pit of her stomach that had not been there in months, if not years perhaps. It was hope.

10 AN INVITATION

Fall was near its end in Woodview. Trees had long since lost their leaves, Halloween had passed, and the gloomy, grey days so characteristic of Western Washington had set in. Paige's life had taken a turn for the better just six weeks ago. She had received all A's on her first quarter report card, and now spent her lunches eating with the "in crowd" at Taryn's lunch table. She no longer spent her lunch hour watching birds out the commons windows or hiding her nose in another novel. She felt included, like she really belonged here. School was becoming her sanctuary as life at home continued to deteriorate. Paige's grandmother, Judith's mom, had been fighting cancer for three years now. Her fight was near its end, and Judith found more solace than ever in the bottle. It was no longer exclusively Friday nights, now it was a random day on the calendar in addition to Friday and usually Saturday night as well.

Paige got to school one morning and found a white envelope taped to the outside of her locker. Her name was written across the front of the envelope in large, bubbly handwriting. She looked up and down both directions of the hallway. At first she thought it might be a joke, but then a smile came to her face, she recognized Taryn's writing on the outside.

"Huh, what's this?" she said out loud, grasping the envelope from her locker and opening it as fast as she could. Inside the envelope was a shiny invitation with the words "Party" splashed across the front in neon pink writing. Paige opened the card up and read it. Again, in Taryn's bubble writing it read, "You are invited to my party, boys & girls of course, on Friday, November 20th at 7:00 p.m. R.S.V.P. to 555-6357. *Oh my God, I'm invited to a party!* Paige thought to herself. She had not received an invitation to anything since the third grade. She read it over and over, memorizing every word of the paper invite.

Paige was so engrossed in the invitation that she didn't hear Taryn come up behind her. "So you like got my invitation I see," said Taryn.

"Like yeah, I did," Paige replied.

"You're coming right? Say you're going to be there. You'll have so much fun. Oh yeah, and you've gotta stay the night after it's over too, k?"

"Yeah, I'll try," Paige said with doubt in her voice. She wasn't sure what her mom would think about a party, especially a boy/girl party.

Taryn gave Paige that look that was becoming so familiar, it was the 'come on, it'll be fun look' that convinced Paige every time she was unsure about something. That same look would resonate in their lives for years to come.

"Okay, I'll for sure ask. I mean, that's like all I can do, right?" Paige assured Taryn.

"Okay, but make sure you call me tonight and like let me know right away what your mom says, okay? Or maybe I'll call you. Well, call me, and if it's busy, well keep calling, okay?"

"Okay," said a joyous Paige.

Paige floated on clouds for the remainder of the day. She played over and over in her mind what it would be like to go to a party with the other kids in her grade, especially a boy/girl party. She was worried Judith wouldn't go for it, but if she asked her at just the right time, maybe she would say yes.

That night Paige waited all evening, doing her homework as

soon as she got home, cleaning up the dinner dishes, and in general walking on eggshells to make sure her mom was in the best mood possible. Unfortunately, Judith hadn't even asked Paige how her day was at school yet. Paige figured that would've been the perfect opportunity to tell her about the invitation.

It was getting late, near bedtime, so Paige decided to go ahead and launch her plea. Taryn had already called twice, totally let down that Paige hadn't found out anything yet. Leaving the sanctuary of her bedroom, she walked downstairs to find Judith on the couch reading the newspaper, glass in hand.

"Hi mom," said Paige easing her way onto the edge of the couch. She held the invitation tightly in her hand. "Anything good in the paper tonight?"

Judith gave a long, heavy sigh, "What do you want Paige?"

"Um, nothing mom. I had a really good day at school today."

Without looking away from her paper, Judith replied, "Yeah, why?"

"Well, I got an A on my Social Studies project I have been working on, and, oh yeah, I got an invitation to a party at Taryn's."

The house was silent with the exception of the sound of Judith turning the pages of the newspaper. Paige's throat was so dry; she could hardly swallow as she waited for some sign from her mom. Paige did that a lot, waiting for other people's reactions.

Still not looking at her daughter, Judith asked when the party was going to be, and Paige quickly responded with the date indicated on the card.

"Is her mom going to be there?"

"Yeah, sure," Paige replied.

Paige purposefully left out the part about the party being boy/girl. She figured if her mom asked, then she'd tell, but not before.

Judith put her paper down next to her and looked around the floor for the next section, still not giving any response. After ten minutes of continued silence Paige knew it was getting to be time to go to bed, so she decided to ask her mom again.

In a small voice, Paige said, "Mom, so, what do you think?"

"About what?" Judith said, sounding irritated.

"About the party?"

"Jesus Paige, do you always have to bug me. I said yes. Don't you ever listen to a thing I tell you?" Judith took another sip of her glass, and started on the next section of the paper.

Paige darted up off the couch, gave her mom a quick peck on the cheek, said "I love you," and went upstairs to bed. Her dreams were filled with mini melodramas that her subconscious conjured up for a restless night's sleep. It was more than she could've ever hoped for, for Judith to say yes. For once, she felt just a little normal, just like the other kids.

The next morning Paige asked her mother if she could ride the bus to Taryn's after school.

"Yes, I suppose you can, do you need a note?" asked Judith.

"Yes mom that would be great. I'll make sure to keep it safe in my overnight bag."

"Overnight bag? I said you could go to a party, not a sleepover. They are two different things Paige."

"Yeah mom, I know."

"Don't yeah mom me. Do you want to lose the privilege of going to your stupid little party too?"

"No mom." The lump began to well in Paige's throat.

"Good, then leave your damn bag here. You're lucky I let you ride the bus there. I'll pick you up from her house at 10 o'clock when it's over. You'd better call me as soon as you get to her house after school; you know how I worry about you."

"Yes mom." Paige looked down at the ground; Judith's voice fading into the background of carpet and furniture.

Paige turned to walk toward the door, hoping she hadn't missed the bus. Tears welled in her eyes. She tilted her head back as not to allow a single drop to fall.

"Paige?" called Judith as her daughter had one foot out the

door. "Have a great day at school. Think about me while I'm here all alone. I'll miss you."

There was no response from Paige, either verbally or in her mind. She was a hollow being walking the concrete path to the large, yellow school bus, one foot in front of the other. By the time Paige had reached school, she had thankfully put the morning behind her.

Of course Taryn was waiting by Paige's locker, eager to talk to her friend. A smile came to Paige's face.

"Hey, so like are you totally stoked for tonight?" asked Taryn.

"Um, yeah," replied Paige.

"What do you mean 'um yeah'? I want to like hear a 'Hell yeah'!"

Paige cocked her head to one side, raising her voice only slightly more, repeated Taryn's request.

"That's more like it, now come on, let's go hang out in the freshman hall and see what my big bro is up to."

Paige followed Taryn's footsteps down the halls anxiously awaiting the school day's end. She felt so cool when she was with Taryn. It was a false sense of popular security though. Paige knew in the back of her mind that she only associated with the cool crowd and upperclassmen because of her friend in the fringed coat.

Last bell finally rang and Paige burst into the hallway following the masses to their respective lockers. School hallways were a bit like human bumper cars, bodies jumbled together, legs and arms maneuvered by a complex system of nerve bundles and synapses executing movement as determined by the brain. It didn't cost a quarter to take this ride however; it cost bravery, ingenuity, and sometimes one's dignity.

Paige made it to her locker and exchanged her books for her coat. Taryn came up to Paige's locker shortly after with a broad smile across her face.

"Ready Freddy?"

"Yes, I am. I've got my note right here."

"Ah yes, my Paige, always prepared," Taryn laughed haughtily at Paige.

Before Paige could respond, Taryn grabbed her elbow and practically drug her smack down the middle of the hallway amidst waves of Friday goodbye hugs and "call me's" toward the exit doors. Once outside they got to bus number 14. Bus 14 was known as the "fun bus" with the "cool" bus driver. Just as Paige did every day, she nervously stood at the bottom of the bus stairs and waited her turn to get onto the steel carriage. This time was different though, as she was standing behind her fringed coated friend.

Paige handed the bus driver her note and moved forward after receiving the acknowledging smile. The two girls sat near the back of the bus, chatting and giggling the entire thirty minute ride home.

Taryn's mom worked full-time, and Reed wouldn't be home until the evening, so the girls arrived to an empty house. Taryn took her key out from her backpack and unlocked the door. The girls threw down their backpacks in the foyer and headed straight for the kitchen.

"You hungry?" Taryn asked Paige.

"Sure, I could eat. Watcha got?"

Taryn rummaged through the fridge, pulling out cold chicken, mayo, tomatoes and lemonade.

"Here, this oughta do us," she said with satisfaction plopping the food down on the counter.

"Um, like, what are we gonna put these on?" Paige asked.

"We're…not," replied Taryn, searching Paige's face for a reaction.

"Oh, okay."

"Psshh, it's NOT ok. Jesus Paige, I was totally kidding, you're so gullible," said Taryn grabbing a loaf of bread from the cabinet drawer. Turning around, Taryn poked her head into the deep freezer and pulled out a carton of double fudge ice cream. She plunked it down onto the counter next to the bread and triumphantly proclaimed, "This is dessert!"

The girls made sandwiches and dished up heaping bowls of chocolate ice cream. It was 3:30pm, only 3½ hours left until the party started. Paige and Taryn sat down on the large couch in front of the television.

"We can eat in here?" Paige asked Taryn.

"Like why couldn't we?"

"I dunno, my mom doesn't let me sometimes. Some of our furniture is only for good."

"Hmm, well, not here, now eat," said Taryn turning on the television.

The television screen glowed with entertaining images of men and women embattled in custody fights, affairs, and secrets only fitting for daytime t.v. fodder. It wasn't long before the phone rang…and rang…and rang. Parents constantly complain their teens don't communicate but they do – only with their friends, not the adults in their lives.

Paige stared in wonder at Taryn. She was in complete awe of Taryn's social ability. "Yeah, oh, I know. What? Oh my God! No, so what did he say…?" Her voice trailed off as Paige again turned her attention to the frosty bowl in her lap and the escalating quarrel on t.v. The room began to feel warm. No, it was actually getting hot. Her hands felt sweaty, even as they cupped a porcelain bowl ringed with frost.

She watched as the young woman with long, stringy hair clearly dressed by the show's staff in slacks and an overly flowered blouse screamed at the person next to her, "You ruined my life!"

"I am not the dad of that kid!" replied the shaggy haired man.

The fight continued on, each person trying to one up the other with verbal insults and cold stares. An image of a little boy with the same coal grey eyes as the foul-mouthed man flashed before the screen. The crowd began a universal cooing for the cherubic image on the screen. The cooing abruptly changed to gasps as the man on public trial had reached his own point of no return; anger had consumed him.

To the horror of Paige, the audience, and the floral print woman on stage, the father in question stood up, grabbed the metal legged chair and hurled it outward toward the spectators. Paige dropped her spoon and reached for the remote. Her heart was beating out of her chest. The man grabbed the next chair, raised it above his head and faced the horrified woman below him. Paige's thumb simultaneously clicked the power button to off. She deftly stood up and went into the bathroom leaving Taryn still connected to the phone.

Paige sat down on the cold, tiled floor, head in her hands, heart still pounding. Several minutes passed before Taryn figured out her friend was no longer perched on the couch across from her. She hung up the phone and proceeded on her search for Paige. Putting her dishes down on the counter, Taryn followed the wooden floor until it turned to tiles. She stopped at the entrance to the bathroom. Looking downward to where her new friend sat on the floor, Taryn made the only decision a future best friend could make – she sat down on that same tiled floor right next to Paige. Taryn had an innate ability to handle almost any personal crisis that would come her way. It wouldn't be until much later in life that she would learn how to find a balance with this gift she was given.

"So Paige, um, this floor is totally awesome, and we could hang out here all night, but, I'm thinkin' like 12 boys and girls wouldn't fit in here for a party. I don't know; call me crazy, but…yeah."

Taryn watched over her friend with the care and tenderness of a mother over her newborn baby. She imagined the horrors her friend must've gone through to be this hurt so young in life. She had no idea. Brushing Paige's hair aside, Taryn quietly spoke.

"Hey, you in there?"

After a long pause she received a reply.

"Yeah."

"Well okie dokie then, we've got life! Woohoo!"

"I'm sorry."

"What do you have to be sorry about? Come on, we've got a party to get ready for dude!"

Paige smiled back at Taryn and stood up. "Ok, let's do this!"

The girls emerged from the bathroom and began preparations for the night's big event. They hung streamers with tape and thumb tacks, moved around furniture, set up the stereo, and blew up neon colored balloons. A square card table was set with paper cups, plates, plastic silverware and napkins.

Taryn looked at the clock.

"Dude we're running late. Big hand on the twelve, small hand on the six. We need to get ready. We've only got an hour!" directed Taryn.

The duo could be seen for the next hour, busily blazing a path between the bathroom and Taryn's bedroom. Taryn cranked up the radio and danced wildly around her room, grabbing Paige's waist and bringing her along for a twirl. Paige didn't know how to respond to such wonton displays of fun.

"Come on Paige, move your booty."

Paige's body was rigid in response.

"Dude, I can't."

"What do you mean 'I can't'?"

"I don't know how."

"You mean to tell me you don't remember? Oh my God, every little girl was in tap and ballet."

With that, Taryn proceeded to put in a mix tape of 80's dance hits. The girls laughed and swayed to the music, Taryn taking her new friend under her protective wing, and Paige relishing in the joy of just being a kid.

Taryn's mom, Anna, arrived home at 6:45pm. She was a tall, thin woman with a crisp voice and pursed lips. Paige would forever reserve a spot in her own heart for Taryn's mom. Anna knew Paige's mom from years ago, and she was to meet her several more times in the coming months, but not always under the best of circumstances. She would eventually play a role in Paige's life for years to come.

Anna poked her head briefly into Taryn's room. "Taryn, did you get your chores done yet?"

Taryn looked at Paige, "Uh, yeah mom." It was a complete lie, but her mom would be preoccupied until the guests arrived with helping to finish the hors d'oeuvres for the party. Her mother was the queen of entertainment.

At precisely 7:03pm the doorbell rang. There on the porch were the first guests of the evening. Two girls, both with hairspray teased hair and name brand clothing, stood there with nervous smiles.

"Oh my God, totally, come in, I'm so excited you're here," exclaimed Taryn to her first guests of the evening.

Next to arrive were the boys, three of them to be exact. This time it was Paige's turn to answer the door, Taryn insisted. Paige awkwardly stood there in the doorway staring at the boy in the center. It was Ricky. The porch light shown directly on him; he was the epitome of perfect in her eyes. He wore white jeans tightly pegged at the ankles, a polo top and leather boat shoes. Paige was pretty sure he didn't even know of her existence, but she didn't mind, she was now in the same room as him and prayed for a dance with him by the end of the night.

In total there were 9 girls and 5 guys that night, dancing, eating and laughing – each having an equal share in the teenage rite of passage – at their first boy/girl party. Paige got her chance, after much coaxing by Taryn, to get a dance with Ricky. Anna was seen twice throughout the night, chronicling events with her camera to place in albums so that as adults, Taryn and Paige could look back on these moments with both laughter and fondness.

This, unfortunately, wouldn't be one of those nights. For at 9:45pm, a pair of headlights shown in the driveway, followed by a slow, steady honking of a car horn. It was Judith. Paige felt the panic seeping in under her skin like oil on sunbaked skin. She went to Taryn's room and looked around for her stuff. The car horn would not abate. Taryn followed her down the hall.

"Hey, what's the hurry? Don't you know there's still a last dance of the night? It's a slow one," she teased.

"I've got to hurry Taryn. Where's my bag? I can't find it! Where is it?!"

"Whoa dude, chill out, it's okay."

"No it's not, you don't understand Taryn. I'm gonna get in so much trouble if I don't find it."

When all hope seemed lost for the bookbag, Paige discovered it under Taryn's bed. It must've gotten shoved under there when the girls were dancing. Paige felt the lump start in her throat. She couldn't look up at her friend. Embarrassment was joining panic. The two were common friends in her world. Her arms filled with belongings, Paige pushed past Taryn and made a beeline down the hallway and out the front door. The glare of the headlights greeted her like the arrival of a movie star at a party.

By the time Taryn made it to the front door, her friend was gone. "Wow, psycho," Taryn said to herself. She no longer felt like partying. It was nearly 10 o'clock anyway, and soon the other parents would start to arrive. The girls that were left helped pick up the streamers and popped balloons, returning the house to its original pre-party state.

Paige stared straight ahead for the drive home. It was going to be a slow one; Judith was drunk, really drunk. Paige rolled the window down for fresh air. Judith had vomited on herself and the floor of the driver's seat. The only sound that could be heard was the whooshing of the air coming in from the window. Paige waited for her mother to speak; she knew this ride home wouldn't be without guilty, insidious statements against her daughter.

"So...were there any adults there tonight to watch you guys?" Judith asked between shallow breaths. "Or, were you guys there by yourselves having a party?"

"No mom, Anna was there."

"Who the hell is Anna?"

"Taryn's mom, she said you know her from a long time ago.

"Do you like her better than me?"

"What?"

"Do…you…like…her better than me?" Judith asked again, this time raising her voice an octave higher.

"I don't know what you mean mom."

Judith began to giggle, and then she was silent. Paige looked out the window, as her mom drove between the yellow lines nearly 15 miles under the posted speed limit. Judith stopped at the red light and waited for the green. Green came and went and still the car and Judith remained motionless.

"Mom, you need to go." There was no response. "Mom, you need to go, the light is green."

Her mom slowly turned her head and looked straight at her daughter. "You think you can get one over on me?"

"What?"

"You think you're smarter than me don't you? Don't tell me what to do. Got that?"

"I'm not."

"You're just like your dad. You know that? You both think you're better than me, smarter. I'm sick of it Paige. Do you hear me, I'm sick of it." By this time Judith's voice was near a scream. Paige hugged the door of the car. Two more rounds of red and green and the car moved on through the intersection towards home. Silence ensued again for the final mile and a half home.

The black car pulled into the driveway a short time later. Judith clicked the button on the garage door opener. Small waves of relief lapped at Paige's fingertips as she felt for the door handle. The car came to rest inside the garage and Paige wasted no time getting out of it. Not giving another glance to her mom, she grabbed her book bag and quickly went up the stairs to her room.

She listened intently for the sound of the garage door closing, which it did just a few minutes later. But then something unexpected happened – she heard the sound of the door opening back up. She went to the window and looked outside, expecting her mom's car to back down the driveway – but it didn't. In fact, Judith's car wasn't to move the rest of the night, only the heavy steel door of the garage was involved in this dance macabre. Repeatedly Judith pushed the grey button on the plastic opener and the door responded in turn, up, down and back up again, over and over. Paige was in a type of fearful awe. The sound of the phone ringing downstairs broke her trance.

She picked up the phone handle from its receiver on the wall. Breathing into the mouthpiece she managed a weak, "Hello?"

It was now almost 11 o'clock at night, and the sound of her friend's voice on the other end brought her quickly back to reality.

"Hey Paige, its Taryn. I was really freaked out tonight, are things okay dude?"

For once Paige was not able to cover it up. No, things were not okay, and they were only getting worse. Paige began to cry on the phone. "Help me Taryn, it's my mom."

"Okay Paige, we'll be right over."

"Hurry."

"I will, I promise." Help was on its way.

Paige went down to her room and slipped into her closet. Huddled down in the corner, she could feel the rhythmic pulsing of the garage door opening and closing beneath her. Her legs tucked close to her chest, she lay her cheek softly down on her knee. The darkness of the closet faded away as Paige let go of the reality around her. Like a clock without hands, time was suspended. Flowers quickly filled her room. Rays of sun danced along green stemmed daisies with the wind playing conductor of this whimsical symphony. Paige walked along the flower-filled path, a smile on her face.

"Paige? Paige. Hello, come back to me sweetie."

It was Taryn. She again spoke her best friend's name. Paige looked up at her through blank eyes. She blinked, sighed and then turned her head away from Taryn's penetrating gaze.

Taryn stood up in the center of the bedroom and began to bellow the most obnoxious song she could think of. "Oh c'mon, c'mon baby, oh yeah!" Over and over, louder and louder until words finally emerged from Paige's lips, "Wow, you suck dude."

"Oh my Paigee!" Taryn exclaimed dropping to her knees in front of Paige, "You're back!"

"Never left dude, like whatever."

Just as a sleeping dog awakes from a deep slumber, it took Paige a few minutes to fully grasp her reality. In a whispered voice, she asked a still smiling Taryn, "Where is she?"

"Never mind that, my mom's got it. C'mon dude, let's start packing you some clothes. You're not staying here tonight."

Like a little girl, her friend obeyed without question. Paige stuffed her backpack with clothes, a book and her toothbrush.

"Okay, you ready?" Taryn asked.

"Um, yeah."

"Good then let's go," Taryn said grabbing her friends arm and leading her down the hall. She was careful to herd Paige hurriedly past the bathroom where her mother was ensuring Judith didn't drown in the shower. Anna figured it wouldn't sober Judith up much, but at least she wouldn't go to sleep covered in her own vomit, although, it may serve her right for being this way in front of Paige. Anna looked upon Judith with a fleeting hint of pity. Everybody has something to hide, she thought to herself. Unfortunately for Paige, Judith had quit hiding it.

Meanwhile the two girls had climbed into Anna's car and started listening to the radio. It was a clear night with a sky full of stars.

"There's Orion," Taryn said pointing upward. "And his belt...oh and just below that," she said as her hand continued to draw downward, "is his fuzzy nebula." The two girls laughed hysterically at the connotation which the named star carried. Their laughter helped carry away the drama of the night.

Anna emerged from the lamplit porch securely shutting the door behind her. Taryn turned the radio down and both girls perched anxiously on their seats for news of what happened inside. In her perennially professional manner, Anna said nothing of the night other than to reassure Paige that she would be taken care of for the rest of the night and most likely the weekend.

Paige slumped down in her seat, the belt firmly securing her. She felt warm, relaxed, and safe, for now. Taryn meanwhile turned the radio back up and her mother steered the vehicle out onto the highway. Paige looked up at the night sky past Orion and focused on one barely glimmering star. "I love you mommy. Good night." With that she closed her eyes and fell fast asleep.

11 THE BEAST

As Paige grew older, she became the one to clean up Judith's messes when her mom was too hung over to work; Paige was the one to call her in sick. Making up excuses and lies became second nature; the words rolled off her tongue as fast as her mind could create them. Co-workers, relatives, friends, it didn't matter the name or the face; the words were always the same. "I'm sorry she's sick…no, she won't make it, car problems…no, I'm coming in my mom's place today, dad's ill and she has to take care of him." Paige became the classic scapegoat, hero and caretaker all in one. These terms she would learn in therapy years later.

She continued to be a model student at school. Teachers loved her, so much so she was often nominated for things like citizen of the year and was presented with several academic honors. They didn't understand the picture perfect façade was a vain attempt to hide what happened in her life beyond the schoolhouse doors.

There was an immense amount of pressure placed upon the now fifteen year old. While Paige was adorned by her dear best friend and school staff, she still felt terribly out of place amongst her peers. It went beyond the typical social awkwardness for her. This coupled with the secrets from home brought Paige to a breaking point.

In the two years since moving to Woodview, Paige had

officially entered high school, received her first kiss from a boy, and had even gotten drunk, not once, but many times. Unbeknownst to Judith, she had taught her daughter very well. Got a problem? Drink it away. Paige's reality was increasingly hard to accept, and escape to her beautiful field of flowers didn't always provide the relief she needed. Teens always seemed to find alcohol readily available, and Paige was no exception. Sometimes it was the parents who provided it so they could "supervise" their kids' drinking. Other times it was an older brother or the old guy down the street hoping to still look cool to the younger generation.

It was the latter of the three that was the case tonight. Taryn was grounded so Paige had to find someone else to hang out with. It was Friday night and no teenager, especially Paige, wanted to be home.

At eight o'clock Paige got a call from her friend Kari. Kari was a girl who lived in the neighborhood a couple blocks over. She was two years older than Paige and ran with a different group of friends than she was used to. These kids were the fringes of social outcasts and much rougher than Paige was used to. Still, she liked it, she felt daring and almost high off the danger they exuded.

"Hey Paige, watcha doin' tonight?" Kari asked on the other end of the line.

"Nothin', why?" Paige replied.

"Think your mom would let you come over to my house tonight? Reg and the other guys are goin' drinkin' at the river. We could go too if you want."

"Yeah, I'll figure something out with my mom and call you back."

Paige hung up the phone and did a quick practice in her bedroom mirror. She was careful not to stare directly into it. Lowering her voice, she practiced the request over and over until it was perfect. She went downstairs to where Judith and Dave were playing cards and drinking at the kitchen table. Perfect, she thought to herself. Judith appeared be in a great mood, laughing and chatting with Dave. Paige swooped in, delivered her request with precision and received an immediate, albeit slurred, response.

"Yes, you can go…no boys, no cars…and you call me when you get there. Understand?"

"Yes mom, thank you, thank you!" Paige squealed with delight. She ran upstairs and quickly grabbed her bag. She had already packed it in anticipation of Judith's yes. Hardly a minute passed and she was down the steps and out the door on her way to Kari's.

Paige got to Kari's not five minutes later. She knocked loudly on the front door. Kari opened her front door to an exuberant Paige standing there. "Oh my God, she let you go?"

"Yeah," said Paige, "I didn't give details though."

"Cool, come in, we'll finish getting ready before the guys get here."

Paige's stomach filled with tiny flutters in anticipation of her night filled with freedom. She reserved a certain amount of fear that Judith would find out, yet she was thrilled to be part of the group, so much so she was willing to risk getting in trouble.

The girls donned brown and blue makeup and sprayed their hair just shy of having to place fire hazard signs atop their heads. Kari reached into her purse as Paige stared at herself in the mirror. She pulled out two cigarettes, handing one out to Paige.

"You want one?" she asked.

Paige was hesitant not knowing what to say.

"Come on, it won't hurt, just one. You drink don't you, so why not have a smoke too?" Kari asked.

Paige shrugged her shoulders, "Like yeah, okay, give me that, where's the matches dude?"

Paige and Kari lit their cigarettes, each taking tiny drags, coughing up bits of smoke as they did. Trails of smoke spiraled upward in the bedroom.

Kari opened up a window, "Hey blow your smoke out here. My mom won't figure it out that way."

The girls finished the cancer sticks and popped cinnamon stick gum into their mouths.

Ring, ring, the phone chirrped.

Kari jumped on it. "Hello? Yeah. Yeah. Right on dude. Okay."

She hung up the phone and looked at Paige, "You ready for a rad night?"

"Totally dude."

The girls headed out the door and down the street. They walked down the lamplit road until it was just stars and darkness around them. Eventually a pair of lights shone in what had become a gravel road ahead. It was Reg. The closer the girls got, the louder the heavy metal music became. Reg drove a large, gas guzzling car from 1974. The backseat was as big as Paige's couch in her livingroom. The engine loped as it pulled to a stop, seemingly wanting to keep going and not willing to give up without protest. Reg turned the key to off and got out of the car.

"You ladies lookin' for a party?"

Kari stepped right up; putting her hand on her hip she flashed a huge grin. "Like yeah, that's why we're here."

"Right on," said Reg as he held the heavy blue door open, "get on in, there's plenty of room."

Paige peered into the backseat of the car. An eerie glow emitted from inside, a mixture of green dash lights and smoke combined with the sweet stench of beer. She looked around, as if Judith would be standing right there, but the woods were only filled with trees. Kari practically pushed her into the backseat causing Paige to land next to one of Reg's friends, Dustin; there were three guys, two girls and one case of beer.

Dustin had long, wavy hair, small patches of stubble on his face and smelled out of this world good to Paige. He wore a t-shirt and blue jeans pegged at the ankles with a pair of high top tennis shoes rounding out his look. He handed Paige a white can with the word BEER imprinted in black on the side.

"Want one?"

"Sure" Paige said without hesitation. She flipped open the top and sucked the foam out of the can.

"You're my kinda girl. Hey Reg, turn that music up!"

"I will asshole, hang on, I think we need to change out the order here a bit." Reg nudged his friend out of the front seat, giving orders for him to go to the back.

"Where's my Kari, come on sweet thang, I need ya up here with me."

Kari did as she was told. Paige felt the fear slip back in as the comfort of her friend left her side. It was quickly dissolved as her friend's sweet perfume as replaced by the cologne of a teenage male.

"Alright ladies and gentlemen, I think we're set." Reg turned the silver key back over in the ignition, giving permission for the beast to move forward once again.

The beast moved on down the road, windows down, rushing wind competed with musical notes over teenage voices. Dustin was generous with the beer, handing a new one to Paige before the last one was finished. Friend with no name sitting on the other side of Paige offered her a cigarette.

"You smoke don't you?"

Paige took the cigarette from no name, and put it between her lips.

"Light me up baby," she replied haughtily to no name. She loved the attention and power that she was feeling right now. They were two things she was never allowed to feel at home. The car winded down seemingly endless dirt roads, snorting and searching for a perfect spot to come to rest, which it did, some minutes later.

Paige hardly noticed the car stop. In a matter of a half an hour since meeting up with the boys, she had already consumed two beers and had a third open in her hands. From the front, Kari called out Paige's name.

"Paigee, sweetie, I gotta pee, and since you're my best friend in the whole world, let's go together." Paige bent forward and grabbed the back of the front seat.

"Ugh, whew, a bit harder than I thought," she laughed. Her muscles felt like jelly as a good drunk had begun to take its hold.

"Here, let me help with that." Dustin grabbed her hips and gave her a nudge up over the bench seat causing her to nearly topple out the door onto Kari.

The girls headed off into the wooded night, giggling all the way.

"So Reg, you gonna take Kari, right?"

"Well of course dumbshit, you two can fight over her friend, or both take her, whatever."

The boys laughed.

The girls huddled between branches out of sight of the guys.

"So you think Reg likes me?" Kari asked of Paige.

"Yeah, why wouldn't he? He totally wants you."

"God, he is so hot. I'm so lucky. What about you Paigee, which one of the guys do you like? I think Dustin is hot, don't you?"

Paige started laughing. "Yeah, he's hot, but so is his friend. What time is it Kari?"

"What. I dunno, what's it matter?"

Paige drew in a deep breath and looked up at the stars.

"I guess it doesn't," she started giggling again.

The girls walked back to the car. As soon as Reg saw Kari he walked up to her and put his arm around her shoulder.

"Hey babe, whatd'ya say we go find a spot a bit more private, jus' you and me."

Kari hesitated; she was worried about leaving her friend alone. Reg sensed this and quickly warded off any such thought of Kari's with even more smooth talking.

"C'mon, she'll be fine." Touching her chin, he turned her head towards him and planted a long, wet kiss on her lips. That's all it took. "Let's go baby."

Third white label gone, Paige didn't even realize it was just her and the two guys left alone in the woods. By this time she could hardly stand, and the giggles had been replaced by an eerie silence. She was tired and just wanted a place to lie down and go to sleep. No name walked up behind and grabbed her around the waist.

"Are you just like your friend? Hmmm, gonna give me a little tonight?"

Paige tried to wriggle free, but her body wouldn't listen.

"I don't know what you mean."

"Sure you do. Both you girls knew what you wanted comin' out here with us. A couple of little whores, and now you're gonna prove it to me."

"I'm not...I'm not a...whore." Her words competed for breaths.

"Hey man," Dustin said walking up to no name. "Leave her alone man."

"Mind your own fuckin' business. This here is mine."

Dustin was bigger than no name and apparently no name realized that the closer he got. No name threw Paige to the ground and spit next to her. "You're still a whore." He walked back over to the car and stood next to the bumper, popping open another beer.

Paige didn't get up from the ground. It felt too good. The bare earth was cool against her hot cheek. "I'm so tired, I just need some sleep."

Dustin bent down next to Paige. He brushed the hair off of her face. "Sweetie, you can't sleep here."

"Why not?"

"Like, cuz', you jus' can't." Dustin reached down to pick up the teenage girl. No sooner did he reach the pocket of her jeans than she rose up like a frightened animal scared from its burrow.

"Don't touch me," Paige screamed at him in a shrill voice. She scooted across the dirt, trying to get as far away from him as possible. She didn't stop until her back hit the solid stump of an Evergreen tree.

"Whoa," Dustin put his hands up and slowly walked toward the ball of clothes and hair. "It's okay, I didn't mean anything...I just wanted to help."

Paige sat there, rocking back and forth, making lines in the dirt beneath her. She didn't hear him, she didn't hear the sounds in a forests night; she couldn't hear anything.

Dustin knelt down next to her and started drawing lines next to hers in the dirt. He drew silly faces under the now full moonlight. There was something about her that he couldn't just let sit there and forget. In the swirls of dirt his finger touched hers causing both to come to an abrupt stop. He held his breath, expecting another violent reaction, but instead Paige playfully flicked dirt at him.

Dustin held his arms out for her. "Here, I think I make a much better pillow than the ground does."

Paige studied him and yawned. "Yeah, okay, will you keep me safe from the big bad wolf?"

"You know it, come on." Dustin welcomed her with an opened flannel coat. Paige leaned over and fell like a lump into his arms.

She lay there, snuggled in his chest, looking up at the stars. "Like this feels really good. Thank you. Thank you."

Dustin kissed her on the forehead, "Get some sleep kiddo. It's okay now."

Sleep lasted as long as it took for the sun to rise. In the dead of night this wasn't a lengthy amount of time. Paige awoke to the chirping of birds and the croaking of teenage voices still drunk from the night before. No name was asleep in the back of the beast, drool escaping from the sides of his mouth. Reg and Kari emerged from the woods, neither acknowledging the other. Dustin helped Paige up from the ground brushing twigs from her backside.

"Thank you."

"You're welcome," he replied, a twinkle showing through blurry eyes.

The teens piled back into the animal which led them to their sinful destination and headed into town. The girls were dropped off at Kari's house. Paige went inside and got her stuff. It was 5 o'clock in the morning; she hoped nobody would be awake once she got home. She was tired and looked forward to going back to sleep.

She made it into her house unnoticed, slipped upstairs, replaced her clothes with clean pajamas and crawled into bed. A deep, unusually dreamless sleep wrapped itself around the sleeping girl. This was good; it was what she needed after the long night. It wasn't long before her restful slumber was interrupted.

Drop...drop...SPLASH!

"I see my little slut is home." It was Judith standing above her daughter pouring beer over her head. Paige awoke with a start. It took a moment for her to fully grasp what was going on.

"Mom, what are you doing?!" Paige jumped up out of bed, sopping wet with beer. She began to cry.

"Mom, why?"

Judith stood there staring silently at her daughter. "You think you're so perfect. You're not you know. You're not."

"I don't think that mom."

"You don't love me Paige. You only love yourself. You are selfish, just like them."

"Mom, stop...please."

Insult after slurred insult was hurled at Paige. She was defenseless against her mother's verbal assault. As suddenly as it started, she stopped. Judith stood there; unaware of the damage moments like this would cause long term with her daughter.

"Change your sheets; your bed is a mess." And with that Judith turned and left the room. The young teen turned toward the rectangular bed and crawled under the covers. Never mind it was sopping wet, never mind the smell and confusion. Paige didn't feel a thing; she couldn't, far away in her protected field.

She slept until the phone woke her up early in the afternoon. It was Taryn on the other end.

"Hey bud, what's up?"

"Nothin' much," Paige replied flatly.

Taryn ranted on for nearly five straight minutes until she was forced to pause for air.

"Hey, what's wrong, are you okay?"

"Yeah, I'm fine, just tired."

Apparently irked by the one-sided conversation, Taryn turned short on her friend.

"Well, you know you can tell me anything dude, if you can't, it helps when I write things out. Okay?"

"Yeah."

Paige hung up the phone and lay on her bed, starting intently at the ceiling. Her mind blinked like a red, flashing light...off...on...off...on. She didn't want to go downstairs and deal with Judith, not yet.

Instead she decided to take Taryn's advice. Digging through her closet, Paige plucked an old diary. It had been buried in a corner, under old shoeboxes and magazines, for safekeeping. She grabbed a black ink pen from her desk drawer and plopped down on the floor next to her bed.

Nothing happened when she first put pen to paper. A few minutes passed...still nothing. Reaching over to her tape deck, she flicked the on switch and pushed play. Guitar chords and piano keys filled the room. Yes, this is what she needed. The ink flowed from her pen filling the blank lines on the starched, white paper.

Nearly two hours passed. The sun had gone down, changing places with an anxious moon. Paige smelled food dipping its fingers under her door. She shoved her diary into her backpack for another day and ventured closer to the source of the smell.

"Hey Paige, pizza just got here. Are you hungry?" Judith asked of her daughter. Paige squeaked out a cautious 'yes.'

This was Judith's official entry into the "kiss and make-up" stage with her daughter. Pizza and pop were expensive, yet classic signs of things looking up. It was the good stuff from Pizza King.

"There's ice cream in the freezer if you want for later."

"Okay," Paige said as squirreled away three pieces of pizza and a can of pop back upstairs to her bedroom. This was classic Judith, provide gifts for her daughter that just hours before had been her nemesis. Once Paige finished eating, she grabbed clean linen from the hall closet and changed her bedding. Her cleaning didn't stop with her bed. Slowly and methodically Paige put her room back together, tidying up even her surviving row of stuffed animals. Yes, even at 15 she still had her stuffed animal friends, although she no longer entertained them in her make-believe world.

The rest of the weekend was comparatively uneventful, if not downright boring. Paige spent Sunday doing homework and talking on the phone to Taryn. She felt both exhausted and restless at the same time. She couldn't concentrate on her homework; her mind kept drifting to the lyrics coming through the round speaker on her radio. She put her pencil down and ran her fingers through the long, felted fibers of the carpet. Sleep again discovered her in an unusual position, curled up on the floor, textbook for a pillow.

Paige awoke the next morning to the sound of her alarm clock going off. She was still on the floor with a blanket somehow finding its way around her. Although stiff from her unconventional bed, she muddled through her morning routine slower than usual.

At school Paige didn't feel much better. She unloaded the contents of her backpack into the shared locker without so much as a 'good morning' to her best friend.

"What's up chuck?" Taryn asked Paige.

"Nothin'."

"Really?"

"Yeah."

"Doesn't seem like nothing to me dude."

"I don't feel like this right now Taryn, please."

Taryn was offended by her friend's rejection of ceremonial Monday morning greetings. Monday's were the most important. It was a time to catch up on nearly 72 hours of combined gossip and news.

Taryn studied Paige's expression and then watched her friend turn and abruptly walk away. "Wow, what's up with that?" Taryn muttered under her breath. She turned her attention to their overstuffed locker. Pulling books for her first class caused an avalanche of paper to fall to the floor. Included in those papers was Paige's journal – flipped open to where she left off.

Dear Diary,

> Please help me. I don't want to do this anymore – I can't do this. I'm scared. Please just kill me…I want to die. I hate my life. I feel like nothing inside.
>
> Paige

Taryn re-read the tattered notebook page from her best friend's journal. She flipped through a fistful of pages, all of which reaffirmed Paige's intent on leaving this earth. Taryn grabbed the book, crammed the rest of her stuff into the locker, and marched directly down to the counselor's office.

"Mrs. Burke?"

"Good morning Taryn."

"Mrs. Burke, I'm really freaked out. I found this in my locker. It's Paige's."

Mrs. Burke reached out with long, spindly fingers and took the notebook from Taryn. Glancing over the scrawled words, she confirmed Taryn's concerns with short 'ahems' and 'I see's' coming from her mauve toned lipsticked mouth. She raised a thinly plucked brow at Taryn.

"I'll take care of this. Thank you Taryn."

The teen stared back in disbelief. "That's it? My best friend wants to kill herself, now head to class?"

Mrs. Burke towered over Taryn. What she lacked in girth, she made up for in height. The other eyebrow was raised up, "Take your excuse and head to class Taryn. We are finished here."

Taryn slumped her shoulders and headed to first hour. Mrs. Burke turned to the office aide and asked, "Will you please look up

Paige Miles? I need to see her right away." The doe eyed office aide responded with a sheepish, "Okay."

Paige was called out of first hour math. She didn't mind being called to the office; she wasn't the sort of kid that did bad things at school. She was surprised to hear she was being summoned to the counselor's office though. Her schedule was fine.

Mrs. Burke stood there in the office door peering at Paige over the rim of her glasses. "Come in Paige, we need to talk." She walked into the office, completely unaware of what was about to occur, until she saw her notebook sitting on the office desk. Her legs suddenly became heavy, like lead weights; the smile on her face quickly diminishing. The young girl sat down in the chair adjacent to the desk, hands shaking, she shoved them deep into the pockets of her sweatshirt.

Mrs. Burke took in a deep breath and exhaled an equal amount. She shuffled some papers on her desk, almost as if purposefully delaying the talk she was about to have with Paige. She took her glasses off her face, folded them neatly in her lap and turned to Paige.

"Paige, I'm concerned here. I read the journal that Taryn found in your locker. What do you have to say for yourself?"

Paige sat there, completely numb. She instantly put up walls around her; solid brick with no way in or out. A small tear rolled down her cheek, but no sound escaped through her lips. The counselor continued to talk, mostly about Paige's responsibility to others and how selfish it was of her to even consider taking her own life. Paige just stared past Mrs. Burke, out the window and on through the cloudy sky. She imagined herself up there in the sky, floating gently among the billowy cloud tops.

"Are you listening to me?" Mrs. Burke asked in an increasingly irritated tone. There was no response from the girl. Paige couldn't, it was physically impossible for her; she had become a master at creating her own private world to escape into.

"Alright then, I have to legally let you know that I have reported your suicidal intentions to the National Hotline. At this point I will not tell your parents if you promise to see our school addictions specialist.

Paige snapped back to reality. "What?" she said almost startled.

"Yes, as a condition of me not telling your parents, I am requiring you to meet weekly with our addictions specialist. Reading your journal tells me that you need more help than you know."

"Me? *I* need the help?" she asked, beginning to become irritated with this whole conversation.

"You don't think you do?" Mrs. Burke inquired back.

"No, I don't. Why don't you go help my drunken mom? *She* needs the help, not *me!*" Irritation had now morphed into full-blown anger.

"Calm down now. We don't need to raise our voices here."

"*We* aren't raising our voices; *I'm* raising mine. I'm done. Can I go back to class now?" Her voice was flat and definite. She was not interested in any more talking with Mrs. Burke or anyone else. She took her pass and headed out the door of the office. Her mind was a swirling sea of anger, distrust and resentment – a powerful cocktail of mortar to build her increasingly taller brick wall.

12 FIRST COMMITMENT

Paige's lifetime of therapy had been born on that day, and just like a developing child, she learned to manipulate therapists, family and friends, one after another. Over time she learned problems were issues and worries were concerns. She learned about coping skills and how to be a good communicator. What she didn't learn was what to do when all those things she had been working on quit working. That's precisely what happened one fateful day in the midst of winter's grasp.

Derek was at work, and although Paige had the day off due to weather, she had still asked him to take the kids to daycare. She craved peace and quiet – some bit of solitude in her chaotic life. It was the first time in nearly six months Derek had taken the kids to daycare himself, yet he grumbled as if it were a daily chore. Paige still got up with the kids, fed and dressed them, and ensured they were safely in Derek's vehicle.

She watched through the frost-paned glass as the car drove off. Putting her coffee down, she swished in slippered feet back to her bedroom. Crawling back under the still warm sheets, she pulled the covers up to her chin and stared at the cream colored walls. Her eyes followed every detail of the bumpy finish, cracks careening across plains of plaster, running headlong into wood chair railings acting as bumpers.

Memories and images of various events in Paige's life fluttered across her eyes like an old-time slide show. This was not how she had imagined life turning out – none of it. She felt a failure as a wife, with a husband who no longer committed to the intimate bonds of their marriage. Her breathing increased as she began to feel trapped. There was no way out of it. This was, is, and always will be her life, no matter what. Paige knew she must be dying.

She sat up in bed and put her head down into her hands. Her breathing began to slow, as she swung her legs over the edge of the bed, dropping down until her toes touched the cold, wooden floor. She didn't feel it though; she felt nothing, her body was just a hollow shell. Paige walked to the living room and sat on the couch. She stayed for a few minutes and then walked back down the hallway. Up and down she paced, running her hands through her hair, then clenching and unclenching her fists. Her paced increased at a feverish rate. If her feet were matchsticks, they would've struck the wooden floor on fire.

On her last turn around she stopped in her tracks. A sliver of sun had pierced the kitchen window shining rays of light upon the butcher block of knives. Like a bug to light, Paige turned and headed toward the cutlery. Her hand reached out for the silver handled clever clinging to its metal like an industrial strength magnet. She held the knife outward, turning it from side to side in admiration of its glaring sharpness. Paige ran the tip of the knife up and down the inside of her arm. With each pass she became bolder with the blade, holding back an urge so deep inside her it hurt. She pointed the knife at a blue, raised vein, pressing its sharp tip closer to breaking the skin.

Rrrinngg…rriinnggg. The phone rang right in front of her, pulling Paige from her trancelike state. She dropped the knife to the floor, startled by the sound. It was Derek on the other end of the line.

"Hello?" he asked, but there was no answer.

"Hello? Paige? Paige is that you?" he asked with more

certainty.

His wife couldn't talk. The lump in her throat acted as a worn tarp, allowing bits of air past it but no words.

Derek was really beginning to get irritated. He had only called home about a check that apparently hadn't cleared the bank yet and he was getting the annoying debt collector calls at work. He didn't need any more crap today.

God intervened, filling Paige's lungs with a burst of air that allowed her to speak again. "Help me," she managed to say with a soft squeak.

"What? Help you what Paige?"

"Please...please...I...I...."

"Paige? Paige, honey, answer me please!"

Beep, beep, beep, beep. The line had gone dead, Paige disconnecting the other end.

Derek was terrified. He knew his wife hadn't felt well from time to time, but had never experienced anything like this. He grabbed his coat and briefcase from his desk, stopping briefly by his boss's to explain he had a family emergency. He got into his car and sped down the highway toward home, not knowing what he would find.

He made it to their house in half the time it usually takes. Derek parked the car, not bothering to even take the keys out. He headed up the stairs, his heart thumping hard in his chest. For all of his shortcomings, he was extraordinarily level headed under the worst of circumstances.

He found Paige in the front room, crumpled up next to the couch, her legs drawn up tightly to her chest. She was still in her nightgown, feet bare on the floor.

Derek walked up to his wife slowly, putting his hand out so as not to frighten her, much like one would do with a stray dog. He crouched down within a foot of her and speaking in whispers, called out her name.

"Paige? Hon? Come on sweetheart, it's me."

Her eyes looked right through her husband of eight years. She was too far away to hear him.

He put his hand on her shoulder, first one, and then the other. Inching in closer to her, he got into position to pick her up.

"Honey, I'm just gonna pick you up, okay? We need to get you some help."

Paige's stiffened body went limp as Derek tightened his grasp on her. He picked her up and carried her in his arms, just as he had done when they first met. He headed back out the door and down the stairs, the reverse of what he had done just a few minutes ago. This time though he held precious cargo in his arms. He put his wife in the car and shut the door.

Derek got in and started the vehicle up, heading down the road as fast as legally possible. He put his hand on the back of Paige's head, feeling the long strands of hair.

"Honey, it's going to be okay. We're gonna get you to a doctor, okay?"

Paige couldn't hear him; she was locked away in her own world. This time there was no field of flowers, only a blank, sterile room. She screamed inside her white walls, but no one could hear her. She felt along the bumpy stucco for any sign of an exit. Her hand rested upon something cold and metal. This must be it; this must be the way out. She pulled as hard as she could, but something kept blocking her.

Derek swerved the car into oncoming traffic. Paige had her hand securely on the door handle trying to jump. "No!" he screamed at his wife. A surge of adrenalin came to the rescue as he dug his fingers into the flesh of his wife's arms. Tiny bruises would be left to explain later on.

Paige's vision cleared and a window opened up in the white room. She peered outside and watched as Derek pulled into the hospital parking lot and escorted her inside the brightly lit emergency room door. He sat his wife down in the cloth covered wooden chair and went up to the admission clerk.

"Yes sir, may I help you?" the older woman said in a nasally voice.

How was Derek to answer this? It's not every day you take your wife to a psych ward because she's gone plumb crazy.

He lowered his voice to answer her, "Um…my wife needs…she needs…to see…somebody."

"Who would that be sir?"

Thank God Derek was in emergency mode or else he would've gone off on this lady.

He looked around the room and drew in another breath. "This is an emergency room, right? People see doctors here, right? My wife needs to see a *doctor.*"

"Sir, if you would please calm down and take a number a *doctor* will be with you when he can" the clerk said pointing to the red ticket machine at the end of the counter.

Derek stomped over to the plastic machine and hit the top of it so hard that not one, but two numbers popped out. An insane chuckle escaped from his lips. He figured by the end of the night maybe he'd need a number too if this continued on. He walked back over to his wife and sat down next to her. He gently nudged her head onto his shoulder and stroked her hair. She was like a child in his arms. His breathing slowed to match hers; it felt as if the storm was slowly ebbing.

He was brought back to reality by the callous clerk calling out the next number. He went up with Paige and sat down in front of a grey computer. He politely complied with the requests for identification and insurance cards.

"So, what brings you here tonight?" the clerk asked next.

"Well, my wife is having some problems."

"Sir, your wife needs to answer me, not you."

"Ma'am, what brings you here tonight?" the clerk directed at Paige.

Paige pressed her face tightly to the glass paned window inside the room in her mind she was still trapped in. "I need help!

Please help me!" she screamed. Her cries for help fell on deaf ears. They couldn't hear her.

"Ma'am, what is the reason you're here for?" the clerk repeated.

Still there was no answer. Derek thought to himself, "How many different ways is this lady gonna ask her before she figures out she can't answer?"

"Listen, my wife is sick, but not medically, it's something wrong with her mental state. She's not going to answer you."

The clerk promptly put her pen down and pulled out a green file folder from her desk. She ran her fingers down a long list of names finally resting on the one she apparently needed. She picked up the phone and dialed. "Yes, this is Sharon down here in admitting. Yes, I'm good, how are you. Oh yeah...."

"Come on," Derek thought to himself, "this is not time for a social phone call."

"Yeah, listen, I've got a potential new admit down here. Can you send someone down for a consult? Thank you."

The clerk hung up the phone and proceeded to give Derek a folder with a list of verbal instructions. He took his wife's arm and led her down the hall following the blue arrow until he came to the first room on his left and then the red arrow to a dimly lit area of the hospital that hardly anyone goes to. They sat down in the double chairs outside the curtained door and waited. Soon enough an older man came clicking down the tiled hall.

He stopped right in front of the couple and spoke, "You must be Mr. and Mrs. Hanes."

"Um, it's Hayes," Derek corrected him.

The doctor pulled the curtain back and motioned for them to come in, "Please Mr. and Mrs. Hanes, this way."

He asked Paige a litany of questions, some personal, some routine. "How old are you? What brings you here? Do you have thoughts of harming yourself or someone else?" Paige watched his lips move like a tug boat through a blurry fog. She was tired and felt confused by the line of questioning. She looked at Derek, "Can we go home now?"

"No hon, we can't. You're going to stay here and get some rest for a while, okay?"

She looked back down at the hard parquet floor, swinging her slipper socks back and forth. The doctor scribbled more notes on a paper and then walked out of the room. The time passed slowly until yet another nurse came from behind the curtain. This time she was accompanied by a tall, male orderly dressed in classic white.

"Alright Mrs. Hayes, it's time to go upstairs."

Paige gave Derek a kiss on the cheek and hugged him goodbye. He watched as the nurse escorted his wife by the arm out of the curtained room and down the hall. He wanted to feel relief, but all that came to him was dread of having to go back home and take care of the kids by himself.

An equally hesitant Paige shuffled down the hallway in fern green slipper socks. She laughed to herself as she thought about the worst Christmas gift ever now attached to her feet, shepherding her toward the locked steel doors ahead of her.

The nurse passed a photo badge in front of a square box and the doors clicked open in return. She stood behind Paige, ensuring her patient was securely inside the unit before proceeding. "This way hon. I'm jus' gonna ask some questions. I know it's late and you want to get to bed. Jus' have a seat there," she said pointing to a stiff backed plastic chair.

Paige eased down into the chair and stared listlessly downward.

"We'll skip the strip search tonight, okay hon?" Paige thought she was kidding – she wasn't. She raised a brow, not breaking her floor gaze.

"I'm thinking, no hoping, you don't have nothing hidden in that gown." The nurse was half joking and Paige was only half listening. She went down a list of questions. Sheet after sheet of paper was filled with checks and marks. Many were answered by nods and shrugs. Paige felt as if she were at an intake session with yet another therapist.

"Were you abused as a child? Do you smoke? Ever tried to commit suicide?" On and on she went for nearly an hour. Paige wondered what this woman's perception of long was if this was short. Finally the nurse stood up and like a child Paige followed without asking. She led her down the dimly lit hall to a heavy wooden door. She took a bundle of keys from her pocket and unlocked the door latching it open against the wall.

"If you need another blanket or something else, just let someone at the desk know. Try to get some sleep hon', you've had a long night."

Paige crawled into bed between starched white hospital sheets which provided no relief for the polyester cotton blend hospital scrubs she was wearing. Her head barely hit the crisp linen pillow and she was asleep.

Staff came around every fifteen minutes and checked on those who were at high risk to harm themselves. Those at risk to harm someone else were labeled AP for 'assault precautions', but not checked as frequently.

Paige only slept a few hours, she just couldn't stay comfortable. She sat up in bed and looked around the room. The floor was cold, hard tiles tucked into the stark, white walls with rubber edging. There was a bathroom in her room with a fake mirror and metal toilet with no lid. The shower had no curtain or door. There was a window in her room that ran the length of one wall. Louvered blinds were sandwiched between two pieces of plastic faux glass.

The fog of disorientation began to clear and its replacement was no better. An anger was brewing in her for being locked up in a psych ward. She jumped off the bed and stormed her doorway. She looked both ways, just as an obedient child does when crossing the street, before proceeding back down the dimly lit hallway. Paige spotted a younger man with a buzz cut reading the newspaper at the desk. She figured this was her guy, some college intern working the night shift – should be easy. She walked up to him and stood squarely in front of the desk. There was no acknowledgement.

She cleared her throat, "Um, excuse me."

Intern put his paper down and looked up. "Can I help you?" he answered in a bland, unconcerned voice.

"Yeah, I need my clothes."

"What's your name?"

"Paige."

"Paige what," intern inquired.

"Really, how many Paige's do you have on this unit? C'mon. Paige Hayes."

Intern reached over to a stack of grey charts and pulled one from the very bottom. He flipped through it briskly and then placed it back on the counter.

"A nurse will meet with you in the morning."

Paige looked at the clock on the wall. "It's 4:45am. It is morning," she said to him.

Intern was apparently not up to earning his pay by talking to patients this morning because he seemingly became irritated with Paige's request.

"You get your clothes when it's morning on the unit. Right now it is still night. Go back to your room and get some sleep."

She wasn't satisfied with his answer. "I can't sleep because I don't have my clothes. Don't you understand?" she stammered.

By now intern was clearly irritated. He stood up, fitting his shirt into his waist. Behind him appeared yet another overpaid, underworked orderly looking equally menacing at their non-compliant patient.

"Ma'am, Gary here has been really nice. I believe he asked you to go back to bed. The doctor will see you in the morning and you can talk to him about your clothes."

With one last triumphant sigh, Paige again declared it was morning, yet resigned herself to returning to her room. She stomped down the hall like a child who was denied a candy bar at the store checkout line.

She did get back to sleep, eventually. In fact she slept through morning meds, breakfast, groups and lunch. It wasn't until late afternoon when a nurse came in to check vitals that Paige finally awoke. The nurse announced the doctor was ready see her now. Paige was still groggy from her long slumber. She wondered almost if she had been slipped something to make her sleep like she did. She made a mental note to herself that from now on she would keep all cups to herself and in her direct sight at all times.

The nurse showed her to yet another wooden door in the corridor. She stepped through the doorway and motioned for Paige to sit down. Moments later a middle aged man in his 40's with milky white skin and a thick accent stepped into the room followed by a mousy looking woman in a white lab coat. They sat down simultaneously in chairs opposite of Paige and her disinterested nurse.

The doctor spoke in an almost accusatory tone at the young woman sitting across from him.

"I am Dr. Klaus Kristoff."

Paige recognized his name from her client's files at work. He had a reputation for an air of arrogance, especially toward women. He wasn't really interested in solving patients problems, just popping a pill to keep them quiet and send them on their drug induced way.

"So tell me Paige, why are you here?"

"Isn't that supposed to be what you *tell* me, not *ask* me? Don't ask don't tell. He-he."

Dr. Kristoff cleared his throat and spoke once more, louder this time as if his patient had a hearing problem rather than a mental problem.

"I would like to know what brought you here."

"Isn't it clear?" The lump in her throat started and tears welled in her eyes. "I'm dying. I'm here, in a hospital...in the loony bin...because I'm dying. Satisfied?!" she answered back emphatically.

"And how do you know you are dying?"

Paige shifted in her chair, become uncomfortable with his line of questioning. Her brain felt fuzzy and confused. It was as if she was on a trip, knowing her destination, but not the path to get there.

"I just know I am. I can't explain it."

"Who's your psychiatrist?"

"I don't have one."

Dr. Kristoff paused while raising an eyebrow. "No psychiatrist? How about medication? What do you take?"

"Nothing, just an allergy pill."

"Nothing for your anxiety or depression?"

"No, I can't take those. Do you know what can happen to you? Do you know the side effects?

"How do you expect to get well if you don't take the medication?"

Paige wanted so badly to continue the protest, but she couldn't organize her thoughts well enough to do so. The doctor continued to scribble notes on his yellow steno pads in front of her. He put down his pen and clasped his hands in front of him.

"So tell me, you are obviously depressed. What else do you think I might diagnose you with?"

She looked up at him in disbelief. "You're the expert. Isn't that your job? Diagnose them and dope them?!" she replied back.

It was funny that of all the human emotions trapped inside the minds and bodies of so many mentally ill people, anger always found a way to rear its ugly head. In Paige, that anger usually morphed into its evil twin – sarcasm.

She abruptly stood up, which prompted the nurse to jump just a little.

"Okay there Doctor Quack, I'm done here, and so are you. Couch time is over."

And with that, she proudly strutted out of the room believing full well she had won the battle and her release was imminent. That wasn't quite so. In fact, she would spend the next five days in here, sullenly wandering the halls. The staff described her mood as "labile" – alternating from happy to sad to somewhere in between, but never on one for very long.

She spent some time in "groups" talking about feelings and events in people's lives that paled in comparison to hers. She mostly sat in the large chairs and stared at the other patients, wondering if that was her destiny, in and out of mental wards, losing family, friends, and eventually her mind.

Her sessions with the good doc never did improve. In fact, at one point, he tried to convince Derek to proceed with commitment papers. Derek declined, but not out of the goodness of his cold, little heart. No, he didn't want his wife gone any longer than necessary. She was essential to the raising of his children, shopping and meal preparation – all of the things he loathed. He felt it was the duty of his wife to take on, not his.

He did visit her quite frequently while she was in the hospital. It looked good to others, caring, wonderful husband, seeing his wife who had just had a mental breakdown, staying by her side just like his vows had promised. He would tenderly kiss her forehead and assure her everything was going to be all right. He told her how he would pick up the slack around the house and become a more devoted husband. Unfortunately, Derek was just as cunning as he was intelligent, and Paige bought every word of it.

He called Taryn at one point, something that was a total surprise to her. She hadn't talked to either one of them for a couple of years. Then one day Derek's name showed up on her caller I.D.

"Hello?" she answered hesitantly when the phone rang.

"Um, is Taryn there? This is Derek...Derek Hayes."

She wasn't sure if she should even answer. Why was Derek calling and not her best friend Paige? Oh no, something must be wrong.

"Yes, Derek, this is Taryn. Is everything alright with Paige? The kids?"

"The kids are fine. It's Paige. She...she." He couldn't finish his sentence. He cleared his throat and tried again.

"She's in the hospital."

"What?! What do you mean? What happened? Is she going to be okay?"

"Jesus Taryn, calm down. She's fine, she's just stupid, you know?"

"Listen Derek, I didn't even need to continue this conversation once I knew it was you. Tell me what's wrong with my friend dammit!"

"Taryn, don't start with me. I'm only calling because I can't handle this. She's gone crazy or something. She's locked up in a psychiatric ward and quite frankly, I don't want her to get out. I don't want to take care of this shit. That's for you to do. She's *your* best friend, not mine."

"No Derek, you idiot, she's your *wife*!"

Derek collected his thoughts and presented Taryn with an offer. "Come out here tomorrow. I'll fly you out from Montana and you can be with your friend when she gets out."

Taryn didn't trust him as far as she could throw him. Given his girth, that wasn't too far.

"Listen Derek, I want to come out there, I really do, but I can't right now. I'm in the middle of taking care of a very sick woman. She's only got a few weeks left at best. I can make it out after that, if you want."

The other end of the line was silent. "Derek…Derek, are you still there?"

Derek was seething. "Yes, I'm here. Thanks for nothing Taryn." And with that, he hung up. Taryn was ticked, and the more she thought about her conversation with him, the angrier she became. She would take Derek up on his offer, just not yet.

Paige awoke on the morning of Day 5 in the hospital to the nurse wheeling her cart into the room just as she did every day at 7am.

"How do you feel this morning?" she asked Paige as she

placed the blood pressure cuff around her arm.

Paige looked out the window and noticed the sun was up. She managed to feel its warmth on her face through the heavy paned window. "Pretty good I think. Thanks."

"Well, that's a big difference from earlier this week," replied the nurse.

"I know, it is, isn't it?" Paige said. Her own words surprised her. Maybe she was ready to go home.

"The doctor is seeing patients this morning about nine o'clock. I think breakfast is out in the day room, you should go."

"Yeah, I think I will," Paige replied. She got up took a shower first. The water fell softly on her skin. She felt an energy that she hadn't had in such a long time. It was a weird feeling. She put on clean clothes, brushed her teeth and proceeded down the hall to breakfast in the day room. She hoped this would be her last day of the grey trays and plastic spoons.

Paige was hardly finished with her scrambled eggs when she heard her name called from the nurse's station.

"Paige, the doctor is ready to see you," said one of the nurse's. "Follow me."

She did so, this time with a little more urgency to her step.

It wasn't Dr. Kristoff this morning; it was another psychiatrist from a neighboring hospital. During weekends and some holidays the doctors floated, or took turns, filling in for each other so the other may have a break. This doctor appeared to be in a hurry, not even taking the time to offer up his name. Paige wondered if he even had the right file in front of him.

"So how do you think you are today, Ms. Hayes?"

"I think I'm doing much better. In fact, I'd like to go home," she replied with a smile, straightening up in her chair.

"Do you have a psychiatrist to see once you leave here?"

"Yeah, I know of some. I'll make an appointment." Paige knew full well that of all the questions she had to answer, this was the most crucial, even if she had to lie.

"Are you still feeling suicidal?"

"No," Paige looked away, "I feel really good. I really just want to go home."

The doctor scribbled some more notes on his yellow pad. It looked just like the one that Dr. Kristoff had been using. Paige wondered if some notepad company had a monopoly on doctor notepad usage.

"Well then, I see no reason for you to continue staying here. I think that there are sufficient resources for you to continue treatment on the outside."

Paige felt a little elation beginning to build. This had worked. They were really going to release her.

"Hmm, one more thing, what about your medications?"

"Medications?"

"Yes, what are you taking? It says here an antipsychotic, anti-anxiety and anti-depressant were suggested. I have no records though for what you've been taking in here. What about that?"

Shit, Paige thought to herself, *she was so close. She had to think up something quick.*

"Um, I tried a couple of things and had a reaction. I'll talk it over with the psychiatrist when I leave here and see about getting something else."

The doctor paused a few more moments. "Okay then, I'll go ahead and sign your discharge." Just like that, no verifying, no second guessing or checking, just sign and release. Either Paige was that good, or this guy was just that dumb.

Once she was finished in his office, she almost trotted down the hall to the nurse's desk. She asked to use the phone so she could dial Derek. She got him on the first ring.

"Hey hon, it's me, I'm released! Can you come get me?"

"Sure," he hesitated, "the doctor didn't call me. You really get to come home?"

"Yes, it's all better, just get here!" she said in a pressured voice to her husband on the other end of the line.

Paige busied herself with packing her belongings out of the grey and white room. She fixed her hair once last time in the faux mirror and waited on the edge of her bed until the nurse came around the corner doorway of her room to announce Derek's arrival.

"All right Mrs. Hayes, he's here. Time to go home."

The nurse stepped aside to reveal Derek, standing there in blue jeans, a white t-shirt and athletic shoes. He held his arm out to his wife and enveloped her in his broad chest. She felt warm and safe, something that she would feel one last time with her husband, only now.

13 DENIAL

It is true that behavior is purposeful and willful. That is, we are each our own agents of change in a world that holds rewards and disappointments. In Paige's world, those disappointments often outweighed the reward. Despite the efforts she placed upon the actions she produced, the next two years would hold this unbalanced proclamation true.

Paige spent the next couple of weeks after her "breakdown" explaining her absence to family, friends and her children. She was honest with where she had gone, even to her children. Lindsay was six years old now, defiant and wild as ever. Paige looked at her with tears in her eyes, knowing full well that the genetic demons that plagued her would most likely do the same for her little girl.

She spoke carefully to Lindsay, "Honey, you know where mommy went?"

Lindsay didn't look away from her doll, but spoke anyway. "When mommy?"

"Last month honey. I went away because I didn't feel good." She hesitated and continued. "Sometimes grownups don't feel very good in their head. They need a break, and there's nothing wrong with that." She spoke to her daughter in a half child, half grown up manner like she always did. "Mommy took a break, and now she feels better."

"Okay mommy," Lindsay replied changing her gaze from her doll to her mother standing in front of her. That was it; that was the beauty of a child. They didn't hold onto things like adults did. They hadn't learned that little trick yet. The forgiveness of a child was the most powerful thing in the world.

Ding Dong. Ding Dong. Ding Dong.

"Holy crap, hang on a minute," Paige hollered from the back room.

Still the doorbell continued on. *Ding Dong. Ding....* Paige grabbed the doorknob and flung the door open. Instinct would've dictated her looking out the window first, but she ignored her gut for once. The door stood open and in its path was Taryn, all the way from Montana.

"Holy shit!" Paige exclaimed with a big smile on her face. "Oh my God, what are you doing here?" she said, hugging her best friend.

"You know me, can't stay in one place too long. It'd been awhile since I got to get on a plane, and, well, I thought now would be a good time."

Paige dropped her hands to her sides and took a step back. She looked down at the ground, the smile on her face following her movements. "You know, don't you?"

Taryn wasn't one to mince words; in fact, she'd only grown more brazen as time had passed. "Yes, I know you just got out of the loony bin," she said tongue-in-cheek. "It's kinda cool having a crazy friend you know," she said enveloping Paige back into her arms.

"How did you know? Who told you?"

"Derek. Can you believe it? Derek actually called me. He must've been desperate to actually have to say more than two words to me. Hey, you got a lighter or matches?" she asked pulling out a pack of cigarettes from her satchel.

"Um, yeah, hey, let me check on the kids and we can go in the backyard."

"Oohh, just like when we were thirteen. Is there a shed we can hide behind too?" Taryn asked haughtily.

Paige checked on Lindsay, who was in a coma-like trance over cartoons on the t.v. Aaron was still at Judith's house. He stayed there a lot, especially since Paige had been in the hospital.

Taryn made her way to the back of the house and settled on an old wooden chair parked on the sun porch. She took off her sweatshirt and hiked up her pajama pants a bit more.

"Ugh, how do you handle this weather Paige? It's hot, it's cold, and speaking of hot, my boobs are sweating, and I think I even have sweat dripping down my ass crack. This weather is crazy, ice cold out there," she said pointing to the world beyond the panes of glass, "and blazing hot here, on your, what do they call this thing?"

"A sun porch," Paige replied.

"Oh, well la ti da then. I thought only rich people had those."

"Maybe I am one of those people," Paige teased back.

"Um yeah, and I'm the President of the United States. How do you stand it here?" Taryn replied.

"I don't know; we just sorta get used to it around here. It's either ass drippin' hot or ass freezin' cold."

"Hmm, nice place to live," Taryn said sarcastically. She took another drag of her cigarette. "Too bad there are not even hot guys to be around that make it worth it." She looked at her best friend's face. "No, Derek doesn't count in my book either. By the way, when does his smiling face come home for the day?"

"Around six or so; just depends what he's got going on at the office."

The two girls, turned women, talked for nearly an hour straight catching up on old times. Lindsay came out of the house and onto the porch every seven minutes, which marked each commercial in her television shows.

"How long are you planning on staying?" Paige asked, standing up and showing Taryn back inside and upstairs to the guest room.

"Long enough to get my best friend back."

Paige paused briefly on the stairwell, not looking back at Taryn.

"What do you mean?"

"Jesus Paige, you live in a flippin' beige house. There is no color here, none!"

"What's that supposed to mean?"

"Never mind, let's just have some fun. We can talk about all of that stuff later."

Taryn threw her bags on the bed and looked around the room. There was a standard queen size bed with a half dozen throw pillows and matching comforter, all of various shades of brown. There were matching beige lamps resting on end tables tucked up to the sides of the bed. The walls were a crème color with a few scenic pictures that matched. She wandered out into the hall and looked at the pictures of various friends and family on the wall. She took down the picture of Paige's wedding to Derek and walked back to her room with it. She put it down on the end table and walked back out of the room and headed back downstairs.

Paige was working on dinner in the kitchen with Lindsay darting back and forth underfoot. "Makin' dinner for the hubby? You're quite the little housewife" Taryn teased.

"Oh you know me, Miss Housewife Extraordinaire."

"That's the problem, I don't know you anymore. This isn't *you*. This is crap, and you know it. What happened to *you*?"

"I don't know what you're talking about. This is *me*. Maybe *you're* the one who's changed, not *me*," Paige replied.

"Wow, I don't know how to get through to you. You know what? We need a girl's night. When's the last time you had one of those?"

"Um…um, let me think. Hold on. I know this answer. I can do it." A small smile escaped Paige's mouth. "Ooh, I got it! I'm thinking it was back in the Middle Ages, no, wait, the Industrial Revolution."

"Oh whatever," Taryn replied.

"I know, and I wasn't even with a girl. But I was out, doesn't that still count?" Paige said.

"Uh, not with a girl? Does that mean a guy? I'm not sure I like where this is going."

Taryn was cut off from any further interrogation. The front door opened and Derek came through the doorway, closing the door slowly behind him as his eyes locked on to one of his mortal enemies – Taryn.

Taryn seized the opportunity to be the first to say something. She liked being in charge and she especially liked being first. "Oh hey there," she waved a hand at Derek from the kitchen.

"Um, hi. This is a surprise," he said back loosening up his tie as he talked.

"Really? How can that be? You're the one who invited me." Taryn opened the fridge and grabbed two beers. She opened one for herself and then offered one out to Derek.

"Beer? This is how a good housewife does it right? Husband walks through the door, exhausted from a tough day at work, and his wife hands him a beer."

"Thank you. Don't mind if I do," Derek said grabbing the beer from Taryn's hand with a twisted smile on his face. He hated that bitch, with every fiber in his body. He didn't understand what she was doing here. He had called her in a moment of weakness, and now regretted it.

"Oooh, manners and everything. Good job with this one," she said looking at Paige.

"Hon, dinner will be ready in about 20 minutes. It's your favorite, roast beef with gravy over mashed potatoes." Paige tried her best to placate her husband in light of her friend's arrival and flippant comments.

"Yeah, I'll be in my room." Like a child Derek walked heavy footed down the hall to their bedroom. The less time he had to spend around either one of those women, the better.

Paige finished making dinner and served up a plate for Lindsay. She disappeared down the hall with it and came back into the kitchen. She then dished up a plate for Derek and again, went down the hall for a few moments and returned empty handed.

"Hey, don't dish up my plate, cuz each time you do, you disappear down the hall and don't bring it back" said Taryn laughing.

"Yeah, they like to eat in their rooms so they can watch t.v."

"You mean your kid and your husband each eat in their own bedrooms while you sit in here?"

"Yeah."

"Doesn't that seem weird to you?" Taryn asked Paige.

"What? Where we all eat?"

"Not just where you eat. That's secondary weirdness. This whole set up isn't right. You're just playing house. It's like sitting here watching a movie. You're a character on the silver screen. Soon enough, there won't be anything left that is real."

"Did you want gravy on your mashed potatoes?" Paige asked.

"I forgot just how stubborn you could be Paige. That's good. That's really good. At least there's still something left for me to work with."

The two ate in silence. Taryn stared intently at her friend, watching every bite, every flinch. Paige sat and thought about what she needed to do next, check on Lindsay, call Judith. Crap, call Judith. She hated to do that, but she couldn't trust Derek to watch the kids on his own.

"I need to call my mom," Paige said breaking the silence.

Taryn dropped her fork. "Why?"

"If we're gonna go out tonight, I need to get my mom to babysit Lindsay."

"Doesn't she already have Aaron?"

"Yeah."

"And isn't Derek the *dad* to both of them?"

"Yes. Is this a quiz show? What are you getting' at?"

"What I'm getting at is Derek is her dad, and he has responsibilities. You don't make him do enough. My God, you've kissed his ass since the moment he's gotten home. He needs to do *something* on his own!"

"He does do something. He works long hours; he needs a break when he gets home."

"So do you Paige. When is your break? You work just like he does, and then you take care of these kids."

Paige stood up at the table and walked down the hall toward her room, leaving Taryn sitting at the table gape mouthed. She returned a few minutes later and sat back down. She picked up her fork and continued eating her roast beef. She could feel Taryn staring at her.

"What?"

"What do you mean what?"

"Okay, I've let you screw with me long enough. Now why are you staring at me?" Paige asked Taryn.

"You're amazing my friend. What time do we get to leave?"

"Nine o'clock. Lindsay should be asleep by then. I get to pick the place."

Taryn looked at the digital clock above the stove. "Okay, we've got two hours to get you ready. Ooh, I'm excited!"

Taryn offered to do the dinner dishes while Paige tended to Lindsay. She gave her a bath and helped her get fresh pajamas on for bed. Paige combed and braided her daughter's hair, just like she did every night. She tucked her in between purple and pink sheets and put a movie on for her. Just before she stood up, she placed a kiss on her daughter's forehead.

"I love you kiddo." It was Paige's vow to ensure she told her children she loved them every day. She wasn't sure when the last time she heard those words escape Derek's lips in the presence of his children.

"Love you too mommy."

Paige went across the hall to her room. Derek was laying there on the bed, staring at the television set, remote in hand. She opened the closet door and began thumbing through some clothes. Pulling down a pair of brown, hip hugger cords from the top shelf, she found a matching peasant top on a hanger.

Derek didn't say a word to his wife. He was sure she was

144

cheating on him, but he couldn't' prove it. He wasn't interested in talking to her at this point about that or anything else. His curiosity though, got the best of him.

"What time you say you'd be home?"

"Not sure. You shouldn't have to do anything. Lindsay's had her bath and she's in bed. I'll make sure she's completely asleep before I leave." Paige walked out of the bedroom before Derek could respond to him. This pissed him off, and she knew it. She also knew not to be overtly confrontational with him, thus she chose the passive aggressive route – something he had taught her very well.

Paige went out of the bedroom and back down the hall. She passed by the kitchen, which was now quiet. She headed up the stairs to the guest bedroom where Taryn was humming to herself. The humming stopped when Taryn saw Paige standing there in the doorway.

"Alrighty, let's see what kinda hoochie momma clothes you got in your hands there."

Paige laughed, "Far from hoochie momma, but I think my butt looks good in these pants."

"Well, get them on, let's see!" Paige slipped the rust brown cords onto each leg, up over her hips, and snuggly fastened the zipper. She turned in a little circle for Taryn.

"Nice. Very nice! Now the shirt." Paige complied and put the peasant top on over her head and slid it past her collarbone, carefully covering her bosom. Taryn stared at her friend.

"Something's wrong here."

"What do you mean?" Paige asked.

"Your ladies are hiding. If we're going out, your ladies need to be part of that experience too." Taryn went behind Paige and slid the shirt down over her shoulders. Then she went under Paige's chest and squished her bosom together so it was only now slightly covered by the top of the shirt that promised them security.

She took a step back, "Now that's more like it. Just a couple more things and we'll be already to go. She put a swath of blush and glitter across Paige's cheekbones and a swipe of cinnamon raisin lipstick on her mouth. She spun her friend around and showed her product in the bureau mirror. Paige slowly drew her breath in and out, her gaze fixed on the person that stood in front of her. She watched as Taryn pulled her hair up in funny, twisted knots, securing it with various hair ties.

"Voila, another masterpiece by me!" Taryn proclaimed. "Okay, time to get going," she said, gently nudging Paige out the door and down the stairs before she had a chance to protest. Paige peeked in on her daughter who was fast asleep. She turned off her television and gave her one more kiss on the cheek. She walked past her own room and saw Derek, still awake, staring at the television.

"I'm going now."

"Where you going?" he asked, without looking away from the bright screen.

"Probably a pub or something; gotta show Taryn the crazy nightlife," she said with a nervous laugh. I'll be home as soon as I can. Lindsay is asleep. She shouldn't wake up." With that, she quickly walked out of the room, not waiting for a response from him. She didn't want to know what he thought, it scared her.

The two women got into Paige's truck and headed down the road filled with tract homes. Everywhere Taryn looked, it was the same. Square houses, with square yards and rectangular people; nothing out of order, nothing out of sorts. This is the way it was meant to be, perfect on the outside, all messed up on the inside. They headed across the river into the city. Omaha was part college town, part Midwestern values and part melting pot. Taryn just saw it as a reason to fill up for gas when a person had to go from the West coast to the East coast or vice versa. Paige saw it as escape from everything that defined her home. They continued on into the heart of the city until they finally reached a hole-in-the-wall pizza joint. Music made its way out of the door and down into the city streets where Paige parked the truck.

"Ready for this my friend?" Taryn asked, throwing out the

omen at her friend.

"Yeah, of course," Paige replied nervously. Anxiety crept into her blood, fighting against the musical vibe already coursing through her veins.

"After you," Taryn said holding the door open for Paige.

"Well thank you."

They got inside and looked around. Small wooden tables and chairs dotted the room like flowers in a field. The walls were dotted with a conglomeration of lights, pictures and trinkets. The air was abuzz with conversations, some intense, others filled with laughter. Beer flowed from the bar into frosty mugs that was whisked quickly to awaiting tables. This libation was the lifeblood to the flowered landscape. Front and center of the room was a stage. Tonight's entertainment consisted of four men, each with an instrument, one being the lead singer and the others playing backup. Near the stage was another guy, dressed like the rest, but not playing any instrument. He just sat there, tapping his hand on his knee to the beat of the music. In his other hand he held some tattered papers.

Taryn ordered a couple of beers along with a pepperoni and black olive pizza while Paige found a seat toward the back of the pub. Taryn came over to the table a few minutes later boasting two large mugs of beer.

"Here you are, one for you and one for me. Who ever said I don't like to share?" she said, putting a beer in front of Paige.

"Thanks," Paige said, taking a small sip of the beer. She turned her attention to the band, her heart rate increasing with every beat of the drum. What her best friend didn't know is that a member of the band was also her co-worker, Nate. He didn't actually play, but during breaks, he got up and read his beatnik style poetry to the rowdy crowd. Never mind that, more importantly, he was her lover, and nobody else knew.

It had all started innocently enough. It involved two married people, still in their twenties, still in their sexual prime. Each one of them was lonely for something, a void that no other could seem to fill. They met for lunch one afternoon, in a park near work. Nate got into Paige's truck and they drove around, what seemed like in circles. Eventually they ended up in a cemetery – morbid, but very secluded. People only go to cemeteries on holidays or other occasions deemed important, but the traffic isn't as busy as a park or other public places one might expect such an affair to occur.

The cemetery was huge, covering nearly thirty acres of land. Lush green grass, clipped short, tucked in neatly against marbled headstones, filled the area. Area signs eclipsed the park at intervals of a hundred feet. The cemetery was divided up by family or religion; there was even a section just for baby souls. They drove until the hill dropped off into an area that couldn't readily be seen by passerbies. Paige stopped the vehicle and turned off the ignition, leaving the radio on. This wasn't her first affair, but at least she was in her own vehicle, with a man she knew and liked.

Nate looked at Paige. "Well, what do you want to do?" There was an understandable uneasiness in the vehicle. She pulled her hair back into a clip and looked straight into Nate's eyes. Her voice lowered, "You know what we're here for." He pulled the lever on the seat and reclined backward.

Paige provided something that every man craved, sexual energy and fulfillment, no strings attached. In turn, Nate provided her with affection, attention and confirmation that she was effective at giving both of those things. In tradition with her perfectionist ways, it was comforting to know she could still do this too.

When they finished, Paige adjusted her hair in the rear view mirror and proceeded to drive out of the cemetery. Her co-worker didn't know what to say, other than a sheepish thank you.

"Yeah, no problem," Paige replied. What was she supposed to say, *Thank you, come again? And by the way, thank your wife for not knowing about this? Oh, and while we're thanking each other, let's thank my husband too?*

From that day on, they continued, for months, throwing flirtatious remarks to each other at work, filling voids that had been created for one reason or another. This led up to tonight, the music pulling Paige back to the present.

"This is a pretty good place my friend, do you actually get to come here often?" Taryn asked of Paige.

Um, not really. I mean, I've never actually been here, but one of my friends from work is in the band, so I guess I kinda know about the place, I mean the band. Oh crap, I'm rambling, huh?"

"Yes, you are, but it's good, it's a good sign to see out of you. Now we just need to throw in some useless facts and we're back to normal," Taryn teased her friend.

Paige smiled and fixated her stare and attention back on the band. She tapped her finger against the cold glass mug to the beat of the music. She closed her eyes in anticipation of actually talking to Nate once this set was over. Her heart fluttered at the thought.

The pizza arrived and both girls dug into it. The hot saltiness of the meat and cheese melted the tang of the beer's aftertaste. She shoved a big piece of Italian goodness into her mouth as Nate came strolling up to her table. She jumped up, pizza slice and all still half hanging from her mouth.

"Hey Paige, I didn't expect to see you here," he spoke between deep breaths as he came down from his combo musical and slightly drug induced high. Beads of sweat dripped from his brow.

"Well, you announced you were part of this benefit tonight, so, you know the philanthropist in me wanted to contribute to my community," she replied, finishing her mouthful. Bits of tomato sauce clung to the side of her cheek like a five-year-old child.

Nate put his arms around her, squeezing tightly, "You know you don't need to make up excuses to see me." His sweaty shirt clung to her like a second skin.

"I have a reputation to uphold," she laughed. His hug energized her, sweat and all.

Taryn stood up at the table, "Do I get to be involved in this happy reunion?" she asked.

"Oh, I'm sorry, Nate, this is my best friend Taryn. She's

from Seattle, well, I mean Montana right now, but we grew up in Seattle together."

"Nice to meet you," he smiled, extending his hand out.

"I don't get a hug? Paige got a hug. Why don't I get one?" she taunted back.

Nate didn't quite know how to take her. She was much bolder than he was used to from her best friend. He opened his arms and came toward her.

"Geesh, I'm just messin' with you. You're too sweaty anyway. Anyway, it is very nice to meet you. I'm sure you're a great guy if you're a friend of Paige's. That's what you are, right…a friend?"

Nate ran his hands through his hair. "Yeah, friends. Well, we were co-workers, and yeah, friends. Hey listen, it was nice to meet you. I need to get a refreshment before the next set. I'm on in just a few minutes. I've got some new material here and I'm excited to share it. You ladies enjoy." Nate slipped away before Taryn could continue her interrogation of him.

"Oh, we will, and I'm sure she has," Taryn said as Nate walked off.

"Taryn, crap, don't say that."

"It's true isn't it? You two have something going on. I could see it all over your faces. I bet you've seen more than that of him, huh? Give me the scoop my friend. I didn't fly halfway across the country just to be met by some boring housewife story, I want soap opera!"

"There's nothing to tell, we're just co-workers," Paige replied.

"Um yeah, well, I think you forget that I'm your best friend, and I know when you're lying. Oh, and by the way, you're lying."

"I don't know what you're talking about. Okay, maybe I do. Maybe just a little bit. Okay, yes, I kinda like him," Paige said with a smile.

"Like him? I didn't ask if you *liked* him. I asked if you've done the naughty with him."

"Define naughty," Paige countered.

Taryn furthered her line of questioning. "Geez, if I have to define naughty, you really do need to go back to the funny farm. Give me the lowdown, c'mon. You did him huh?" Taryn said, finishing off her second beer. She raised the empty glass into the air signaling to the waitress that she needed a refill.

Her friend still refused to come right out and say anything. Several months prior, when she met her first tryst online, Taryn had been extremely outspoken toward her best friend's affair, in part, due to the betrayal of her own father against her mother. Hearing the details of Paige breaking the bonds of marriage was almost too much for Taryn to handle at that point. Now, having almost lost her faithful sidekick, she stepped down as judge and jury, turning instead to just a member of the audience.

Paige smiled, and in a rare moment of strength in an often lopsided friendship, she sat up in her chair and looked at Taryn straight in the eyes. "Yes, we had mad, passionate animal sex in the woods like two gazelle's."

"Gazelle's?" Taryn asked.

"Yes...gazelle's," Paige volleyed back.

"What the hell? How do gazelle's have sex?"

"Wouldn't you like to know," Paige replied. She revisited her now lonely beer glass and turned toward the stage. "Nate's comin' back on, ssshhh, I want to hear him," she said with a triumphant smile. And with that the conversation on that topic ended.

The junior high turned lifelong friends soaked in the words of Paige's secret lover, the music and the atmosphere that accompanied all of it. They talked about everything from the weather to politics and religion. It was an involved conversation about nothing at all really. They continued to skirt the real topic, the whole reason Taryn flew out – Paige's continued reluctance to change the way she both viewed and lived her life. It was self-destructive, not in a way that most people would think, but in a more covert manner. Unlike a drug addict that leaves needle marks or a compulsive gambler that loses their house and car, Paige's life looked relatively perfect on the outside. To those who knew her intimately, primarily Taryn, she was a ticking time bomb, ready to implode again at any moment.

The now grown girls made their way back home shortly after midnight. As Paige's truck rounded the corner of the street, she peered up the row of street lamps until she found her house. She breathed a sigh of relief noting that the lights were all out on her home. She was relieved to think that Derek would not be awake waiting for her, ready to interrogate her on the evening's events.

She nudged Taryn in the seat next to her. "Alright sleeping beauty, time to awake from your slumber." Taryn blinked heavily as she adjusted her eyes to the bright dome light of the vehicle. She giggled.

"What are you laughing at?" asked Paige.

"You."

"What about me?"

"You're just so darn cute. You look just like we did in high school. In fact, this feels just like high school. You driving us home, me a little bit drunker than you. Except this time, it's not your drunk mother waiting for us inside. Instead we get the psychotic husband, yippee!"

"I'm going to ignore that comment," Paige responded curtly. "You've been drinking."

"Yeah, and so have you, but unlike you, I'm aware of reality." Taryn spoke without even thinking. The comment hadn't been meant to hurt her best friend, only to wake her up.

Paige's mind was sent reeling. It was not in her nature, or the realm of any of her relationships to engage in argument or debate. She simply shut down any display of emotion on the outside as a flurry of feelings set off a firestorm on the inside. Her heart thumped inside her chest. "It's late and you need some sleep," she said to Taryn through gritted teeth.

"That's great Paige, just like Judith taught you. If you don't talk about it, it didn't happen."

Paige ignored Taryn and made her way into the house through the basement door with Taryn in tow like an ankle biting yap-yap dog.

Taryn grabbed Paige by the sleeve of her coat, "Just listen to me for a minute dammit! For once don't be as stubborn as everyone else in your life! Look at yourself, look at your life. It's a joke!"

"Please lower your voice, you'll wake up Derek," Paige said looking past the frustrated friend in front of her.

"Screw Derek!" Taryn replied lowering her voice into a barely audible hiss. "He's killing you, and you don't even know enough anymore to recognize that!" Her voice wavered, nearly breaking into a soft whimper. "I'm terrified for you...please...you've got to believe me. Listen to what I'm saying. He's not good to you, or the kids. He treats you guys like crap and you let him."

Then, like a fortune teller's voodoo, Taryn squeaked out one last warning, "This won't end well for anyone, and when it does, you'll just be happy to make it out alive. There, I've said what I need to. I'm done."

She grabbed her friend and held her close, tears welling in her eyes. She whispered into Paige's ear, "Please believe me, if not for you, then for Lindsay and Aaron. You have to leave him." She couldn't see Paige's reaction in the dark night, but felt her trembling as she held on to her. She reluctantly let go and turned to go upstairs to the guest bedroom.

"Just remember my love for you and your babies."

Paige stood there, her knees trembling, the room spinning. It was all too much for this young woman that just a few months ago had been doing the slipper shuffle on a psych unit. Her mind shot off like a bottle rocket on the 4th of July. Sparks of thoughts seemed to launch in all different directions, each with an uncertain landing. Her body instinctively walked up the stairs and turned down the hall to the room she shared with her husband. She listened to his breathing, snore and stop, snore and stop. She changed into her gown and slipped into bed, coming to rest on her back with a birdseye view of the shadows dancing on the ceiling.

The next morning was very different for Paige, because in fact, it wasn't morning at all. She rolled over in bed, noticing first she was alone, and second how quiet the house was. She attempted to sit up in bed, but was immediately struck down by a pounding headache. The room spun with a relentless vengeance. The only way to stop it was to lie back down. She closed her eyes and fell back to sleep, totally unaware of the events that had occurred in the morning hours that she had slept through.

Late into that evening, she was awoken by her husband. "Hey honey. Hey there hon. Time to wake up," Derek said gently to his wife.

Paige peered at the room through heavy eyelids. Her vision was still a bit blurry, but she was able to make out the silhouette of Derek perched on the end of the bed, and what appeared to be a lunch tray laying on the down comforter in front of her. Her tongue filled her mouth such that she could hardly speak. She reached out for the glass of fizzy soda on the tray, but didn't have the strength in her arm to pull it to her.

"Just a minute hon, let me go get you a straw." Derek brought back the green and white striped plastic straw and plopped it into the tall glass. He lifted the drink up to her lips, helping guide it to her mouth. Paige sucked the liquid into her mouth, waves of bubbles riding on her tongue and teeth, splashing and filling every crevice. Like a machine in need of a long overdue oiling, her jaws moved back and forth forming words with a newfound ease.

"Wow, thank you. What happened? I feel like hell."

"I think you had a bit too much to drink. You came home with Taryn a couple nights ago raising all sorts of hell…you couldn't hardly keep your clothes on or your mouth shut," Derek replied with a triumphant sound in his voice.

"Oh," Paige cleared her throat, "I didn't know that. I'm sorry." She cowered down to her husband, not wanting to fight. Her mind was too fuzzy to question anything he said. She fully believed his only intention was to take care of his wife who needed her husband to nurse her back from a debilitating hangover.

"Did you say a couple days ago?" Paige asked.

"Yes, you've been in bed for three days," Derek responded.

"Oh my God," she paused, "What about the kids? Where's Lindsay and Aaron?"

"They're at your mother's. We figured you could use the rest. Don't want you ending up back in that hospital you know. Gotta build your strength back up."

He continued to purposely cultivate the idea in his wife's head that she needed him for her very survival. It was better that way, less questions and certainly less resistance. Paige was oblivious to his tactics, fully believing in the vows that bound their marriage together – in sickness and in health.

She took another drink of soda and started to make an attempt to sit up. "Here, let me help you," Derek said reaching out to help his wife. He wrapped her up in a fluffy, white robe and stood as her brace while she swung her legs down. Her feet landed on the hard wooden floor, which in turn promised support of her body as she navigated the path from her bedroom to the bathroom. Derek helped her over the threshold, gave her a peck on the cheek and assured her he would be right outside the door should she need him.

Derek continued his duties for as long as Paige needed him. He received praise for having done the laundry and dishes. Dinner arrived in the same fashion as lunch had, on a tray lined with cloth and accompanied by a red rose. How could a wife ask for anything more?

She could ask for more, a lot more, and it would start with the truth. They did talk about the prior days' events that evening, but it was as far from the truth as Earth was from Mars. Derek spoke of Paige's poor behavior until she asked him to stop out of sheer embarrassment. She simply didn't want to hear any more. She was curious about Taryn, thinking over and over in her mind how she would bring up the subject. She didn't like to speak of Taryn in front of Judith or Derek, but he hadn't spoken of her best friend and she wondered why.

"So when did Taryn go home?" Paige asked broaching the topic with an innocent question.

"She left the very next morning after your night out on the town, something about a cheaper flight and needing to get home to her family."

"Huh, did you take her to the airport?" Paige asked with an uncertainty to her voice.

"She insisted on taking a taxi. She seemed in a hurry to get out of here. She got a phone call late in the night and left early in the morning. She was pretty rude, didn't have a lot of nice things to say about you. That's about all I know."

"What do you mean rude things?" Paige asked.

"I'm not going to go into detail. I'm guessing she's just jealous of what you…what *we* have. Look at her, any man she dates won't stay with her longer than a couple of months. She's never settled down, and she lies. Besides, she obviously doesn't care – hasn't even called since she left." Derek headed off any further questions by insisting that his wife had enough for the day and any further talk would only make her recovery that much longer.

"It's just a silly hangover," Paige pleaded with Derek.

"Yeah, a silly hangover that lasted three days," he replied firmly. "Now come on, get back into bed and tomorrow we can start brand new. We'll put all of this behind us. We sure have enough practice at it."

Sensing the anger that was brewing in his chest, he quickly walked out of the room. He didn't need his wife asking any more questions. Questions only led to more questions, and he worried he might run out of answers. That was the trouble with liars, the more tales they spun, the greater difficulty they had not getting stuck in their own web.

14 FEAR AMONG US

Derek kissed his wife goodbye the next morning before heading off to work. "You look so much better hon, remember to take it easy today. I called in to work for you again, they understood."

"Oh crap, work, I totally forgot," Paige replied. "You think of everything, thank you." Flashing his signature smile, Derek nodded in agreement and then left the room. She listened as he went out the front door and down the steps. Satisfied he was gone; she reached across the bed for the television remote, instead her hand land on the phone. Paige scrolled through the caller id list, and was surprised to see that there were no phone calls since Taryn had arrived last week. She quickly dismissed it as her search for the TV remote resumed. The blankets would not give up the device easily however, and boredom finally nudged the young woman out of bed.

Paige got up and started her daily routine, cup of coffee, read the paper, bowl of cereal. Once finished, she went over to the sink to put her dirty dishes in it, but stopped short of doing so. Realizing the sink was empty, she pulled the dishwasher door open with a begrudging groan, as if its protest might somehow deter her from using it. It too was empty. She placed her cup and bowl on the empty rack and shut the door back up. She paid no attention to the details of her morning, as she would normally do, as her mind skipped on to the next task at hand.

Paige went down the hallway to the shower. The water felt good, as if it were rinsing the sins of the past week right down the drain. She still felt ashamed for her actions, completely convinced that what Derek had told her was true. Why would she have any reason to doubt him? After all, it was she that had broken the bonds of their marriage, unbeknownst to him. It was she who had come home at night, lying next to her husband in their bed while she thought of the other man she had just been with only a few hours earlier.

After getting dressed Paige spent time on the computer, playing games of solitaire against an imaginary opponent. As she moved the mouse over to click on the next card, she was startled by the *ding* of the instant messenger window popping up on the screen. It was Taryn.

"Hey there stranger, have a good vacation?" Taryn typed on the screen.

"Vacation?" Paige clicked back.

"That's what your answering machine said."

"Weird."

"What's weird?" Taryn asked.

"Nothing. Never mind. Gotta go." Paige clicked the "x" at the corner of the webpage, closing the internet and eventually shutting down the computer. She sat in the highbacked chair, staring at the wall above the computer desk. Her eyes turned on the row of pictures that adorned the wooden desktop, her grandparents, various family photos, and then her gaze stopped dead in its tracks. Where her wedding photo once stood, there was still the frame, but the picture had changed. It was Paige as a teenager, looking young and beautiful in her senior photo. *What the heck?* she thought to herself. Picking up the frame she turned it on its face and unscrewed the metal hinges in the back. Her wedding photo was neatly tucked in behind the senior portrait. Paige took the picture of hers out from behind the glass front and stared at it. How she missed being that age, when the only thing she had to worry about were grades and a curfew.

Things just weren't adding up. Paige put the photo frame down and reached for the phone next to it. There was a thin layer of dust on the receiver; tucked in amongst the gallery of pictures. Derek had obviously forgotten this check this one. The red light shown zero as an indicator that no messages were waiting. Paige turned around to head downstairs, but something stopped her. She whirled around and marched for the handset once more. This time she pressed the button labeled 'answer' and listened with anticipation as the voice came on over the speaker. It was a computerized voice letting the caller know that no one was available to take their call. She continued to press the button, getting the same result each time. It didn't make sense. When they moved into their house, the phones had been a housewarming gift from Derek's sister. That very evening after taking ownership of their new place, still deeply in love, they had recorded a message together – now it was nowhere to be found.

But Taryn had told Paige that the answering machine indicated they had been on vacation. Paige dismissed this by thinking Taryn was either lying or she had dialed the wrong number. Her mind tried putting the puzzle together, but so far, she only had half the pieces needed to solve the ever growing mystery. The best person to ask would be the source himself – Derek. Paige picked up the phone to call him, figuring she's just redial him by flipping through the caller id. Instead of Derek, the first name she came upon was Taryn. Not checking the date of the call, she decided she had started at the oldest calls first, so she clicked the button even faster. Even still, it was Taryn's name that repeatedly popped up.

This couldn't be. Her name wasn't on the phone downstairs. Paige went down the steps holding the phone under her arm, so her hands were free to grab the other receiver. There was no trace of Taryn's name on that phone. The ID had been wiped clean. Paige's heart began to thump, getting in line to race alongside her thoughts. She sat down at the kitchen table trying to collect herself. She replayed each event of the past 24 hours in her mind. Derek's devoted husband act, his portrayal of her bad behavior, the apparent hangover that lasted three days, the answering machine and caller ID. It just didn't make sense.

She put the phones back on their homes and proceeded on with her fact finding mission. It was a bit after 1:00pm. The day was half gone. She thought about calling Taryn, but at this point, she trusted no one, not even herself. She looked around the living room, staring briefly outside at the neighbor as he brought the trash bin to the street. His yard was immaculate, and his car was washed, without fail, each Tuesday. She counted the driveways along the street, each adorned with their own tan plastic bin, with big black wheels that squeaked when you pushed it. Paige's eyes came to rest on their own driveway. Just like a row of soldiers, there was her own garbage bin, ready to serve the monster refuse truck. *Wow, Derek thought of everything, even the garbage can.*

Something in Paige's mind clicked. *This is too perfect, too much.* She opened the front door and headed down to where the trash container was perched. Her neighbor stopped pushing his industrial sized broom across the concrete long enough to look up at Paige lugging the vessel of suburbia waste back into her garage.

"Mrs. Hayes! Mrs. Hayes, the trash hasn't come yet!" hollered her neighbor. Paige waved and smiled, paying no mind to what he was saying. She was only focused on her loot she had pulled into the garage. The nosy neighbor shook his head and went back to maintaining his property.

Paige laid an old blue tarp down on the concrete floor of the garage. She went into the house, threw on another flannel coat, and grabbed a pair of yellow dishwashing gloves. Over the course of the next two hours, Paige went through every fast food bag, leftover meal, and tin can that couldn't be recycled. She wasn't sure what she was looking for, but figured she'd know when she found it. And then, nearly a full hour into her scavenger hunt, she found it, an innocuous looking brown paper bag. Her heart took a thump as it began to edge out her mind in this marathon of a day.

She slowly opened the bag, the crinkle of the heavy brown paper smoothing out under stiff fingers. Not yet ready for what she might find, but feeling certain this was it, Paige set the bag aside. She didn't want to eat her dessert first. There were other things to finish before doing that. She picked up the blue tarp, folded its contents up like a hobo bag, and dumped it in the trash bin. Satisfied it was all back in there, the blue tarp was returned to its own home – stuffed in a corner under a lantern and gas stove – remnants of a family whom at one time coveted the institution of camping. Paige opened the garage door and returned the trash to its original post. Her nosy neighbor was nowhere to be found.

The time was now 4 o'clock, she had maybe two hours, but more likely just one hour until her husband returned. One hour might be plenty for a person to physically look through a sack, but what she would find would potentially take a lifetime to recover from. With shaking hands, she again proceeded with opening the bag. She was afraid to look inside, so she flipped the sack over and dumped its contents out onto the basement floor. Receipts fell from the brown bag like snowflakes from the sky – no two were the same. She picked up each one not really knowing what she was looking for. Paige checked dates, places, times, amounts. Over and over she read them, consuming each bite of this paper dessert like it was her last.

The receipts were the last part of the puzzle that Paige had been so desperately looking for. There were some from take out, dry cleaners, gasoline – all of which would seem innocent enough – a man trying to cover up for not really having done all the things he said he had. That would explain the clean house and empty sink. There was even a grocery store receipt for chicken soup, soda and ice cream. Derek had simply paid for everything to be done for him.

When Paige was a child, her favorite dessert had been Baked Alaska, a delicious treat with an ice cream center. She got a special dinner out at the restaurant each year. Taryn would usually come with her and the two girls would order fancy non-alcoholic drinks and relish in turning one year older. Paige would always tease Taryn that she was the one who would turn the magic 18 and 21 first. Taryn would quickly come back with how after that, Paige would be the one to turn 40, 50, 60 and so one first. Perhaps the greatest part about this delicious dessert was the way it was delivered to the table – on fire, flames so bright, that the flash bulb on the camera wasn't even needed.

Unbeknownst to Paige, what remained in the bag was her Baked Alaska. This was one time in which her OCD would come in handy. She opened the bag once more, plunging her hand to the very bottom, checking each corner until her hand stopped on a very slight bump. There was another receipt. She pictured the broad smile across the waiter's face as he lit the dessert in the large dining room. As she blew out the candles in her mind, her eyes decoded the words on the paper in front of her, sending messages to her brain down complicated pathways of nerve endings.

The receipt was from a pharmacy in town. The top it had Derek's name, address and telephone number. Below it read the medication, dosage and instructions for use:

Lorazepam, 1mg, take 1 every 6 to 8 hours as needed.

Lorazepam was a generic form of a drug used for anxiety. In high doses it could cause confusion, dizziness and memory loss.

Paige knew enough from living with a prescription drug addict for years, that Derek didn't take these. Judith ate them like candy, but not Derek. This was the center of her dessert; this was the chilling ice cream part that made her whole body shiver.

Paige was pulled from trance-like state by the cuckoo of the clock in the living room upstairs. It was 5 o'clock and Derek would likely be home any minute, she could feel it. Paige shoved the crumpled papers back into the bag, rolling it up into a tight ball. She looked around for a good hiding place, thinking of all the places he might look. She settled on the laundry room, it was her domain, an area seldom breached by her husband. She shoved the bag in the back of a cabinet, behind the iron and spray starch. She hadn't used either of those items for several months, and doubted Derek would either, especially since she had found the dry cleaning receipt.

Paige turned around to head upstairs, she needed to think about how she was going to act in front of him, what would she say, should she confront him? Good at masking emotions; she had honed that skill to perfection in high school. Her life had depended on it then, just as it did now. She took a deep breath and turned the basement door handle. To her relief there was no one there, she was still alone. Everything about her felt dirty from the day's events. She had already showered earlier in the day, and figuring Derek was going to be late coming home for work, Paige decided to draw a hot bath instead.

She poured two capfuls of bubble bath under the steady stream of hot water filling the tub. Watching the bubbles as she undressed, she turned off the water just a few inches shy of it reaching the top of the tub. Not bothering to check the water's temperature, Paige dipped one leg and then the other into the accepting porcelain vessel. She lowered the rest of her body slowly into the depths of the tub, until her backside came to rest like a ship at the bottom of the sea. Waves of lilac fragrance ebbed and flowed in unison with their tiny, circular counterparts that tickled Paige's nose when she moved. Her bosom showed through the water like tiny mountain peaks in some far away range. She ran her fingers along the length of her stomach; her skin felt silky soft in the treated water. Beyond that lie an area deprived of all worldly pleasure under the roof in which she lived, one in which she had become guilty at the mere acknowledgement if its existence in front of her husband.

Paige's pondering of the revival of her womanhood was cut brutally short by the sound of keys in the front door. She pulled the curtain closed while quickly summoning more bubbles to cover her exposed areas. It was almost as if she anticipated his next move, for just a few moments later Derek came in to the bathroom. No warning, no hello, no nothing, just a quick rush into the bathroom. He swiftly pulled the curtain back with a look of defiance on his face.

Startled, Paige sat up, drawing her knees close to her chest and looked at her husband with frightened eyes.

"Derek, you scared me!" There was no response, only a glazed stare by a man at his wife.

"Derek? What's going on?"

After what seemed like eternity, he responded, "Oh, sorry hon, I guess I was just surprised that you'd be in the bathtub at this time of day," he said, his face softening into a look of inquiry. She knew where this line of questioning was going, and it made her uncomfortable. She chose the victim role, one that Derek played into best. After all, this was his first choice after nursing her back from the drug induced 'hangover.'

"I'm sorry, the day just got away from me. When you didn't come home after work, I decided to kill some time with a bath. I wanted to keep busy...you know what happens when I have too much time on my hands," Paige responded coyly.

"Yes, I know that all too well. The important thing I guess is that you're safe and well. You are doing better aren't you?" he asked.

"I am, thanks to you. You take such good care of me. I don't know what I'd do without you," Paige replied as she forced a warm smile.

"I'm glad to hear you say that. All I ask is that you always believe it." The misogynistic husband felt a sense of accomplishment, his wife was back where he wanted her, and in his mind, this was the way a marriage should be. "Finish up your bath and get dressed. I think we need a night out together."

Paige played the dutiful wife, draining the tub and drying off before heading to their bedroom. "What should I wear?" she called out to Derek. He came down the hall to answer her.

"How about that black skirt with the green vest you wore to my company dinner last month. You looked good in that." Derek reached over Paige, gently brushing her shoulder with his arm. She recoiled in swift reaction, not thinking how he would respond. But Derek was too involved in his own thoughts, still distrustful of his wife's sudden turn into his own mother: the good wife. She was so convincing though, he dismissed her sharp movement as merely still getting her equilibrium back after days in bed.

He left her in the room to get dressed while he went to the bathroom for a quick shave before they left for the evening. Derek opened up the medicine cabinet and reached for his razor. Tucked behind the shaving cream was a tiny, amber colored bottle. It was the drugs he had given Paige to ensure her compliance while he removed the last roadblock to their perceived happiness – her best friend Taryn. He slipped the toxic vial into the pocket of his blazer, continuing on with his grooming ritual.

The young couple stepped out on the town. With two little kids at home, they didn't get this chance very often. Judith was expected to bring Lindsay and Aaron back home on Sunday, so they still had two more days alone. Derek took Paige to a steak and seafood restaurant in the next town over. It was a favorite of theirs. Paige ordered her steak well done while Derek ordered his the same. They carried on a superficial conversation, each guarded in their own way and for their own reasons.

"So how was work today?" Paige asked.

"Oh you know, same crap, just different day," he replied. And that is how the conversation continued, well past after dinner, dessert and coffee.

"Hey, do you want to go into the lounge for a drink? I heard they have a live band now. It might be good," Derek said, extending the offer of lengthening the evening together.

"Yeah, that would be nice," said Paige. They stood up and walked toward the lounge entrance together. It was a heavy wooden door with huge brass railings for handles. Derek held it open for his wife as she walked in ahead of him. She was struck by the smell of the room – it was just like that of the liquor store she spent Fridays in as a child.

Derek put a hand against his wife's back, gently nudging her in the direction of an open booth. "Here hon, have a seat and I'll get us something to drink."

"I'll just have a cup of coffee with cream. Given what happened earlier in the week, I think I'd better stay away from the alcohol for now."

Derek nodded in sympathetic understanding at his wife's request. Little did she know it wasn't the alcohol at all, but that was okay, what she didn't know wouldn't hurt her. He went over to the bar while she sat down, taking in her surroundings. There were couples, single men, and what appeared to be single ladies. Some were in groups, others were by themselves. Derek's back was to her as he ordered her coffee and his beer. She turned her gaze away from him and instead, focused on a couple that was in the booth directly across from theirs. They looked to be in their late twenties, nicely dressed, and obviously very involved in only each other. Paige felt a twinge of jealousy, wishing that were she and Derek in the booth, hardly able to keep their hands off each other. The jealousy quickly subsided when she saw the shiny gold band on his left ring finger in sharp opposition to the naked ring finger of the woman in his arms.

Derek brought the drinks back to the table, a routine he would repeat throughout the night. They listened to the band and held hands from the quaint booth in the darkest corner of the lounge. Derek had his hand on Paige's thigh, rubbing it up and down to the beat of the music. Although not drinking, she felt intoxicated by the music and atmosphere. She giggled to herself as she drew in another sip of warm coffee. It coursed through her veins, warming her from the tips of her toes to the end of her nose. A never-ending smile eventually took over the giggle.

"It sure is good to see you smile," Derek said to Paige, squeezing her thigh even harder, inching ever so closer to forbidden fruit. She couldn't help but smile, she couldn't say why she felt so happy; she just knew she did. Derek apparently noticed the difference in her too, because he kept asking her how she felt. It didn't bother her; he was just showing how much he cared. Her mind filled with a fuzzy vague familiarity as she tried to recall where she had felt like this before. But try as she might, she just couldn't do it. She again succumbed to the Gods of Happiness, the muscles of her neck relaxing as she leaned on Derek's shoulder for support.

The band was finishing up their last set, so Derek invited Paige out onto the dance floor for a slow dance before the evening was finished. She agreed to follow him, holding securely to his arm as they walked in tandem onto the lighted parquet floor. He held her close, placing her arms securely around his neck. Their bodies moved together just as they had so many years ago when they conceived each of their beautiful children. As the song played on for what seemed like eternity, Paige moved her arms down closer to Derek's waist, much like the position of two kids at a middle school dance. Adjusting her hand one last time, Paige came to rest on the pocket of Derek's blazer. Instead of the smooth pocket lining, there was a bump, a bump that felt much like that of a pill bottle. The lights and music became too much for the already dizzy woman. All at once she felt sweaty and somewhat nauseous.

She leaned back and stared into Derek's eyes. Taking a labored breath, she managed to speak, "I think I'm going to be sick. I really need some fresh air...it's so hot in here."

Worried, he led his wife to the bar and sat her down while he went back to the table and gathered their coats. After paying their tab he went back to Paige. "Alright hon, here's your coat, let's go."

"I don't think I'll need it." She wiped the hair from her face, "I'm hot."

"*Yes you are*," Derek responded slyly.

"No, not that kind of hot. I mean I'm really warm; I need to get outside." Derek led Paige through the maze of doors leading out of the lounge, back through the restaurant, and finally out to the nearly empty parking lot. Paige sat down on the bench outside, as if it were a hot summer evening. The temperature had dropped down to the freezing point, and Derek was certainly feeling it.

"Come on; let's get you to the car. I think maybe it was just too soon to get you out again." He took Paige's hands in his and helped her up off the wooden bench. Securing her in his car, he walked around the other side and got in the driver's seat. Derek took the long way back home, twisting and winding across back roads that were hardly used anymore.

"Why are we going this way?" Paige asked.

"I thought we'd make use of the most of this night that we could. I didn't want it to end."

Paige fought against a response that would suggest questioning Derek's intentions. "That's very thoughtful of you. I'm jealous."

"Of what?"

"Of you and how smart you always are. Have I told you lately how much I love you?"

"I love you more," Derek replied.

"No, I love you more." Paige wasn't distracted by their banter; her mind was clearing as she kept a watchful eye on the road ahead of her. "Are we going to get home soon, I'm very tired."

"Yes honey, I just wanted to check out one more part of this county at night. There's a place out here I remember from years ago that you can see every star in the sky for miles around."

Paige didn't want to go stargazing with the psychotic man in the vehicle that had to drug his wife to have a good time. She just wanted to go home. She looked through the window at passing empty cornfields. Rows and rows of unplowed dirt, waiting for the spring thaw so the cycle of planting, growing and harvest could continue. It was a way of life around here, one that families had spent generations involved in. It was some measure of comfort knowing there wasn't a shovel hidden in the backseat, and even if there was, the fields were too frozen to dig in anyway. Paige looked behind her shoulder just in case her husband had taken up gardening in the past few weeks. It was empty except for a few empty pop cans and candy bar wrappers.

Derek brought the car to a rest at the end of County Road 54. He shifted the transmission into park, leaving the engine running for some measure of protection against the cold, night air. Paige found it odd her husband didn't talk. He brought her out here on the premise of looking at stars, yet not one mention of even The Big Dipper. The hollow feeling returned to her stomach. The clock radio on the dash glowed 2:34am. Next to it was the instrument panel, whose needle on the gas gauge flirted precariously close to the large 'E.'

"Oh wow, looks like we'd better be getting back, I think we're getting pretty low on gas," Paige commented with complete surprise in her voice.

Derek didn't respond; his mind was apparently in a far off place, away from the cup of trouble he continually brewed and poured in his own life. His wife now shared from that same cup of poison.

"Derek? Derek, did you hear me?" Paige leaned over into his seat, "We're about out of gas," Paige repeated.

"What?" Derek asked, straightening up in his seat. His mind was in a faraway place, and it wasn't a good one. He pictured himself pushing his wife out of the car right here, her body thumping to the ground as he backed up, perhaps not quite missing her in the course of it all.

"Look at the gas gauge, we're about out."

"Oh, I guess you're right, we'd better head back to town." Derek shifted the lever into drive and turned the car back toward the glow of the city. Paige was relieved, feeling as if somehow she had averted a major crisis, maybe even saving her own life.

15 DAY OF DECISION

Paige drove to Judith's on Sunday to pick up Lindsay and Aaron. It felt like forever since she had seen her kids – long enough to miss the noise and business of child's play. She parked her SUV in the driveway, got out, and hopscotched her way across the icy path to the front door. She hesitated for a moment before turning the doorknob. Although this was a different house than the one she grew up in, numbered metal doors still haunted her. She grabbed the brass colored knob and tried to turn it. Of course there was no give; no matter where her mom lived, everything was locked tighter than an armored truck. Paige fumbled through the keys in her purse, finally landing on a dull, pewter one. With cold hands, she pushed the key into the lock, manipulating the tumblers inside into position so the door could be relieved of its bondage to the frame.

Paige hardly stepped over the threshold, when Aaron came teetering around the corner. "There's my big boy!" she said, stretching out her arms to scoop up the chunk of a growing boy. Once securely in arms, she held her face close to Aaron's head, breathing in the sweet smell of a toddler's soft hair. "How are you? Mommy missed you!" she said, planting yet another kiss on his ruddy cheek. Aaron flashed his mom a wide grin, sporting yet another new tooth. "Look at you, you got a toofers! Yes you do." After another prolonged hug, he pushed away from Paige, wriggling to get down. She set him gently on the ground, and like a wind-up toy turned loose, he scooted back down the same hallways he had appeared in just moments ago.

She had a pretty good idea where to find Lindsay. If it was summer, she was usually outside on her tire swing or playing in the blow up pool. But it wasn't summer, far from it. Paige headed down the same hallway her son had been in displaying his magical ability of appearing and disappearing in. Following the trail of squeals and animated computer sounds to the back room of Judith's house, she found her daughter twisting back and forth on an oversized office chair. Lindsay clicked the mouse with a rhythmic chirp, maneuvering her way through shamrocks and hearts on the multi-colored screen. Aaron was nearby, entranced in his train set. Paige wondered if Lindsay was watching her brother.

"Hi kiddo!" Paige got no response. She touched Lindsay's arm this time, "Hey kiddo, its mommy!"

"Hi mommy," Lindsay replied without breaking concentration on her game.

"What are you playing kiddo?"

"Mouse in the House," the little girl replied still feverishly clicking away on the mouse.

Paige backed out of the room, still pondering what shamrocks and hearts had to do with the title of the game. Maybe Lindsay had just made it up. She was glad to have greeted her children first. *Think happy thoughts* she told herself as she looked for her mother. Sunday mornings before noon usually meant her mom would still be in bed.

The final door in the hallway belonged to Judith and Dave. Their room was cold and dark, like a vampire's lair. Paige envisioned the two of them for a moment, long teeth like fangs, pale skin…nope, it just wasn't happening for her. She opened their door and tiptoed across the cluttered floor to the right side of the bed. Clothes were strewn everywhere, looking like extra-terrestrial pods in the glow of the television set. Dave never turned the tube off, and it drove Judith crazy that she couldn't completely control her husband. A little part of Paige appreciated Dave all the more for that. *Good for him* she thought.

Judith's snoring was like a rescue beacon deep within the piles of blankets. Paige touched her mom's shoulder – it felt like a dead fish. *Ugh!* "Mom," she whispered in a part hiss, "Mom!"

The sleeping woman moved, slowly at first; and finally completed rolling over to face her pestering daughter.

"Whatttt?" Judith groaned.

"Mom, it's almost noon. It's time to get up."

"Come on, let me sleep."

"No mom, we have to talk." That line, that line right there was the surefire way to get her mom's attention. Judith always perceived this as code for some great opportunity for insight into her daughter's emotionally private life.

"Okay, just give me a minute. I've got to get dressed."

Paige dutifully left the room and headed for the kitchen. It was getting close to lunchtime, and she guessed that her kids hadn't eaten. She made noodles and fruit, setting out a sippy cup of milk and a pink plastic cup of apple juice onto butcher-block style table. Just as she had the kids seated together at the table, Judith came into the kitchen. Immediately she began making excuses, nearly knocking her daughter out of the way as she headed toward the refrigerator.

"I was up with your kids all morning. I had just laid down five minutes before you got here," she explained to Paige.

"I know mom."

"Okay, I just wanted to make sure you didn't think the kids were by themselves over here. I take care of them."

Paige shifted her weight from one leg to another, rocking slightly back and forth. She didn't want to continue down the road they were going. Her mom would continue on with the 'poor me' excuses until Paige became so frustrated; she'd have to pack up and leave prematurely. That wasn't going to be okay today. Today Paige actually needed her mom.

As the kids feasted on their noon-time meal, the two women proceeded to the couch in the living room, sandwiches in hand. Bite by bite the sandwiches slowly disappeared, along with Paige's chance to talk to her mom. Judith didn't stay still very long, and this was a conversation that she needed to sit through.

Always the faster eater, Paige finished her sandwich, and with hardly the last bite consumed, she dropped the bomb on her mother. "I'm filing for divorce from Derek." There, she had said it. It felt so real finally getting out of her head and into the air. The words hung like a thick fog though for Judith. She recalled saying the same thing to her own mother nearly thirty years ago. Although for Judith, she wasn't a woman trapped by a manipulative husband, she was a woman trapped by her own mind.

"There's too much to explain right now, I just need to know that I can have your support in this," Paige asked of her mom.

"Yes. You know I am here for you, whatever you need. Will you please just tell me something about what's going on?"

Paige believed her mom's sincerity, and in that, also felt that her mom deserved to hear some of what brought Paige to this point. Over the past couple of years, the two of them had sat together in much the same fashion. The seasons had changed, but the conversation had not – until now. Judith always made her feelings heard; she didn't like how Derek treated Lindsay and Aaron, and she certainly didn't trust him.

"I've always told you you'll just know when it's time. I'm guessing you've reached that finally."

A tear fell down Paige's cheek, and then another. She swallowed hard, not expecting this reaction from herself. "I'm so scared mom. I don't know what he's going to do next."

"What do you mean?" Judith asked.

"Mom, he's been drugging me."

"What the hell! How do you know?"

Paige explained what happened in the days following Taryn's

arrival and sudden departure. She even included what occurred last night when Derek took her out to dinner.

"Oh my God mom, I don't know what he'll do next! Will he go after my kids next, or just continue to slowly kill me?" Panic began to set in for Paige.

"Do you want the kids to stay with me again this week?" Judith asked.

"No, I don't want things any different until I get everything worked out with the lawyer. Derek will get suspicious fast if it isn't life as usual at home."

"I don't want him around my grandchildren."

"I don't either, but right now I don't have a choice in the matter." Paige felt so trapped.

Lindsay hopped down from the kitchen table and tore back down the hallway to the play on the computer. Aaron kicked at his high chair, clearly upset by his sister abandoning him. "Alright big boy," Paige said to her son, heading over to help him as she brushed the tears away from her face with the sleeve of her shirt, "I'll help you down." She wiped his smashed noodle moustache clean with a damp cloth, unbuckled him from the seat, and slowly lowered him to the ground. Much like his sister, he took off down the hallway to play in the same room as her.

Paige began cleaning the table off, when she was stopped mid-swipe by Judith. Her mother stood there, the distinct lines around her mouth quivering in anticipation of catching the tears that were welling in her eyes. She reached out for a rare hug from her daughter, grasping on so tightly, Paige took in an extra breath. The two embraced, communicating only love. It was such a rare, but bonding moment. For all of the bad history between them, they were still bound by the same genetic makeup. Their enduring relationship truly proved the old adage that blood was thicker than water.

Judith helped her daughter pack the kids' clothes. She stalled for time, looking through baskets in multiple rooms for their clean clothes. When she ran out of rooms, she moved on to how taking the playing children away from a computer game or television episode may somehow affect their ability to get into college.

"You know, it's really no bother if they stay here another day, or week, or whatever you need," Judith offered.

"It's good mom. I can take care of my kids."

"I know you can. I'm just worried about what *he'll* do."

"I don't want him to get suspicious."

"Jesus, he won't even probably know they're gone."

Paige walked up to her mom, their noses within inches of each other. "Mom…please…let me handle this. If I think my kids are in any kind of danger, I will let you know and you can be their great protector."

"Don't be sarcastic with me. You know I'm right." Judith deployed the death stare at her daughter hoping she would cave. No such luck.

Paige disappeared down the hallway, leaving her mom to putter around the kitchen with nothing to really do other than appear busy. Plates clanged against cupboards making their own harmonious music with the sink faucet. The music stopped when she returned with the kids, bundled up in their winter gear, cherubic faces appearing from behind tufts of cotton and polyester linings.

Judith didn't want to watch. In her view they were like tiny lambs to slaughter. Of course she tended towards the dramatic at various points in her life, but she felt overcome with fear at what was to come.

Paige had already warmed the vehicle up, so it didn't take long to leave once everyone was buckled in. Not looking up to see Judith in the window, she focused her attention instead on the rear view mirror, ensuring no one was behind as she shifted the selector to 'R.' Judith watched as they backed down the driveway and drove off out of sight. She stood there at the window for the longest time, wishing against all hope that the SUV would return, but it didn't. The aging grandmother said a small prayer as she sunk down into the cushions of the bargain shop couch. Her only wish was for her daughter and grandkids to make it out alive. All she could do now was to wait; for something, only she didn't know what that was going to be.

The SUV made it into the Hayes' drive just before dusk. As soon as the hum of the engine was silenced, the kids woke up, ready to be ushered out of the warm vehicle and into the house. Once they were safely in, Paige went back out the garage and unpacked all of their belongings. Of course there were new items that Paige hadn't seen before. Judith was a sucker for her grandchildren, never denying them a new movie or fun pair of pajamas. Paige put a bag on each shoulder, blankets under her left arm and toys under her right. She looked like a poster child for a manic shopping spree.

She dropped off Aaron's belongings in his room and then turned to go to Lindsay's room. She hadn't even thought about the possibility of running into her husband, even though his car had been parked in front of the house, and this wasn't a workday. Lindsay was already in her room, in front of the television watching a movie. Paige walked into Lindsay's room, "Okay Lindsay, your suitcase is here," she said, placing the brightly colored bag on the bed, "Make sure you get it unpacked tonight before you go to bed." The little girl was mesmerized by dancing blobs of fuzzy creatures on the square screen, nodding not in agreement with her mother, but in acknowledgement of the request to dance along to the beat of the music filtering through the speaker.

"Do you want a snack before bed kiddo?"

That got her attention, food always worked. "Yeah mommy."

"How about some hot cocoa with whip cream?"

Lindsay squealed with delight, "Yes!"

"Yes what?" Paige didn't know why she did that, prompted her kid to say please. She hated it when adults did it to her as a child, but here she was, being that same hated grown-up.

"Yes, please. Please. Pleeeaasse!"

"Alright, I get it."

Paige went to the kitchen and filled a mug with water from

the faucet. While she waited for the water to heat up in the microwave, she found the hot cocoa in the cupboard and grabbed the whip cream from the refrigerator. *Ding!* The microwave signaled it was finished. Paige took out the steaming cup of water and carefully measured two tablespoons of cocoa flavored powder into it. Tiny marshmallows floated to the top, becoming suspended in sweet, mocha colored foam. They quickly disappeared by the mountain of whip cream sprayed on top of them.

Obviously entranced by the masterpiece she created; Paige was completely unaware that Derek was watching her from the opposite end of the kitchen. He wasn't really watching her, no, that's not altogether accurate. It was more of studying, yes, he was studying her. Watching is a passive activity while studying has purpose, and Derek had purpose. He was on to his wife, and she didn't even know it…or so he thought.

Paige cupped her hand around the hot mug of cocoa in preparation of lifting it off the countertop. "Hey there, didn't know you were home," Derek said.

Paige jumped, nearly spilling the hot liquid, but instead just splashing enough on her skin to sting. "Crap!" she hollered, quickly plunging her hand under the faucet. She turned the cold water on, letting it run over the stinging red streak, waiting for the relieving numbness to take hold. "Why'd you scare me like that?" she said accusingly to her husband.

"I didn't mean to scare you. I think the better question is why didn't you tell me you were home?" Derek responded with a sly smile.

The anger was quickly replaced with the same humbling tone used by a whimpering dog when their master was upset. "I'm sorry dear, I thought you were sleeping and didn't want to wake you. There was just so much to do with getting the kids settled in and unpacked, that I figured you didn't need to be bothered by it."

She turned and faced him, her gaze locked into his, not like two lovers ready to engage in a tango of pleasure. Instead, she briefly flashed a challenge to Derek's authority. It was a look that he hadn't seen before, and it felt downright uncomfortable to him.

Derek cleared his throat, "Okay. Okay, yeah, thank you. I wasn't asleep; actually, I was just watching a movie. It must've been good because I didn't even hear you guys come home."

He moved toward his wife, a smile on his face. She didn't trust him, not one bit, but played along with the "nice Derek." He reached out and pulled his wife into him, wrapping his arms around her so that his hands came to rest clasped on the small of her back. She so badly wanted her husband back, the carefree and trustworthy one that she met all those years ago. It wasn't going to happen though, and she knew it. The blinders were off. She had been at the helm of a perpetual cruise down the river denial for all too long. It was time to debark and landfall was set to occur tomorrow.

Sleep came surprisingly easy for everyone in the family that night. Lindsay had dozed off watching television and Aaron was easily coaxed to bed by a warm bottle of milk. Unlike his sister, weaning had been a pretty easy process with him, except for his night bottle. Paige was okay with that; Lindsay had begged for one until she was nearly five years old. Derek had his usual hot shower and had actually opted to not watch a movie before bed. It all felt a bit too perfect for Paige; it was like the calm before the storm, and this one was going to be the storm of the century.

The next morning clicked by without a hitch. Routines were in place and Derek appeared to be a man on a solid foundation. He had a devoted wife, who just like a dog, was easily controlled by her master. He left the house just like he did on any Monday, to an unfulfilling job in a cubicle that he hated, collecting a check just so his wife could spend it, or so he believed.

Paige dropped the kids off at daycare and then headed across the bridge to work. She hadn't been there in over a week and all she could think about was how much there was going to be to catch up on. She walked in the back door of the building just as the clock struck 8:02 a.m. She knew her boss would have one eye fixated on the clock and the other at the stream of staff who walked in late. She didn't need to hear that lecture this morning; enough time had already been spent feeling like a child with Judith and Derek this past week.

Not wanting to be rude, Paige shot a quick "good morning" to her co-workers. She sat down at her desk with her back to everyone else, shuffling papers and making phone calls, clearly letting them know that wherever she had been was not going to be a topic of conversation this morning. There were calls to return and calls to be made, but each time she reached for the phone, the book of numbers made the loudest call directly to her. Unable to ignore it any longer, her hand took a slight right, landing on the soft bound book next to the phone. She thumbed through the pages until she they turned from white to yellow. It didn't take long after that, since what she was looking for was at the beginning of the alphabet. She scrolled up and down the lists of names until finally landing on one that felt, well, powerful. Paige had to go with her gut feeling; it wasn't like she could ask co-workers or families for a good divorce lawyer reference.

The office was fairly empty; the weather had kept many clients from coming in today. She picked up the telephone receiver to dial the attorney, playing with the pigtail cord as she waited for someone to pick up on the other end. She didn't have to wait long.

The pleasant tones of a receptionist answered on the other end, "Good morning, Kline, Berg and Stallings, how can I direct your call?"

Paige hesitated, feeling somewhat strange that her heart wasn't racing. The calm was still there. "Yes, I'd like to know if any of the attorneys are taking new clients?" she asked the voice on the other end of the line.

"What type of case are you needing an attorney for?"

Paige opened her mouth to reply, but nothing came out.

"Ma'am? Ma'am? What kind of case?"

It felt as if someone had put the young mom on pause. In

179

that same instance, her boss reached over her shoulder and put a small piece of blue-lined steno pad paper down in front of her. The supervisor stood there only long enough to ensure that her employee had read it. A head nod of acknowledgement was all she needed.

Paige turned her attention back to the sounds filtering through the mouthpiece on the phone. "Um, yes, I'm sorry. I need a divorce attorney. I need to get a divorce."

"Thank you ma'am. Let me just get a little information from you and I'll get you scheduled. When would it be convenient for you to come in?"

Paige clutched the steno paper in her hand, "I could actually make it this afternoon." She squeezed her eyes shut, waiting to hear the answer on the other end.

"Ma'am?"

"Yes," Paige answered.

"I actually happen to have a cancellation. Can you make it in here by 2pm?"

"Definitely, thank you." Paige answered the woman's questions, being careful not to give personal information that would allow Derek to find out what she was doing before it she was ready for him to.

"Okay, I think that's about it. Do you know where we're located?"

Paige looked at the phone book again, "Yes, 5th & Boyer, right?"

"Yes ma'am, that's right. Parking is in the garage to the east of the marble building. Your parking ticket will be validated by our office, so don't forget to bring it in with you. We'll see you at 2 o'clock then."

Paige hung up the phone and finished typing up case notes on various clients for the day. She planned to leave by 1:30, giving her plenty of time to navigate traffic jams or anything else that might come up. The long hands of the clock finally edged onto the '1' and the '6', signaling it was time for Paige to leave. She grabbed her purse and keys from her desk drawer and headed back out the door she had come in this morning.

The attorney's office wasn't hard to find, it was one of the biggest buildings in all of downtown. Beautiful white marble, intertwined with flecks of gold and silver granite created a landmark that put many resident and visitor in awe of its regal beauty. Long brass handles adorned the front door, daring those on the street to take the challenge of coming inside. Paige pulled the right door open, shifting the weight of her body backward so as to give some leverage against the heavy door.

Inside was no less disappointing then out. A flurry of activity came in every form, barista's brewing masterpieces to her left and a bank of elevators shuttling workers and consumers from one level to another on her right. The herd of workers was clearly different from their consumer counterparts. Workers wore blue and black pin-striped suits, with only the height of the heel on their shoes and style of satchel in their hands separating the males from the females. The consumers were a bit more of a curiosity. Their dress did not separate them by gender, but rather by class. Some wore tattered blue jeans and ball caps headlined with a long grease stain brought on by hard work and a lack of caring about what others thought. Others were just as majestic as the building they were standing in, carrying purses adorned with designer symbols to signify the money they had to spend. Paige fit somewhere in the middle of all of them.

She looked for the highest concentration of people, not near the coffee stand, but rather near the middle of the steel boxes with doors that open and closed. A directory was placed for convenience right next to the up and down arrows. She looked up and down until finding the law firm's name. It was on the 22nd floor. Paige didn't much care for elevators, in her dreams they would twist and turn uncontrollably, creating a fear that transcended from her nightmares into a fuzzy reality. The doors opened welcoming the next crowd. Paige stepped in, making sure she was as close to the door as possible. Promptly upon the doors closing, the steel cage shot straight up, leaving her stomach on the floor while her eyes remained glued to the numbers above the door. Although the entire ride to the 22nd floor was less than a minute of her life, it felt like an eternity until she finally got there.

Ding! Ding! After a brief pause that matched the skip of Paige's heart, the doors opened and she gladly stepped out onto the plush carpeting. Each step felt like she was walking on a cloud of cotton. The office was set up in such a way as to obviously impress those who carried the symbolic purses. She walked over to a long counter that served as the receptionist's desk. It was heavily paneled in a cherry wood, capped with black granite. A mix of sounds could clearly be heard as Paige got closer to the greeter: clicking of keyboard keys, buzz of the phone's speaker from demanding attorneys, and the soothing voice of the employee managing it all.

"Hello, may I help you?" the receptionist asked.

"Yes, I'm Paige Hayes. I have an appointment with an attorney at 2pm. It's for a…a…a divorce."

The lady behind the counter smiled warmly, clearly seeing that Paige was nervous. "No problem, I have you down. Would you like a cup of coffee or something else to drink while you wait?"

"No, thank you." With that, she went over to the waiting area and sank into an overstuffed, leather chair. Not faux leather, no, this was real. This was the kind that you *didn't* stick to in hot weather. Not to worry about that today though, not this time of year. The longer she sat, the more difficult it became to get a breath. Her throat felt dry and scratchy. Every breath she drew in felt like it was being run through a filter of broken glass.

She got up and went back over to the counter. "Would that offer of coffee still be available?"

"Certainly, I'll just be a moment."

Paige sat back down and waited. Thankfully, it wasn't long before the smiling woman appeared again, steaming hot coffee in hand. The mug was just as professionally adorned as the office she sat in. Swirls of steam danced above the rim of the cup in tune to the music that was piped in to the office from the speaker on the ceiling above. The first swallow barely squeaked past her vocal cords, but each subsequent sip went down smooth.

It was 2 o'clock, and right on cue appeared the attorney Paige had been waiting for appeared from around the corner. Her name was Dara Stirling. She had a pocketful of credentials and a pit bull reputation. Her hair remained suspended in a tight, perpetual bun, so much so that people claimed the only reason it looked like she was smiling was from her face being pulled tight from her hairdo. Dara spoke in a no-nonsense tone of voice, clearly commanding an audience wherever she went; her speech always carefully measured syllable by syllable. This woman was going to be Paige's advocate in the Courtroom, and Paige couldn't be happier.

"Come this way, my office is toward the back."

Paige dutifully followed the woman, past grey fabric cubicles emitting the same tones as the front counter had. Dara's office was in the back, but it was for good reason, she had an almost 360 degree view of the city.

"Wow!" said Paige. She hadn't meant for it to escape, but it was just so breathtaking.

"Yeah, I know, most people think that way, unless they're in my line of work. I look at the world down there so much different now," Dara lamented. She didn't expound on her view, clearly feeling uncomfortable that she had even said that much. It wasn't professional in her viewpoint; focus must remain on the client, not on one's own personal opinions about life.

Dara motioned to a matching set of plush, blue linen chairs in front of her desk. "Go ahead and have a seat. Do you need more coffee?"

"No, thank you."

"Alright then, let's get down to business." Dara opened up a leather bound notepad and positioned her ballpoint pen on the very first line. "Okay, what do you have for me?"

Paige wasn't sure where to start. This felt a little bit like an interview where the employer starts with, "So tell me about yourself." She decided to start where she was and work backward; it was a bit like reverse osmosis. Paige even handed over a manila file folder full of information. At the top of the stack was an outline of their assets and debts, resumes, medical records, what she would like to keep and what she would not. There was even a timeline of events, the same ones that she had just explained.

Dara didn't flinch once; she had heard plenty of different stories in her career. This one was no different. It did raise red flags though. "Okay," she said, flipping through the multitude of information in the file given to her, "I will take your case. There are a couple of things you need to be aware of though."

"Okay," Paige answered hesitantly. "What are they?"

"I require a retainer; it's pretty significant, $2,500. Do you think your husband will protest the divorce?"

"I don't know. He's not a man that hates to lose. I truly think he'll only protest if he feels like he's not getting his way."

"Yes, men are a bit like children, but we can deal with that." Dara clasped her hands in front of her, placing them meticulously centered on her desk. "What is the most difficult to deal with at this point is the danger factor."

"Danger? I'm not sure what you mean. I mean I know what you mean, but not completely. What are you thinking?" Paige asked.

Dara took off her glasses and placed them in a pinstriped case inside the top drawer of her desk. She leaned back in her chair and sighed, for once unsure how to proceed. The silence was uncomfortable for both of the ladies.

"Listen, I've been in this business for probably longer than you have been alive. I've seen and heard enough to fill an entire volume of encyclopedias. I tell you this first, because what I tell you next you must believe. Does that makes sense?"

"Um, yes," Paige replied, still confused.

Something inside of Dara's head caused her to take a sudden U-turn on the conversation. "You know what," she said, putting her glasses back on, "it doesn't matter. How about this, you look so organized, why don't I adjust my retainer? If you can come up with a $1,000, we can get started."

Paige opened up her purse. She counted out $850 and put it on Dara's desk. "This is what we got back from our tax refund. I can get the rest for you on Thursday when I get paid."

Dara didn't bother counting the money. She gathered it up in a pile in front of her and set it aside. "That will be fine. The receptionist up front will write you a receipt. Do a favor for me though?"

"What's that?"

"Will you please call me every couple of days and check in?" Dara spoke matter-of-factly. "It's a common practice. I have a large client load and want to make sure I keep on top of everything. So, if you don't hear from me, please call."

"Yeah, sure," Paige replied standing up, coffee mug still in hand. She shook Dara's hand once more and then left her office. It was a bit disorienting, nothing but grey everywhere. By the time she got back up to the front desk, the switchboard operator was busy fielding phone calls from all directions. Hardly glancing up, she pushed a square receipt, along with a validated parking pass at Paige as she whispered, "Have a nice day." She grabbed both pieces of paper and shoved them into her purse. Another ride down the elevator, and she would be back out through the huge doors that sheltered those on the inside from the world on the outside. It was just before 4pm, perfect time to head back across the river. For once she was going to beat rush hour traffic.

Paige drove her vehicle up to the toll booth at the exit of the parking garage. She reached into her purse to get her ticket out, pulling out instead a fistful of miscellaneous papers. The receipt from the lawyers office was on top – it was written for $1,000. *What the heck?* Paige hadn't given her that much money. She counted it out loud for Dara. Just underneath that was the blue lined steno paper that her boss had slipped her. Paige smiled as she read it again,

"Do whatever it is you need to do. Only you know what that is. We're behind you all the way." Lastly was the parking ticket. Paige handed it to the attendant and just a few moments later, the red and white striped barricade was lifted. The clouds had given way to blue sky, and for once, in a very long time, Paige felt hope in her future.

16 SLEEPLESS

By Thursday of that same week, Paige had received the initial papers to file for divorce. They arrived at her work, in a plain white envelope with a simple return address in the form of a post office box. Seeing it there in front of her, the blank ink in stark contrast to the white parchment paper, felt all too real. The first steps were the easiest part; the toughest was yet to come.

Paige called her attorney and confirmed everything was in order. Dara asked whether she'd like to have the papers served on Derek at home or at work. "Can't I just do it?" Paige asked.

"Do what?"

"Serve him? Can't I just give him the papers? I just don't want him to be any more upset at me than he already will be."

Dara thought for a moment and then agreed, "That will be fine. Just make sure that he understands that he has ten days to return the documents, whether that be through his own attorney or by himself. If he chooses to do nothing in those ten days, then it all defaults back to you."

"That would be wonderful," Paige said with false optimism.

"That would, but it won't happen. Sorry to burst your bubble. Besides, it's a lot more fun this way."

"What do you mean *fun?*"

"There's nothing better than beating someone at their own game; and that is precisely what you…what *we* are going to do. Now, enough of this. Give him the papers tonight, and call me tomorrow. Sound good?"

"Yes, it does, but can't I wait until tomorrow? I just think it will be easier to do on a Friday. That way if I'm up all night arguing about it, I won't have to worry about work the next day. I'll even check and see if my mom can watch the kids."

"That's fine, whatever day you choose. Paige?"

"Yes," she responded.

"Just make sure you call me the very next day – even if it's a weekend," Dara said.

"Will do. Goodbye."

"Goodbye." The line went silent. Paige pushed down the plastic piece on the phone to hang up. She let it back up and a dial tone returned. She called Judith next and explained what she needed from her mom. Judith hadn't slept well all week. Paige called her every night with updates; some conversations were more involved than others.

"Hey mom, it's Paige."

"Yes, I know the sound of my own daughter's voice." Judith couldn't help sounding irritable, but then let a little giggle escape.

"Mom, what's so funny? Oh Jesus, are you drinking? I really don't need this right now."

"*You* don't need this right now? Why's it always have to be about *you?* All these years I have asked that question, but nobody can answer it. What about *me?* Hmm? Answer me that why don't you."

Judith continued on, but what she didn't know is that Paige had already hung up the phone. The daughter sat motionless, hand still on the receiver of the phone, not sure what to do next. Maybe it was better if the kids were at the house when she told him. Her mind swirled with thoughts. She would have to decide something soon. For so long she had let her husband make all the decisions, except when it came to her kids. She had to remain strong for them.

Paige tucked the envelope back into her desk drawer and finished out the rest of the workday. She tried her best that evening to carry on like nothing was different. It truly wasn't that difficult. Derek stayed in the basement all evening, watching movies on the television. Lindsay and Aaron had supper and then each got a warm bubble bath. It was a surefire trick to coax them to sleep early. Paige did the same, closing her eyes in complete exhaustion shortly before 9pm. Tomorrow was a big day and she had to make sure she was well rested for it.

The next day flew by. Paige transferred the envelope from her desk to an oversized purse she brought to work just for the purpose of carrying the important documents home. She had hoped to purposefully avoid speaking with Nate today, and luckily for her, he had called in sick. She couldn't avoid her boss however, and it was probably good she didn't. Paige spent the last hour of the day with her employer, covering details of nearly the entire past month. The experienced supervisor practiced active listening, nodding in empathy and asking questions as needed. At day's end, Paige felt ready to head home and face the night's events. It felt good talking about what was going to happen, sounding ideas off of people she trusted. Unfortunately it wouldn't be this easy once she got home.

Derek called Paige at work about ten minutes before she was due to leave for the day. "Hey hon, how bout' I pick up the kids for you tonight? I got off work a little bit early and thought I could help you out."

She didn't know what to say. All she could wonder was why was he being so nice. "Um, yeah...yeah that would be really nice. Thank you," Paige managed to stammer. This was too weird, and it definitely wasn't part of the plan that she had rehearsed over and over.

"Okay then hon, we'll see you when you get home. Love you."

"Love you too." Paige put the phone down and grabbed her

keys, while clutching the purse slung over her shoulder. She felt awkward now, hoping the drive home would reveal a how to get around this diversion that Derek had thrown her way. He was a smart man; he had to know something was up. Niceness was not in his repertoire.

By the time she got home, Paige decided she would fight fire with fire. If he could be nice, then so would she. She got out of her vehicle and headed into the house. She was immediately hit by the smell of pizza. Derek was in the kitchen slicing up triangles of cheese and meat covered crusts. The kids were standing nearby, like two puppies waiting to be fed.

"Hey hon, good to have you home!" Derek smiled at his wife.

"Mommy!" Lindsay said, echoing her dad's sentiment. Aaron smiled big at his mom, mimicking his sister's excitement.

Paige walked over to her son and daughter, giving them a large bear hug, "Hi kiddo's, mommy missed you today!"

"Me too," said Lindsay. "Oh yeah, and Aaron missed you too mommy."

"I know he did sweetheart, I love you." She kissed Lindsay on the forehead, "And I love you too," she said, giving Aaron his own kiss.

"Mommy, look, daddy bought pizza!"

"I see that." Paige turned to Derek, "Thank you for doing all of this. It isn't even my birthday."

"I know that," Derek said, moving toward his wife. He grabbed on to her, holding her tight at the waist. He looked at her in the eyes, staring almost to her soul. Paige knew what he was doing. He was trying to read her; get any thought he could, but it was useless. She might not be good at exercising her own self will, but she was the master at hiding emotion. "You deserve to have *every* day be just like it's your birthday."

"Oh Derek, you're too good to me."

He held his wife tighter and whispered into her ear, "I know I am." His comment sent chills up her spine.

Derek quickly switched his attention back to his kids. He dished them up each a slice of pizza, being careful to cut Aaron's up into tiny bits. What Aaron didn't outright chew, he could gum with a mouthful of child's saliva until it deteriorated back into its original form of flour and water. Derek took a piece of pizza from a second box and offered it to his wife on a paper plate.

"Are we out of regular plates?" she asked.

"No, I just figured it would be easier to not have to dishes for once," Derek replied.

Paige was suspicious and quickly looked for a way out of eating the pizza. She grabbed her stomach, "Oh gosh, hang on hon, I need to go to the bathroom." She went down the hall and closed the door behind her. She sat down on the closed seat and waited until Derek came to the door and knocked.

"You okay in there?" he asked.

Paige strained her voice as if she were in dire straits. "Yeah, I'll be fine, just give me another minute. I'll be out soon, promise."

She stayed in there until satisfied her husband had moved beyond the pizza issue. She turned the faucet on and ran it, washing her hands even though she had done nothing. Emerging from the bathroom, Paige was surprised there was no one around. The kitchen light had been turned off and the pizza boxes were nowhere to be found. The first thing she did was check on her kids. Lindsay was in her room playing dolls with Aaron. He had a doll in each hand; joyfully tossing them up in the air and watching them fall back down to his lap. He repeated the same scenario, over and over.

The rest of the house was dark, except for the light that shone from under the basement door. Derek had to be down there. Paige looked around the kitchen before going downstairs. She needed to get the papers out of her purse. She looked everywhere, but there was nothing; it was nowhere to be found. Suddenly her heart took a hard thump in her chest, *Oh God, he's got it!* She stood frozen in the kitchen. This isn't the way it was supposed to work out. The only thing left to do was go down to the basement and face whatever was going to come. She turned the brass knob on the painted wooden door and proceeded to descend the stairway. It felt like she was a dead man walking.

Derek didn't even look at her when she finally got down to the last step. She sat down on the couch right across from him.

"I kinda feel like I'm in the principal's office." She tried making a joke, but he wouldn't look at her.

He just stared at the neat little pile of papers resting squarely on his lap. To his left lay his wife's purse. He had gone through it when she was in the bathroom. Her diversion had completely backfired. After what seemed like an eternity, Derek finally looked up at his wife. His eyes were red and glossy. She couldn't tell if he had been crying or not.

"How could you?" he asked his wife. "How could you do this to me? I've given everything to you. Do you understand what this will do to me?"

Paige was dumfounded. She didn't know how to respond. "Answer me dammit! I deserve an explanation of this!" he said, shaking the papers at his increasingly terrified wife across from him.

Derek stood up and began to pace the room. Back and forth he went, fists opening and closing. After what seemed like the hundredth time he had circled, his feet suddenly stopped dead in their tracks. It was their daughter at the top of the stairs. "Daddy?" she asked.

"What honey?" Derek replied, running his hand across his head.

"Can you come tuck me in?"

"Sure, I'll be right there." He looked over at his wife, ordering her to stay put until he returned. "We're not finished here."

She listened as he headed upstairs, following the echo of his footsteps as he went down the hall. As she waited for him to return, waves of nausea threatened her ability to remain glued to her spot on the couch. Her muscles began to ache from their forced stillness. It was almost as if she rationalized not moving into not being noticed –

as if somehow he'd forget she was there. No such luck, he was hardly gone longer than the time she had spent faking ill in the bathroom. The sound of his footsteps slowed as he approached the basement door, and then they stopped altogether. Paige strained her head to hear what she could. What was he doing? Part of her didn't want to know.

Curiosity finally got the best of his wife. She stood up and grabbed the papers off the larger couch that Derek had been sitting on. Firmly clutched in her hand, her mind willed the rest of her body to go upstairs. This had to be finished; the waiting was killing her. Judith used to do this to her as a child. Paige would get the "notice" that Judith wanted to talk to her later. It always had to be later, that way Paige had time to imagine all the things she had done wrong that her mother had found out about. People often say that girls look for men to marry that are like their dad's. Paige was quite the opposite, apparently she had found someone just like her mother to marry – they both had passive aggressive as their middle names.

Derek hadn't gone to bed, he only changed positions in the house, much like chess pieces on a playing board. He had settled into the recliner in the living room. Upon seeing his wife, he sent the first strike, "What do you want bitch?"

Ugh, she hated that word, but she would be relieved if that was the worst he did this evening. "Well, I think we should talk," she said as she slowly lowered herself down onto the ottoman across from Derek.

"Apparently there's nothing to talk about. You've already made up your mind, these papers tell me that," he replied.

"We can't go on like this."

"Correction, *you* can't go on like this. My life is just fine. You're the one that's screwed up, not me. Did you forget *you've* been in the loony bin? You didn't think this through too well did you?"

"What do you mean?" she asked.

"What I mean is you didn't realize that the only thing you're gonna get is the clothes on your back. That's it! Don't think for a minute that you're taking my kids away from me!"

The idea of Derek wanting the kids hadn't even crossed her mind. She felt certain that when her attorney asked about Derek contesting the divorce, it referenced material things, not human lives.

"You'll get to see your kids."

"Damn right I will. I'll get to see them all the time. It's *you* who won't get to see them!" Derek fired back at his wife.

Somewhere deep down inside of the woman who fought her way through a horrific childhood was a bit of spark left. It lit just at the right time. Not even the tears that had begun to stream down her face could put it out.

And then she began, "You know as well as me that this cannot continue on. We are broken Derek. It's not either one of our faults. It is what it is. We've tried. You need help just like I do, and two sick people can't help each other in a marriage. I'm just doing what you've wanted to do all along." Paige shifted her position on the couch, crossing and uncrossing her legs.

Derek hadn't heard a word his wife said. He was deep in thought, organizing his next move, looking for one that would permanently end this. He had hoped to put Paige into checkmate just by virtue of pawning the kids, but it hadn't work. She was stronger than he had anticipated. He decided to move the knight next.

"You know how much I love you. Look at yourself. No one will *ever* accept you the way I have. You're going to be alone the rest of your life if you leave me."

Hoping she would respond to some desperate need to stay with him, Derek stood up and walked over to the couch where Paige sat. He stood perched above her, waiting for a response. There was nothing, not a word, a sob, or a sigh, nothing. The only way he could even hear her breathing was by having to sit down right next to her. This was better than he could hope for. Put her back over the edge, back in the hospital, then he would be a sure bet for keeping the kids.

Sure enough, in her mind Paige was walking through a field

194

of beautiful daisies, sun shining. It was the greatest feeling in the world. But she couldn't stay. The fire shone brightly from inside, overpowering the sunlight in her made up world. Paige was thrust back into the dark of the night, still on the couch in the living room. It was quiet except for the hum of the refrigerator in the other room. She was alone and uncertain as to what time it was. What she did know is that it was late, and the kids would be getting up early in the morning. As she did any night, Paige compulsively checked all the outer doors to ensure they were locked. The basement television emitted a telltale glow signaling the whereabouts of her husband. She didn't care really, all she wanted to do was go to sleep, and she went to their room and did just that.

Saturday morning began like any other, Lindsay standing at her mom's bed, her eyes just barely able to see over the top of it. "Are you hungry sweetie?" Paige asked her daughter.

"No mommy, I already ate."

"What a big girl! What did you have?"

"Daddy made me pancakes." Lindsay gave her mom a kiss on the arm and disappeared out the doorway.

Curiosity got the best of her, so Paige decided to get up and follow the aroma of breakfast to the kitchen. It smelled wonderful. The kitchen table was occupied by several brown, paper bags from the grocery store. Derek had gone out before anyone else woke up this morning. The fridge was filled with orange and apple juice, various sandwich makings and a couple packages of meat for supper. On top of the stove were several metal containers covered with foil. Each one held a different breakfast item, bacon, pancakes, scrambled eggs. Paige's stomach growled in protest as she resisted taking part in the feast. What man in his right mind makes brunch for his wife that just served him with divorce papers? That was it; he *wasn't* in his right mind. She carefully scooped portions from each of the containers and ran them through the disposal. He moved his pawn, and so could she.

Paige took a bowl down from the cupboard and rinsed it with

195

hot water. She took a spoon from the drawer below and did the same with it. She wasn't taking any chances. Breakfast consisted of a packet of oatmeal and juice box, all things that were sealed so no one could sabotage her food. Paranoia has incapacitated some while saving others. Paige hoped she could use it for the latter of the two.

The phone rang once and then was silent. A few minutes later Lindsay came into the kitchen and handed it to her mom, "Here you go, its nana."

Paige took the phone from her daughter. "Hello?"

"How's it going?" Judith asked.

"Oh fine."

"Just fine?"

"Yeah, just fine. What should I say?"

"Do you want me to take the kids today? We're not doing anything."

"That would be good. I can bring them over. What time?"

"Any time after noon. Bring their sleeping bags and extra clothes. I'm sure they'll stay the night. Do you have any microwave meals or something for dinner?" Judith had grown cheap over the years, most likely a bi-product of living with her husband.

"Yes mom, I have some. I'll pack some snacks too. See you in a couple hours." Paige hung up the phone and started packing up the kids. Lindsay was excited to hear she was going to her grandmother's house. She liked being the center of attention over there. Aaron didn't know much difference, being happy just to be held and fed. Shortly before noon Paige wrote a note to her husband, explaining where she was going and when she would be back. She left it on the kitchen table, figuring that would be the easiest place for Derek to find it.

Over at her mother's, it wasn't long before the conversation turned from niceties to the down and dirty details of last night. Judith hadn't wanted to pry, but was profoundly curious. Paige figured that was why her mom offered to have the kids over. In reality Judith just wanted to see her daughter in person, she worried terribly that Derek would do something to change that.

"So everything went okay?" Judith asked.

"As good as can be expected. I just hope he signs the papers and we can get on with this," Paige responded.

"What happens after that?"

"My lawyer said once he signs them, she will file them at the courthouse. After that, we have to attend some kind of class about the kids. The divorce can't be final for at least 90 days after it's filed. There's some kind of cooling off period that is in place by the courts."

Judith tried to do the mental math, but it wasn't working. She walked over to the calendar on the wall and counted off the days. "Kids will be out of school by then. That's good."

"How come? Why's that good?" Paige asked.

"In case you need to move, or Lindsay has to change schools for some reason. At least you won't have to do it mid-year and interrupt her education."

Paige hadn't thought that far ahead. Losing her house would be tough, but if it meant gaining her independence back again, it would be worth it. "I need to get back home." About ready to head out the door, Paige suddenly remembered she needed to call her attorney. She picked the phone up and dialed the number. She had already memorized it.

She got Dara's voicemail. "Hello, this is Paige Hayes. I was just calling to let you know I did give my husband the papers last night, and surprisingly I woke up to a full course breakfast this morning. I will let you know more when something else changes. Hopefully he'll decide one way or another to sign them and we can get the clock started on getting this finalized. Thank you for everything."

Paige hung up the phone and headed out the door. She left quickly, not knowing what to expect when she got home. A warmth from deep inside fueled her anticipation – it had continued to smolder from the fire that had been lit last night.

There was no one there when Paige returned back home. The house was filled with an eerie silence that hung in the air like low lying fog. Hungry, she opened a can of stew and sat down at the kitchen table to eat it. In the same spot where the note had been left just hours earlier, were the divorce papers. She flipped absentmindedly through the papers, slowly realizing that all the blank spaces had been filled with ink pen. Derek had signed them.

With no one home, and nothing on the television, Paige went upstairs and got on the computer. There was always something to do on the internet. She logged on, bringing up the internet home page. As she started to type in the web address, the square, white box populated with a popular dating website. It had been months since her online tryst, and she had always been careful to cover her tracks. Feeling the need to pursue this further, she typed in the search parameters features and characteristics that would be similar to her husband. She got back 82 hits. Face, upon face scrolled past her on the computer screen, and then, like hitting a jackpot on a slot machine, the screen roll stopped on an all too familiar face – Derek. *Oh my God!* There, in living color, was the smiling face of her husband. A picture that had just been recently hung on the wall behind her now stood juxtaposed on her computer screen. The title gave a brief overview of his vital statistics – age, race, who he was looking for. But it was his introductory sentence that was the killer. It read: "Divorced, full-time loving single father of two, successful business man, seeks woman who wants to be spoiled." It hadn't even been twenty-four hours and he was already out searching for the next woman to trap. It wasn't her that couldn't be alone, it was him; Derek didn't want to be alone. He needed a woman in his life to take care of his own narcissistic needs.

The phone rang, taking Paige away from her detective work. The caller ID flashed Taryn's name. Knowing her friend wouldn't give up, Paige took the call. "Hello?" she said.

"Well hello there! I'm surprised anyone answered," Taryn replied.

"Yeah, I'm sorry, it's just been super busy."

"Sorry? Geesh, why do you always have to apologize for everything you do? So tell me, what's going on?"

"Nothing much, just the same old stuff."

"Really? We haven't spoken to each other in over a month and that's all I get? Come on, spill it, I deserve more than that."

"Hey, I have a lot to do around here today. My work never ends you know."

The girls developed an understanding very young, whenever the two of them were talking on the phone, and there was a potential for their conversation to be overheard, one would start to stall so as to clue in the other. It was exactly what Paige was doing now. She didn't want anything to be said over the phone for fear that Derek was somehow recording her conversations. He wasn't savvy enough to review the computer history, but he could certainly do something to the telephone. Fortunately for Paige, Taryn it didn't take long to pick up on what she was doing.

"Okay, I can hear that you're busy with work…or something. You enjoy that and we'll talk to ya later." She didn't even wait for a good-bye from Paige. She knew something desperate had to be going on, but now had to wait until her best friend returned to work on Monday to find out.

Paige went back to the computer, doing a quick search for other dating websites. She knew them all too well from her days of looking for love in all the wrong places. Each site she turned to provided her a hit; her husband's name and face repeated itself over and over. It was like trying to turn the pages of a book to read a new part, only each page was the same in this chapter, 'loving father' blah, blah, blah. It was almost too much to look at. The past forty-eight hours had been draining on the young mom, but she didn't realize it was just the first mile of this marathon. Paige gazed out the window, coming to the reality that the sun was getting lower in the sky, and at any time her husband would possibly be returning.

Derek did return, but it was far after sundown. He came into the house, using the glow of his cellphone to light the way rather than turn on the lights and wake someone up. He went into the kitchen, opening up the fridge and staring blankly at the shelves of food. There were various plastic containers of food from the week prior, cans of fruit waiting to be opened and jugs of 1% milk. Tucked behind all of it were the same aluminum tins that he had put out for his wife this morning. He picked up each one individually, lifting the lid to peer inside. Noticing the food had been eaten, he smiled, feeling satisfied that his wife had done exactly what he wanted. "This is going to be easier than I thought," he muttered under his breath.

"What's easier?" Paige asked from the entrance to the kitchen. Sleeping was no longer her strong suit; she had heard her husband's vehicle and had been waiting for the right moment to approach him.

Derek froze, his body poised halfway between the fridge and the open door. His fingers stiffly reached around a glass bottle of beer. *What the hell was she doing awake?* He straightened his back, slowly shutting the door to the refrigerator. "What was that?" he asked his wife.

"Easier, you said easier. What was easier?" she responded, eyes fixed on every move her husband made.

"Huh? I don't know what you're talking about" he said, trying to play dumb.

He turned his back to her, rummaging through the silverware drawer until he came upon a bottle opener. God she was relentless, he needed to do something quick to divert this conversation. He was tired and not so sure that he could keep it together like he needed to do. This was the most crucial time; any stupid move he made that she could figure out would go straight against him in divorce court. He didn't want the kids, but he also didn't want her to have them either. She didn't deserve anything but hell. He popped the top off of his beer and turned back toward his wife.

"Sorry, I must've been talking to myself," he said through a forced smile.

Paige didn't know why he tried to fake anything. He may have been a well-rehearsed liar to some, but to her, every syllable caught on the forked tongue that filled his mouth.

"No problem. I just heard something and thought I'd better make sure it wasn't an intruder." As she spoke, Derek headed for the basement, her words trailing his footsteps. "Okay then, I'm gonna head back to sleep," her sentence finished to an empty room.

Paige went back to the bedroom, but didn't sleep, she couldn't. She grabbed her pillows and headed down the hall, taking a sheet and a blanket from the closet as she went. She ended up at the couch in the living, making the cushions into a makeshift bed with sheets and blanket. This would become her routine each night, after the kids went to bed, for the next two months. Paige no longer wanted to lie down next to the same man that bore her two children. The simple thought of doing so made her skin crawl.

17 CHECK PLEASE

Sleeping on the couch was just one routine Paige developed over the next two months. Suddenly everything became methodical – bordering on neurotic at times. Her life became a system of checks and balances, ensuring she ate nothing at home that didn't originate in a sealed container while trying to maintain some sense of normalcy both at work and at home for Lindsay and Aaron. Taryn remained a constant source of support, making daily check-in phone calls to Paige at work. The two women no longer communicated by computer, no paper trails Paige insisted.

"Heck Paige, whatcha gonna do next, start taping lines of thread to the door to see if it's been opened? Dusting for fingerprints even?" Taryn asked during one of the phone conversations.

"Hey, that's not a bad idea! I might give that one a try!" her best friend replied.

Taryn laughed, "Seriously I'll be so happy when this is over and you're home where you belong. It's gonna be so fun, just like old times, and I get to help you with your babies. I've been looking around and there are a bunch of cute little houses for rent. I'll start making a list and you can check them out when you get here."

"That sounds awesome, I can't wait. I bought towels today,"

Paige replied.

"Uh, okay, towels? Are you going to use them to mop up the blood from Derek's dead body when this is all over?"

"Oh my God, really? You really just suggested that? How'd you guess?" Paige teased.

"That's just me, I'm magical I guess!"

Paige got silent for a minute. "Are you still there?" Taryn asked.

"Yeah, I'm still here. You are magical, but even more, you're a lifesaver. I mean that from the bottom of my heart. You've been there ever since we were in junior high, looking out for me when no one else would or could. I thank you for that my friend, I really do."

"You're welcome. You know, I really think it's what God called on me to do, kinda like a guardian angel."

"You've definitely earned your wings," Paige said.

"And I think you're about ready to earn yours, just in a different way. You're about to be set free. Are you ready for that?"

"Yes, I opened up my own bank account and everything is done with the courts, now I just wait another thirty days for everything to be finalized."

"I'm not talking about all of that stuff Paige; I'm talking about *you, your mind.* How's that doin'?"

"You know, I alternate between the daisy filled fields and the River Denial. It works."

"Okay, it might be for now, but promise me that if it stops, I'll be the first to know."

"Yes, okay," Paige replied.

"*Promise* me," Taryn insisted.

"I promise. Satisfied?"

"Yes, thank you."

"Okay, I need to get going to get the kids from daycare. Listen, I only have two weeks left until I leave, and tomorrow is my last day here at work. This is it for now. I'll call you again when I'm on the road – headed home. God it feels good to say that word. I love you."

"Love you too my friend."

Paige hung up the phone and finished putting the last of her desk ornaments in a small cardboard box. She walked over to Nate's desk and slipped a small, red tube of cinnamon gel into the drawer. It was a souvenir of sorts, something only shared between the two of them. She wrote a note to place underneath it:

To my loving twin brother. You are the best. I will never forget you.
Love, your loving twin sister.

Paige felt a lump rise up in her throat. She heard the familiar click of the clock striking the five o'clock hour in the background. It was time to leave. Tomorrow was technically supposed to be her last day at work, but she planned on calling in sick on her last day of work – good-bye wasn't her thing. She tucked the box of personal belongings under her arm and headed out the back door. Setting the alarm for one last time, she stepped over the threshold and out into the bright sun. She mentally checked off one more event in her mind. The list was growing shorter day by day causing her body to fill with nervous anticipation.

The last thing to do was pack up her belongings. Things had cooled down between her and Derek. She still didn't trust him, but her anger had slowly been replaced with pity; for whatever reason she actually felt sorry for him. He was a shadow of his former self, once physically strong and loving he was now morally weak and bitter. He no longer threatened to take the kids, only because she had made a deal – a deal with the devil himself. Paige agreed to only move as far away as Judith's, a short drive down the interstate away. Derek had insisted that she not take the kids more than an hour away from where they lived now, or else he would fight. Paige couldn't take the chance of losing that one, the risks were too great. She hadn't told Taryn, she wasn't strong enough emotionally to take that on right now.

A final custody arrangement had been worked out with the courts; Derek would get every other weekend and Christmas with Paige taking primary physical custody of the kids on the remaining days. The hardest part of all of it was yet to come – telling their precocious daughter that mommy and daddy were no longer going to be together. Telling her would be like swimming through a marshmallow goo of guilt.

Derek was actually home before his wife this evening. She found him in the kitchen rummaging through the freezer for something to eat.

"I can order us some pizzas if you'd like," Paige offered.

"What us are you referring to? You and the kids? Me and the kids? Because there certainly isn't a you and me 'us' anymore, is there?" he shot back.

"All I wanted to know is if you wanted me to get something for dinner. Please don't read into it, I wasn't trying to start anything, I promise," his wife responded back, her voice faint, but steady.

The two adults were cut short by a presence greater than the animosity that brewed between them – it was Lindsay. "Hi daddy, hi mommy!" the little girl said to her parents, greeting each one with a brief hug before tearing out of the room in search of her next adventure.

"When are we going to tell her what's going on?" Paige asked Derek.

"Here you go with this us and we stuff again. How bout this, how bout when are *you* going to tell *my* daughter what you've done to *us*?" he replied.

Paige knew enough to let it go. Avoiding conflict was paramount to her very survival at this point. "I'll call and order some pizza for tonight's supper. Just let me know when you want to talk to Lindsay with me, or if you want me to do it alone."

"Yeah, okay," Derek said to his wife without looking at her, "go ahead and talk to her, I'm sure you'll do it better than me."

He turned and walked away, leaving Paige to be alone with

her thoughts in the now empty kitchen. She walked over to the table and rummaged through the newspapers, looking for pizza coupons. Each piece of paper looked like the other, letters floating across the page, organizing themselves into words meant just for her – traitor, guilty, whore, bitch. She dropped the newspaper, reaching for the phone book instead. Thumbing through the white, and finally yellow pages, she ended up at the pizza section and picked up the receiver to dial the number. The numbers on the keypad didn't look normal. They floated, just like the words on the newspaper. Paige didn't stick around to see what they were going to tell her. She grabbed her keys and purse and told Derek she was going down to pick up the pizzas.

"What, they don't deliver anymore?" he asked.

Paige thought quickly and responded, "Yeah, but it's cheaper to go pick it up, just trying to save some money. I'll be right back." Aaron and Lindsay were playing in the room with their dad, so it was a perfect time to leave without having to say anything else.

She returned forty minutes later to Derek playing with the kids in the living room. Laughter, so seldom heard, filled every square inch of air space. Paige watched the interaction of a seemingly normal, middle-class family. Moments like these stung with painful regret at the decision she had made to leave. That had been Taryn's responsibility all along, to remind Paige that there would be times of hope, but it was false hope, tricking her into believing all was well. She pulled her thoughts together and brushed her face with a fake smile.

"Hey guys, I'm back with dinner," she said, purposefully looking only at her kids.

Paige got the kids seated at the table, each one eager to dive into the thick, cheesy crust. This might be the right time to have the talk she so desperately needed to get done. "Hey kiddo, I've got something to tell you," she began.

"What mommy?" her daughter responded, eyes fixated on the strings of cheese flecked with tomato sauce.

"So there's been some things going on between daddy and

I….” She stopped. The look on her daughter's face, the absolute innocence, was almost more than she could bear.

“Daddy and I aren't going to be living in the same house anymore.” The words hung thick in the air, taunting those around with their power.

“Where's daddy gonna live?” Lindsay asked.

“He's going to live right here sweetheart. *We* are going to be moving.”

The little girl stopped chewing her food, slowly putting the piece of half-eaten pizza back on the brightly colored plate. She looked up at her mom, little tears forming in her eyes. “What about my friends mommy? What about my school? Where are we going?”

The questions came in rapid fire succession, almost faster than Paige could manage. “You'll make new friends, and you'll get to see your old friends when you come to visit daddy. The same goes for your school. I think you'll really like it where we're going. It's going to be right by your nana's house.”

Just as the first tear made its way to the kitchen table, Lindsay's little lip suddenly stopped quivering. “Nana? Are we going to live with her too?”

Paige laughed a little bit and smiled, “No sweetie, we're not going to live with her, but maybe we can live by her. Would you like that?”

“Yeah, can I be excused? I want to go tell my friends I'm moving.”

“Yes, you can be excused, but it's getting late. You can go outside and play, but please don't leave the yard. You can talk to your friends tomorrow, there's still time.”

“Okay mommy.” Lindsay stood up from the table and pushed her chair in. She made a beeline for the front door, opened the screen door, and stopped just short of going over the threshold and stepping outside. She turned around and flashed her mom a toothy smile. “I love you mommy.”

“I love you too sweetie.” It had been easier than she thought, telling her daughter that she wouldn't be seeing her daddy every day. Maybe Paige had overestimated the connection between this father and his daughter. Then again, maybe this would play out some day when Lindsay was a rebellious teenager with daddy issues. Paige wiped her son's face with a warm washcloth, thankful that he was far too young and disconnected from his dad to understand what was going on.

Two more weeks passed, each day filled with a new routine, checking food packages, making the couch into a bed at night, unmaking the same makeshift bed in the morning, and packing, lots of packing. Cardboard boxes in all shapes and sizes slowly replaced piles of toys, closets of clothes, and drawers of utensils. In order to save money in lawyers' fees, Derek and Paige had each drawn up a list of the things they wanted to keep and another list of items that didn't matter. Paige marveled at the value people placed on objects. She had read about people who spent thousands of dollars fighting over a set of towels, it was crazy.

Paige's father rented a moving van for her, but wouldn't come out to help. His stance had always been one of distant support; emotions were not part of the parenting deal for him. "I'm sorry you have to go through this Paige, why do you think I never got re-married?" That was all he had said to her.

The sound of the doorbell was deafening on the final morning Paige was set to move. The kids were at her mom's, and Derek had left the house before sunrise, leaving her alone for the day. She threw some sweats on, put her hair up in a ponytail, and answered the door.

"Hello ma'am. Are you Mrs. Hayes?"

"Yes."

"We're here to move your stuff ma'am."

"Sounds good, but please don't call me ma'am, that's what people call my mom," she said opening the door to the young men dressed in matching blue t-shirts and hats.

They made quick work of the house, moving like a well-oiled

machine from room to room. The house began to lose its life, its character turning gloomy. There was no longer any love in it.

"Okay ma'am," the young man paused realizing he had again called her ma'am. "Um, Mrs. Hayes, would you please come verify the contents in the moving van for me so we can get this signed off and transported to the storage unit for you?"

Paige gave a quick glance at the tightly packed van and signed her name on the blue line next to the large "X." In return for her signature, she received four page copy of all the disclosures she had just signed for.

He then handed her a business card, "Okay, just call this number on the bottom of the card when you're ready to have your belongings delivered to your new residence. Your contract includes 30 days of free storage from today's date."

"Yeah, thank you. I'll let you guys know as soon as I have my address. Thanks again."

She stood there and watched the moving van drive away. It was all she could do to go back into the house for one last look. She stood there, waiting for something, some feeling, some sign, anything, but nothing came. She was devoid of any emotion, completely exhausted and empty. This was checkmate, but who was the winner?

She thought long and hard about everything that had happened in the last several months on the way out to her mom's. Her thoughts turned to Taryn, her loyal friend that was, at times, solely responsible for her still being on this earth. *Shit, Taryn, I forgot to call her.*

Paige dialed her best friend's number on her cellphone and waited for it to connect on the other end.

"Hello? Is this my best friend in the whole world calling to tell me that she is on her way home with her babies?"

"Yes, this is your best friend," Paige began, "but I'm not with my kids, they're at my mom's."

"Oh, what happened?" Taryn asked, suddenly worried.

"Nothing, nothing at all, they're fine, and so am I."

"Fine, hmmph, I know what that word means. What's going on?" Taryn inquired.

"Listen, I'm not sure you'd understand right now. I've decided to go stay with my mom for a little while. Things just got super complicated, I'm sorry, we're not coming out."

The line went silent. "Are you still there?" Paige asked.

"Yes, I am," Taryn replied, her voice flattened. "This is absolutely stupid, you know that right? You need to be *here*. You can't be the mom and woman you need to be while you're still at Judith's. Living with her instead of Derek is the same thing as you've already been doing, just a different name and face."

Taryn continued on, pleading her case, but her words fell on deaf ears. There was going to be no changing her best friend's mind.

"Well then, that's it, I'll talk to you sometime," Taryn finished.

She didn't give Paige a chance to respond, quickly hanging up on her. Paige continued on to Judith's, collecting her thoughts and stuffing them deeply inside her. Her mother was not privileged enough to access that part of her daughter's thoughts.

The next morning Paige got up early and went into town to the public housing office. She had no job, and no savings, but knew she couldn't stay with her mom for long. She pulled into the parking lot, her nice truck sticking out like a sore thumb amongst the other patron's vehicles, dilapidated and rusting sedans. Once inside, she took a number from the wall and sat down in a row of orange and green hard plastic chairs. Women sat with babies, some with runny noses and coughs. Toddlers navigated across people's legs and chair arms, babbling nonsense at their parents. Paige couldn't believe she was here – asking for a handout, that's how it felt.

"Number 33. Number 33!"

"Yes, I'm coming," Paige said standing up. They certainly didn't give a person much time to get up to the window. She got up to the counter and looked for some sign of humanity in the state worker's eyes – there was none.

"How can I help you?" asked state worker.

"Yes, I, um, I just moved here and need to apply for housing assistance."

"Have you filled out an application with us before?"

"No, ma'am, I haven't."

"Okay then, fill these out and return them. You must fill out everything, and when you return them, we will process your application and set up an appointment with one of our housing coordinators." State worker handed Paige a thirty page packet and stared at her blankly.

"Thank you," she said, taking the packet and sitting back down on the hard chairs. It took over an hour for her to fill everything out. State worker was surprised she returned so quickly. "Actually, I have an opening this afternoon at 3pm, can you come back then?"

"Yes, I sure can. Thank you!" Paige replied with enthusiasm.

Paige was approved that afternoon for a three bedroom duplex in a public housing unit just south of Judith's neighborhood. It was a far cry from the life she had been used to, but this was a new beginning, and it had to be viewed as such. With very little furniture or belongings, Paige moved in to her new place the following week. The movers, different guys than last time, weren't as nice as they had been a few weeks before. She wondered if they somehow judged her differently now because of where she lived. No matter, she no longer cared what others thought of her.

Changes were going to occur, slowly, but surely she would become a different person, a transformation long overdue. Her and Taryn were speaking again, though it was a guarded conversation each time, until today, nearly three months since Paige had moved.

The phone rang and Paige was delighted to see it was Taryn. "Hello my friend!"

"Wow, you sound happy," Taryn said surprised.

"I am happy, happy and liberated."

"Ooh, new word, what's the special occasion?"

"I took a shower today," Paige replied.

"Good, glad to hear you're keeping up your hygiene," replied Taryn.

Paige laughed, and then lowered her voice to a whisper. "It's not the fact that I took a shower today, it's what I did in the shower."

"Oh, um, I think that's too much information."

"You didn't even wait for me to tell you *what* I did. Don't you want to know?"

"Okay, I'm ready."

"I drank coffee. I drank coffee in the shower. How absolutely ridiculous is that? And the best thing ever – no one could tell me not to!"

Taryn began to giggle, and her giggle turned into a full blown laugh. "Oh my God, that's awesome. You're awesome, you know that? You're going to be okay, aren't you?"

"Yes my friend, I am. And, I'm going out tonight."

"Whoa there, don't shock me too much at once," Taryn playfully warned.

"My mom actually made me promise to go out. She said I was too young to sit at home every weekend. I told her I would, but I'm not going out to meet anyone. I will only go out if there's a pool table."

"Wow, I think for once in my life, and I hate to say it, Judith is right. Good for her. Good for you! Make sure you call me tomorrow and give me all the details."

"Okay, I will, love you."

"Love you too."

Paige was nervous to go out. She hadn't been out in months, and didn't even know what to wear. She tried on several different pairs of pants and shirts, some were too revealing, others made her look like she was old. She settled on a white shirt with three-quarter sleeves, a pointed collar and bright silver snaps down the front. She chose a pair of light colored blue jeans to go with it. It was comfortable and casual, yet hugged her in all the right spots that gravity hadn't taken a toll on yet. She spritzed her hair once more, put a swath of lipstick on and grabbed her keys to head on out.

The bar was a neighborhood favorite, and not more than five minutes from her duplex. It was smoke filled and loud, and as promised, two pool tables were tucked against the wall. A jukebox shown dimly in the corner, belting out tunes that flowed as well as the beer from the tap. It was the perfect place to disappear from the world for a while, one that you weren't bothered by anybody in, unless it was well after midnight and you were drunk. Paige walked over to the bar, waiting for the bar tender to finish pouring another drink before asking for her own.

"What'll it be?" he asked.

"I'll have whatever lemon-lime soda you have."

"Soda? Are you someone's designated driver tonight?" he asked.

Taking offense to his question, she answered somewhat guarded, "No, why would you ask?"

"I didn't mean anything by it. Just if you're a DD, we give pop out for free, that's all."

Paige relaxed and smiled, "Not a DD, just like to come for the pool, not necessarily all the other stuff."

"That's cool. Hey, if you're in to pool, talk to one of those guys over there, maybe the one in the red and white shirt."

"Okay, thanks."

Paige didn't intend to take him up on his suggestion, she hadn't been a single woman in a bar in all of her twenties, and didn't know how to act. She held her pop in one hand, and reached for a pool cue off the wall with her other hand. Sure enough, the guy in the red and white shirt came right up to her. "Hey there, can I help you pick out a stick?"

Nice pick up line thought Paige. "No, I'm good."

"Okay, how about a game though."

She studied his face and body language. He was pretty short, and looked harmless. "Okay, that'd be great."

The two played for nearly an hour, talking about how Paige had just moved here and some of the challenges she had been going through, without getting too personal.

She noticed out of the corner of her eye a man who just walked into the bar. He had salt and pepper hair, high cheekbones, and a warm smile. Her pool partner noticed her staring across the bar and walked up beside her. "That's my cousin," he said.

"Really?" Paige responded with interest.

"Yup," he said. "Hey cuz, I'm over here" he waived his arm at his cousin. He turned back to Paige. "You see all these trophies on the walls here?"

She looked around, and then back at him. "Yes."

"He's on most of them. He's an awesome pool player. You want me to introduce you?"

"Um, no, I'm good." Her feelings scared her, and the best thing she thought to do was to avoid them at this point.

The man came up to them anyway, holding what looked like an extended, oblong briefcase. He put it down on the table and turned toward Paige and his cousin.

"Hey cuz, this is Paige. Paige, this is my cousin."

His cousin extended his hand out to Paige as she did the same with hers. Their hands locked as she simultaneously looked into his eyes. Her heart melted as his slate grey eyes twinkled back at her.

"Nice to meet you," he said. Something about his voice both excited and calmed her at the same time. She felt flush, her body conjuring up emotions that had been quelled for some time.

"You too. Do you have a name?" she asked.

"Drifter. They call me Drifter," he replied.

"Well Drifter, it's very nice to meet you. And with that, Paige's life began anew.

www.ingramcontent.com/pod-product-compliance
Lightning Source LLC
Chambersburg PA
CBHW070819120626
46556CB00002B/571

9 780989 639002